Also by Jessica Cunsolo

She's With Me

Stay With Me

Stay With Me

JESSICA CUNSOLO

wattpad books

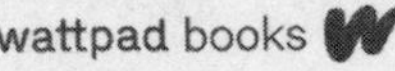

Published in Canada by Wattpad Books, a division of Wattpad Corp.
36 Wellington Street E., Toronto ON, M5E 1C7

www.wattpad.com

First Wattpad Books edition: December 2020

ISBN 978-1-98936-531-1(Trade Paper original)
ISBN 978-1-98936-538-0 (eBook edition)

Library and Archives Canada Cataloguing in Publication information is available upon request.

Printed and bound in Canada.
1 3 5 7 9 10 8 6 4 2

Cover design by Laura Mensinga
Images © Logan Weaver (front cover) via Unsplash and
© Camille Minouflet (back cover) via Unsplash
Typesetting by Sarah Salomon

This story is dedicated to my mom, Carmela Cunsolo.
Thank you for being my number one fan.

Prologue

Life laughs at you sometimes. Perhaps people like me are boring to watch, so every once in a while life goes, Hey, why don't I mess around with Amelia a bit? Don't you think that'll be funny?

And then life's friends, drama, pain, uncertainty, and unfortunate events, say, Hell, yeah, dude! We got your back. Watch the shit storm we can cause.

And they all get to work inserting themselves where they don't belong, stirring up the pot. Then they sit around with cold beers clutched in their hands and some boxes of pizza shared between them and laugh uproariously. At least, that's how I think it happens, because sometimes it seems like my time here on Earth is just one long episode of let's see how we can screw with Amelia today.

There's a man out there intent on murdering me: Tony. He has hurt and killed other people in the name of revenge. And I care very deeply about someone I'm destined to end up hurting—someone who discovered that he was being deceived from the start, and then was promptly arrested for murdering his stepfather, whom he'd been worried about harming his brothers ever since Greg was released from jail. Aiden is not a murderer; he's *not* capable of doing something like that. Or is he? He's a fierce protector of those he loves, and he would do anything to protect his brothers . . . but murder?

Aiden hates Greg with a burning passion—I'm pretty sure he abused Aiden as a child. But I can't see Aiden taking his life then coming over to my house to watch movies like it's any other day.

Why *do* the police think Aiden did it? He was at my house all night, and he was with Mason before that . . . right? When did Greg die, anyway? He's been out of prison for a couple of weeks—wouldn't he want to spend some time with his son, Ryan, and not bother with Aiden?

Ryan.

I wonder if Aiden's stepbrother has heard about the death of his father. I wonder if he's heard Aiden was arrested for Greg's murder. Ryan hates Aiden for being Aiden; I don't want to know what he'll do if he thinks Aiden's responsible for the death of his father. Before, this was just a petty rivalry, but now someone's *dead* and Aiden's in jail accused of *murder*.

I can't lose Aiden. Not right now, not when he's come to mean so much to me. Everyone here in King City has. All my friends are the people I never thought I'd ever have in my life; people who make me feel like I belong, like I have a *family*. I can't let *anyone*, not Ryan, not Tony, and not even the police, take that away from me.

1

The police station hums with activity. Men and women in uniform are all over the place, either walking around like they're in the middle of some important task or standing around talking like they have all the time in the world. An odd combination of disinfectant and dirt scents the air, and the constant ringing of a phone drills at my head. We've been sitting here for hours. No one has told us anything, as the only interaction between us and the officers has been them occasionally glaring at us for taking up practically the entire waiting area.

I hate police stations. I've been in plenty over the past year and it never gets better—the anxiety never goes away, and neither does the pit of dread that sits in the middle of my chest. Police stations remind me of Tony, and every person an officer leads past us in handcuffs makes me cringe. The only reason I'm sticking rooted to my seat instead of flying out of here as fast as my legs can take me is Aiden.

After the arrest, Julian, Mason, and Annalisa picked up the

twins from their friend's house like Aiden asked, and took them to Julian's house for his mom to watch. Everyone else came to the police station, and Julian showed up a bit later with Annalisa and his father, Vince. Julian clearly got his height from his father, as well as his broad shoulders, but Vince has a stern face, and there's a commanding presence about him that makes him feel trustworthy. Of course Julian would go to his dad for help, since we clearly need a responsible adult and it's not like Aiden has another one to turn to. Plus, Aiden practically grew up with Julian.

A bit after Vince showed up, Mason arrived with his dad, Brian. The adults went to talk to the police about Aiden while the rest of us sat worriedly in the tiny reception area.

Mason gets his good looks from his dad, as their dark hair and tanned olive skin are almost identical, but Brian's a bit shorter than his son. Brian's dark eyes also lack that certain spark of mischief that Mason's often hold—but then again, this isn't a happy situation.

As the two dads talk to the officers, I sit straight up and study them intently, and it doesn't look like it's going well. Brian's running his hand through his hair like Mason does when he's frustrated, the gold wedding band sparkling brightly in comparison to his dark hair. My heartbeat hasn't slowed down to normal since we sat down.

After a while, Vince is led by some officers to the back, and Brian comes to sit with us.

"What's going on?" Mason asks his dad.

"They have Aiden in holding right now. He's still a few weeks shy of eighteen, so they can't question him without the presence of an appropriate adult and a social worker, and we're trying to sort out who that is, exactly," Brian explains, pulling out his phone and going through some contacts.

"But they can't question him without a lawyer! Shouldn't we be getting him a lawyer?" Annalisa exclaims.

"He doesn't need a lawyer because he didn't do anything!" Noah defends Aiden. "He has, like, seven alibis! Eight if you count the guy working the counter at the pizza place!"

Brian ignores Noah and stands up. "I'm calling a lawyer now. Hopefully, he'll be here soon."

And with that, Brian walks away to find a quiet place to make his phone call, leaving the rest of us to our unproductive worrying.

Half an hour later, a professional-looking man in a pressed suit enters the police station, and Brian gets up to shake his hand. They talk to some officers, who then hustle the man I'm assuming is Aiden's lawyer into the back room.

Charlotte is sitting beside Chase, and they're talking in hushed tones between themselves. Annalisa glares down everyone in the police station, and looks like she's trying very hard to not punch anyone who looks at her the wrong way. Julian's beside her, talking to Mason and Brian about what could possibly happen to Aiden and what's going on in the back. Noah's beside me, his foot rapidly and incessantly tapping the floor, the sound slowly driving me crazy.

Since moving to King City, I've been lucky enough to meet all these incredible people—friends who have become like a family to me. I've never had friends like this, who have your back no matter what, and who stick by you through hard times. We're all in a police station on a Friday night instead of out enjoying ourselves, and it's all because we care about each other, about *Aiden*.

While I'm grateful to have my friends, I hate that I'm stuck in an uncomfortable chair in a beige room with awful lighting, incapable of doing anything except try really hard to ignore the pit of anxiety and worry building in my stomach.

After a while, I can't take it anymore and slap my hand on Noah's thigh. "Stop!" I snap.

"I know I'm irresistible, Amelia, but now is not the time or place to get frisky," Noah says.

I pull my hand back, in no mood for his Noah-ness at this particular time. His foot has stopped incessantly tapping, but I don't feel any better. What's taking so long? Aiden didn't do anything. All of this all should've been sorted out already. Right?

The minutes tick by painfully. Charlotte's strict parents call, and then her older brother comes to pick her and Chase up, who has his own worried parents to get home to. We promise we'll keep them both updated.

We've been here for how long now? Hours? It's past ten o'clock. Why has the activity in the police station not slowed down? The phone hasn't stopped ringing. I have half a mind to rip every single phone off its cord and chuck them all out the window. The last time I was in a police station this long was when Tony found me for the third time, and I'd had to go from the hospital to the station to give my statement, which was useless, clearly, since he's still out there, searching for me. And just like that night, my flight response is kicking in—I want to run as far away from here as humanly possible, but I'd never leave Aiden behind.

It's just after eleven o'clock when the lawyer and Vince come back out, unfortunately without Aiden. Brian goes over to talk to the other men, and we all sit up, ramrod straight, straining to hear the conversation. The dads talk for a while with some detectives, and then the lawyer and Brian depart with two other police officers, leaving us all staring after them, confused.

Vince heads over to us, looking tired but less frustrated, which I hope is a good thing. We get to our feet as he approaches.

"They're going to hold Aiden overnight," Vince says before any of us can interrogate him. "While they check his alibi."

"Aren't we his alibi?" Julian asks.

Julian's father motions us over to the side of the tiny waiting area for some privacy from the other people here.

"Here's what we know: Greg's body was found dead in front of Aiden's house, and he was pretty badly beaten. They found Aiden's cell phone at the crime scene. Right now the cops have a tentative time of death around six in the evening. Aiden had been at Mason's house since four thirty, and they were there until they left to pick up the pizza around ten to seven, and then they went straight to Amelia's house. The security footage from the cameras in front of Mason's house can prove the times are correct, and Brian just left to get the police the tapes to clear Aiden."

We all look at each other, stunned. Greg's body was found in front of Aiden's house? With Aiden's cell phone?

"His cell phone? I know for a fact that his phone was with him at Amelia's house," Mason chimes in.

"His old phone. Remember, he lost it a few weeks ago, at the Tr—school." My awkward cover-up isn't at all cool, but I'm not going to narc on anyone by saying "Tracks" in front of a parent.

"How did Aiden's phone end up at the crime scene?" Annalisa asks, even though no one knows the answer.

"Never mind that, how did the dead body of Aiden's despised stepfather end up in front of his house? Was it moved there?" Julian ponders.

Vince rubs his eyes. I seriously doubt that he ever thought that being a dad meant having to deal with a murder charge.

"Forensics determined that it was the primary location, meaning that Greg died in front of Aiden's house."

"That does not look good for our boy." Noah grimaces.

"He didn't do it, Noah!" Annalisa snaps.

"Geez, I know. I'm just saying . . ." he replies, then under his breath adds, "Why do I always forget that she's crankier than usual without sleep?"

"Noah's right though," Vince says. "With the location of the crime, Aiden's phone, and the bruising on Greg indicating a recent fight—it doesn't look good. Plus, Aiden and Greg's past doesn't help—it's on record that Aiden petitioned against Greg's parole. It could be reasoned that he had a motive. Even if we have an alibi for him, we have to prove that's enough for them to let him go."

This whole situation is ludicrous. I explain, "Aiden is one of the smartest people I know, book- and street-wise. He has one of the top GPAs not just in the school, but in the entire school district. I think if he was going to kill a guy, he wouldn't leave the dead body in front of his house."

Everyone smiles tiredly and nods at the truth behind my statement. I mean, really. No one can actually be so dumb as to kill someone and leave their dead body chillin' in front of their house like no big deal while they go eat pizza and watch movies at their friend's house.

But if Aiden didn't kill Greg, who did? Why was the primary crime scene in front of Aiden's house? Is someone trying to frame him? But why? There are so many more questions than answers, and that makes me uncomfortable. Oh God. What if they need to question *me*? He was at *my house* when he was arrested. What if they need to dig into me? What will they find?

"Listen, everyone," Vince commands. "They're going to clear all this up and Aiden will be out of here before you know it. You should all go home instead of sitting here worrying about him. He wanted me to assure you all that he's fine, to go home, and that it'll all be okay."

Aiden's *literally* in jail (or in police holding, whatever, there's still bars) and still his first priority is his friends? That man cannot make me like him any more than I already do.

Vince lightly slaps Julian's back. "Come on, son, let's go home and get some rest. Everything will be sorted out soon. Annalisa, I'm guessing you're staying at our house tonight?"

Annalisa nods and pulls on her jacket, and Vince looks at the rest of us. "Do you guys need a ride home?"

"Yeah, I do," Noah says, looking up from his phone. "Maybe I should stay at your house too. I have nineteen missed calls from my mother and don't feel like dying tonight."

Noah's humor breaks the tension. We're all exhausted. "Tough break, kid. Judy's one tough woman when she's angry." Vince looks at me and Mason. "Do you kids need a ride home?"

"I drove here," I say, leaving out the part that I have absolutely zero intention of leaving.

Mason looks at me as if he can read my mind. "I'll catch a ride with Amelia."

"Okay, then, you guys get home safe," Vince says. "Try not to worry, everything will be all right."

We say good-bye to everyone and when they're out of earshot, I turn to Mason. "You know I'm not leaving anytime soon right?"

He rolls his eyes at me and plants his butt firmly in the chair in the waiting area. "Of course I know that. I messaged my dad and told him that I'm hitching a ride with you once this is all sorted out."

Taking the seat beside him, I slouch back, tired. Despite our rocky start, Aiden's been here for me every moment of the last few months. He's helped me out whenever I needed it, even if I didn't ask him, even when I pissed him off or antagonized him. Like when he got Ethan Moore to take down the video of me that he had posted on the internet, without asking any questions about why I panicked so much. Or when he put up with all my attitude and tutored me in calculus, helping me pull up my failing grade. Or when our archenemies Kaitlyn and Ryan trashed my car and he brought me to Charlotte's to sleep while he dealt with the tow truck, the mechanic, and all the repairs, refusing to accept any money. Or like when he won $4,000 racing Ryan at the Tracks and gave it to me to spend however I wanted. Or how he's basically raising his twin brothers by himself. Aiden's such a good person with such a genuinely kind soul. The thought of leaving him in jail is unbearable. He might have told us to go home and stop worrying, but I can't leave knowing that he's here. I'd be abandoning him in a way, especially after he just found out the real truth about me and wasn't scared away.

He knows my name isn't Amelia—he found the shoe box that holds reminders of my past lives; he found out that I am a lying piece of garbage. He opened up to me, something that's extremely hard for him to do, and I betrayed him. I've been lying to him while he's been completely honest and transparent with me. He was so incredibly hurt when he found out that my entire identity is a lie. The look on his face, that flash of realization that I had been lying, loops around my mind like a car on a racetrack—his complete disbelief and betrayal.

But he understood. He wasn't mad and he kissed me. He said that he's all in—so I'm not going anywhere until he's released. Because I'm all in, too, no matter what happens.

"What do you think he's thinking about?" I ask, trying to distract myself from my thoughts.

"Probably his brothers," Mason answers.

"He loves Jason and Jackson more than anything."

"Do you think Ryan found out about his dad?"

"I don't know. But I'm completely certain that this is only going to make the hatred Ryan holds for Aiden so much stronger."

"You don't think—" Mason pauses, hesitating like he can't even say the words out loud. "You don't think Ryan had something to do with this?"

Mason and I catch each other's eyes for a second, letting the suggestion sink in, before shaking our heads to dismiss that notion.

"No way," I say. "Why would Ryan kill his own father at Aiden's house to frame him? Even he's not that psychotic."

"You're right. Ryan might be crazy, but he's not murder my own dad just to frame my archnemesis crazy."

Slinking down into my seat, I lean my head on Mason's shoulder, his familiar cologne giving me some semblance of peace. I'm glad Mason decided to wait here with me. There's got to be an explanation for what happened. And none of us will stop until we know who really killed Greg.

2

When Brian finally strides back into the waiting room with the officers and lawyer he'd left with, Mason and I sit up with hope. But our hopes are dashed as he disappears almost immediately into the back with barely a glance at us.

Forever passes until Brian comes back out, alone, and sits with me and Mason. We've been here for hours now—it's just past midnight. I'm exhausted, still paranoid every time an officer looks at me as they walk by, my head is pounding from the phones ringing shrilly, and my ass is numb from this stupid chair. If it was up to me, I'd ban this chair from every retailer across America—they're literally torture.

"What's going on?" Mason asks. "Where's Aiden?"

Brian grimaces. "It's all more complicated than we thought."

Mason and I share a look. *More complicated?*

"When Aiden was arrested, they contacted his legal guardian," Brian continues, "which was Greg's wife, Paula, who informed them that she hasn't seen Aiden in who knows how long now, and wants nothing to do with him. She painted an awful picture of Aiden, saying he stole from her, did drugs, ran away from home with his brothers, and so on."

Liar. Sure, she wants nothing to do with him, but she absolutely wants something to do with the government's child support checks.

"That obviously led to the question of where Jason and Jackson are, which Aiden refused to answer."

And risk them going into foster care? I didn't blame him. Every minute that goes by means that we're closer to the police calling social services, if they haven't already.

"Not only did my friend Alan have to get Aiden off a murder charge, but also a kidnapping charge."

Mason and I must have matching panicked looks on our faces, because Brian quickly adds, "Don't worry! It's all been sorted out. Aiden's been cleared of murder."

I breathe for the first time since Brian started talking. The weight that's been on my chest since Aiden was arrested lifts and my heart no longer feels heavy. He's not going to jail for killing Greg!

Brian doesn't wait for us to bombard him with questions, but just starts explaining. "His alibi checks out. He's with Alan back there signing release papers and stuff."

"What about the kidnapping charges?" I ask.

"Alan talked Paula into relinquishing legal custody, something about getting her charged with child endangerment for not reporting the twins missing since she said Aiden kidnapped them. I've agreed to be the legal guardian for all three Parker boys until Aiden turns eighteen in a few weeks and can file for guardianship over his brothers. Social workers are going to be checking up on us, though."

Mason throws himself at his father and wraps his arms around him. "Oh my God, Dad. You're the coolest."

Brian pats Mason's back before they pull away. "I wish Aiden hadn't felt the need to shoulder all of this alone. If we had known before about the custody situation, Vince or I would've stepped in sooner."

Mason and Julian's dads are *such* good people. It makes me wonder what my dad would've done in this situation if he hadn't died. It gives me comfort to think that before the fighting with my mom and the drinking started, he would've done the same thing.

"How long will the paperwork take? Is Aiden almost done?"

Brian doesn't need to answer me, because Mason abruptly stands up, focused on the hallway ahead of us, a giant grin on his face.

I practically jump out of my chair, and am beside Mason in an instant. Aiden, in all his intense, tall, confident, broad-shouldered glory, is being led toward us by an officer, Alan the lawyer following them. Even though he's spent a large chunk of the night in jail, Aiden looks irresistibly gorgeous, and my breath stops when his piercing gray eyes meet my hazel ones, his facial expression giving nothing away. Seeing him now, it feels like it's been ages since I've seen him, even though our kiss was only a few hours ago. They stop just behind the reception desk, where the officer says something to Aiden, who still hasn't broken eye contact with me, and the officer gestures that he's free to go.

Aiden takes a few steps toward us and is barely able to rub his wrists where the handcuffs must have been before I launch myself at him. A feeling deep down takes over, demanding I hold him, to make sure that he's actually here and okay. He doesn't hesitate and wraps his strong arms around me, pulling me close. With my head against his muscled chest, listening to the calming sound of his steady heartbeat, I assure myself that he's actually here.

"Are you okay?" I ask.

He releases me and gently tucks a piece of my hair behind my ear. "Of course I am. Why are you guys still here? I told you all to go home and not worry."

He and Mason do their bro hug. "We couldn't just leave you here, man," Mason says. "Everyone else was waiting, too, but in their defense, they were kind of forced to go home."

"You guys didn't need to come. No one needs to worry about me."

This must be weird for Aiden. He's the one who's there for everyone else, making sure that they're okay and taken care of. He's the strong one, the one who holds everything together; having other people worry about him is something I'm sure he's not used to.

"We care about you, Aiden. So we stayed." My cheeks heat up because of the way he looks at me.

"And we never want to see you in handcuffs again," Brian says, and then he hugs him too. A giant, comforting dad hug.

"Thanks for your help, Brian. You, too, Alan." Aiden shakes hands with the lawyer, who tells him that it was no problem, and to call him if anything else happens.

"Come on, man." Mason lightly slaps Aiden's back while his dad talks to Alan. "Let's get the fuck out of here."

Aiden agrees, and we leave the place that almost turned more than one life upside down. As we walk out the exit, I can tell both Mason and I want to ask Aiden about what happened, but we're too scared to. Despite his exhaustion, Aiden notices, and he knows exactly what we're thinking.

"I'm too tired to answer your questions right now," he says. "I'll tell everyone what happened tomorrow."

Makes perfect sense. He was interrogated for hours straight; we don't need to subject him to even more interrogation.

"Need a ride, Aiden?" Brian asks. "Your house is still a crime scene, right?"

Mason's about to offer his house for Aiden to stay at, but before he has the chance to say anything, I blurt: "You can crash in my guest room."

I need the chance to sort everything out with Aiden—alone. He *just* found out literally a few hours ago that my name is Thea and that I'm hiding my real identity from a man trying to hunt me down. We didn't get to talk about it, even though he said he was all in, that he understood, that he didn't hate me. But I still remember how betrayed he looked, how betrayed he must have *felt.* Aiden said that he accepted me, the real me, but it's only fair to him that I tell him my story—the *whole* story. He deserves that.

"Plus," I continue before anyone can object, "your car is already at my house. It'll make things easier for you."

"Are you sure?" Brian asks. "If it's a problem, Amelia, Aiden can stay with us."

"No problem at all. What time is it? One a.m.? My mom will have just gotten home and will be asleep by the time we get there since she has an early morning flight. She won't have time to object." I don't add that I sent her a text saying we were all out watching a movie and that I'd volunteered to drive, and her only reply was *K*.

Either Aiden is so tired he really doesn't care or he's burning for answers, because it only takes a few moments for him to agree to come to my house.

Up until a few minutes before Aiden got arrested, I'd been avoiding him like a kid who'd received a bad report card dodges their strict, high-standards-holding parents. And now I'm practically begging him to come home with me so we can talk alone. Funny how things change in a matter of hours.

After saying good-bye to Mason, Brian, and Alan, we all head in different directions in the quiet parking lot, which is a stark contrast to the loud craziness of the police station. It's a calm, cool night, but I feel anything but. Now that I'm alone with Aiden, sneaking glances at his broad frame as we walk, my stomach squeezes. Will my stomach always do somersaults when I'm around him? Will my heart ever beat normally when I look at him?

Before I can open the driver's side door, Aiden's behind me. Suddenly, we're chest to chest, and he's looking down at me, a lightness in his eyes and a tension in the air.

His deep voice is low and even. "We were interrupted."

His closeness makes it hard for me to think. "We were?"

"Mmm-hmm." His hands tug my hips to his. "I have no problem refreshing your memory if you forgot."

He leans down and kisses me, roughly and fiercely, like it's been ages since we've seen each other and all he needs to feel whole is his lips on mine. I wrap my arms around his neck and pull him closer to me, *needing* to feel him against me. All the worry and tension I didn't even know I was holding vanishes as we come together. He's here. He doesn't hate me. I didn't lose him. The kiss ends way too fast, but I'm still left breathless when he pulls away.

I'm all in, Thea Kennedy. His words play in my mind, making me shiver. His grip tightens. "Come on, let's get out of here," he says, his warm hands vanishing from my waist as he walks around the car to the passenger side.

As I pull out of the parking lot, Aiden calls Julian to see about picking up the twins, but Julian says they stayed up all night asking questions about Aiden and playing video games, and only now fell asleep.

Aiden rubs his temples. "Okay, let them sleep. I'll pick them up in the morning and explain what's going on. Thanks again, Julian." He pauses, listening. "Yeah, I'm okay. See you tomorrow."

We don't talk, and the soft hum of the radio acts as background noise. The road has that late-at-night quality in which the lights are hazy, and Aiden leans back against the headrest, his eyes closed and body relaxed.

His presence fills up my small car, and he almost looks ridiculous with his long legs barely sitting comfortably under the dash. He's sitting *right there,* and he's not pressing me for answers. Not pushing me about Tony. Not asking me about the three people Tony killed. It's equally hard for me to not ask him how he's feeling. I tap the steering wheel and force my vision to stay on the road, not to drift over at Aiden, too nervous to ask him any questions despite the fact that he just kissed me.

"Thea," he says, breaking the silence, his head still relaxed against the seat.

"Yes?" I answer, my heart skipping a beat at hearing my real name in his deep voice.

"The tapping is driving me crazy," he says, eyes still closed.

I stop immediately. "Sorry, I'm just . . ."

"Anxious?" He lifts his head. "I know. How are you holding up? We didn't have enough time to talk about your secret. You know I'd never tell anyone—you don't even have to ask. But I was worried about you being in a police station." He shifts in his seat and runs his hand through his short but messy dark-blond hair. "If those articles are a snapshot of what you went through, then being there must not have been the easiest thing for you."

How much time did he have to go through the news articles of my past lives that I keep hidden in a shoe box? He's either really good at puzzles or he got a really good look, because he's spot on about my hatred of police stations.

"Normally, it would've brought up some bad memories, and I definitely wouldn't want to be there for as long as I was. The smell. The phone ringing. God, even the stupid chairs are all the same. I've been let down so many times . . . but I was only worried about you."

My voice erupts awkwardly, and Aiden asks, "Why are you laughing?"

"You literally spent hours in jail being questioned about a *murder*. You went through that whole traumatic experience of being arrested and interrogated and potentially going to *jail*. Your stepfather is *dead* and your house is a crime scene, and the first thing you do is worry about *me*?"

"I knew I didn't do it, and I knew my alibi would check out. I didn't have anything to hide so I wasn't worried about being charged. But since I had nothing to do but wait, my mind wandered, and I've got to be honest with you—thinking about everything we've been through, I was mad for a moment. After opening up, trusting you, telling you things I've never told anyone. I was pissed thinking that you didn't care, that my feelings weren't being reciprocated."

A tear slips out as my reply comes out in a rush. "I'm sorry. I kept those secrets because I had to. I wanted to tell you so many times, but I couldn't."

"I'm not mad at you, and I mean it," he assures me. "But the more I think about it, the more pissed I get. Not at you, never at you, but at the circumstances. You shouldn't have to go through all of this, not alone. What can I do to help? There has to be something we can do. Please."

I feel like laughing and crying all at once. "You can't help."

"I *can* help. I'm Aiden Parker."

"Not this time, Aiden." I'm staring straight ahead because if I look at him, my heart will surely break. He can't change what's happened, what I've been through. The suburban houses all blend into one another, looking like one generic, mediocre house; every town I've been in the last year just like the others, none of them feeling like home until now, and only because I have Aiden and my friends. We're almost at my house and I need to get out and breathe the fresh air before I burst out in tears.

"I can. If you would just tell me—"

"*You can't help!*" I snap, instantly regretting my tone. "I'm sorry—it's just—there are some things that even you can't fix."

"Why don't you tell me and we'll take it from there?" he says softly, placing his large hand on my forearm.

I pull into my driveway and shut off the car, then turn to look at him in the dark, his face illuminated by the glow of the headlights that have yet to turn off.

"It's late. You're exhausted. Why don't we get some rest and I'll tell you the entire story tomorrow, okay?"

"That's fair." He nods.

I quietly unlock the front door and we make our way up the stairs without making much noise. I'm not sneaking him in, per se, but I'd rather not wake my mother. I'm sure she'll be suspicious when she sees Aiden's car in the driveway when she leaves for work in the morning, but what's she going to do? Move me to a new state? Oh wait, she's already doing that.

Once Aiden's set up in the guest bedroom, which has its own bathroom attached, I leave him so he can have a few moments of privacy, and find him something to change into. When I get back, I give a courtesy knock on the door and he opens it for me.

"I brought you an extra toothbrush and some toothpas—" I stop talking and openly stare at Aiden, who is standing in the doorway *in nothing but his boxer briefs.*

This is not a drill. Aiden Parker is in my house at night in nothing but his underwear.

My God, please tell me I am not salivating.

I force my head up so fast I probably give myself whiplash, and awkwardly thrust out my hand to give him the toothbrush and toothpaste. *Geez, Amelia, can you be any more embarrassing?*

"Thanks," he says, an amused look on his face. Dammit, he knows how hot he is and enjoys torturing me.

"I . . . couldn't find anything for you to change into . . . unless you think you can squeeze into my pj's."

"I'll just sleep in my boxers, it's fine."

"I have a sweater of yours, though. I never gave it back to you after that night we got locked out of the school," I admit sheepishly.

I've been wearing it around the house (in a noncreepy way) mostly because it's nice and big and comfy and warm. But also because it reminds me of him (again, totally not creepy).

He looks at the sweater in my hand but doesn't make any motion to take it. "Keep it. I'm hot anyway."

Hell yeah, he is.

"If you're sure." I am not going to fight that hard to give it back to him. It's a really comfy sweater.

"I'm sure. Good night, Am—Thea."

My breath hitches in my throat. "Good night, Aiden."

3

In the morning, I sit at the kitchen island, not really eating the cereal in front of me. I'm alternately staring at the bowl then using the spoon to lift up the cereal and drop it back into the milk unenthusiastically. My mind isn't on food but on telling Aiden about my past. What if he thinks I'm a coward for running and letting other people get hurt? What if he thinks I have too much baggage for him and decides he wants nothing to do with me? I have no idea how to tell him my mother's forcing us to leave in the new year, and that means he'll probably never see or hear from me again—because whatever my new name will be, I will have to leave Amelia in the past. She'll cease to exist like Hailey Johnson and Isabella Smith before her. When Amelia Collins disappears, she can't bring anything or anyone with her. *I* can't bring anyone with me, and I can't stay here. The court case and everything with Aiden's stepfather is going to be in the news, which will make my mother even more nervous about staying here. She said as much in a few quick words before she left for her flight very early this morning.

Footsteps come down the stairs and I look up to see Aiden, unfortunately fully clothed.

"Hey."

"Morning," I reply as I slide the box of Froot Loops toward the bowl I set out for him earlier.

He bites back a smile at our little inside joke about Froot Loops, but doesn't make a move to pour his own, instead taking a seat beside me at the counter. He's sitting right beside me but he still feels so far away. I pretend to be superinterested in my now-soggy cereal.

"How are you feeling?" I ask, trying not to shift nervously in my seat.

"Better with some rest now. I talked to the twins. They wanted to know why they had to stay at Julian's last night instead of at their friend's like they usually do on Fridays."

It takes me a second but I connect the dots pretty easily. Friday is when Aiden goes to the Tracks and races, which is how he makes most of his money. The twins probably spend that night at their friends . . . free babysitting for Aiden, I guess.

"What did you tell them?" I ask.

"I said I had to go out of town last minute and wanted Julian's parents to watch them. They don't seem to mind, though. They said Julian's mom is making homemade waffles for breakfast and I'd better come quick to get some before they're all gone. I'm so glad they weren't home when Greg showed up, or when whoever killed him was there."

His shoulders tense and there's a tick in his jaw that appears whenever he mentions something that could harm the twins. It's hard, thinking of something terrible happening to someone you love more than anything in the world. He's practically the only father those boys will ever know, and them getting hurt must be Aiden's biggest fear.

"They're okay, Aiden," I say, not knowing how to comfort him. "They're safe."

"There are so many unanswered questions. Why was Greg in front of my house? What did he want? Why did he have my old cell phone? Who killed him?" Aiden rubs his hands through his hair and I refrain from reaching out and soothing the tension from his brow.

"I'm sure the cops are working on it. This isn't really the right way to say this, but at least you don't have to worry about Greg ever again."

"Good fucking riddance."

The loud vibration of my phone against the hard counter interrupts us, and I pick it up to check what's going on. "You probably haven't been checking the group chat, but it's basically been blowing up."

All our friends have been wanting to know if Aiden is okay, how he's feeling about the death of his loathed stepfather, and if he's free and clear of any charges.

"We should all get together and have a conversation after I get the twins," he suggests. "I doubt sending *I'm fine* back in the chat will go over well. Ten bucks says Anna punches me."

I'm glad he's finding humor in the situation. I poise my fingers over the phone's keyboard. "What should I tell them? We can use my house if you want."

"Tell them to come around seven, with some food." He sighs and rubs the back of his neck. "I'm going to go check on the twins, see if I can come up with something to say to explain why we can't go home for a while. Maybe I'll see if they can stay at Tyler's, that way it's more fun for them."

That conversation isn't going to be easy, but neither is the one I'm going to have to have with Aiden, preferably sooner rather than later.

I can't look at him as I say, "We're going to have to have a serious talk too."

"You don't owe me anything, Thea."

But I do. The guilt sits in a pit right in the middle of my chest. I'm leaving this town, leaving Aiden, and if I'm going to go, I need to leave him with the truth. Aiden's been nothing but honest with me. He let me in when he really doesn't let anyone in, so I want him to know me, the *real* me.

"It's not about owing," I say. "I need to tell you. All in, remember?"

I look away from him, willing my face to not turn bright red from his intense and unwavering gaze.

"Before everyone gets here tonight, you and I will talk," Aiden says.

» «

The rest of the afternoon moves slowly while I try to keep busy and not overthink. My mom sends me another text, just like her first one earlier this morning, reprimanding me again for letting Aiden stay the night, but what's she going to do from Canada? I'm not really worried about getting on her bad side since she's already ruining the semblance of a normal life I have by relocating me. When was the last time I had a boyfriend? When was the last time I felt as close to someone as I do to Aiden? The only boy who ever got somewhat close to me was Hunter, which was a few months ago when I was Hailey, but even he never got past a few dates. He never gave me mammoth-sized butterflies like Aiden does. He never made me feel safe and secure and completely at peace with who I am like Aiden does. In comparison to Aiden, Hunter was a blip on my radar while Aiden takes up the whole damn thing.

By the time Aiden texts me to let me know he's on his way, I've vacuumed and mopped the entire house twice.

"Hey," I greet him as he enters my house. "Where are the twins?"

"They wanted to stay and play with Bubba. We're going to stay the night with Julian before we move into Mason's, since we're not cleared to go home. Tyler's parents have some event tonight and some teenage babysitter can't handle all three of them." He laughs a bit as he takes his shoes off and follows me into the kitchen. "So they're spending real time with Julian's dog. They can see how much work goes into taking care of him, since they keep asking me for one."

Laughing at the mental image of Jason and Jackson trying to play with Julian's fifty-pound bulldog, I hand Aiden a glass of water.

"You're moving into Mason's?"

"Brian's our legal guardian. The social workers are going to be checking up on us and stuff. Since my house is still a crime scene, we figured we might as well stay there for a bit until we can sort everything out."

I nod, then bite my lip. The dark circles under his eyes do nothing to take away from the attractiveness of his face. Neither does the hard set of his jaw or the tension he holds in his back. I wish this wasn't happening to him, that he could've been dealt a better hand.

"How did telling them about Greg go?"

"It was hard." He lets out a heavy breath. "I sat them down and told them that a bad thing happened to Greg, and it was outside our home. They kept doing that twin thing where they lock eyes and communicate with each other without saying anything. I told them I'd go back home to pick up some things, but they were kind of freaked out when I told them we'd need to stay with Mason for a bit." He releases a sad, humorless chuckle.

I shake my head. The last thing those boys need is to be worried about anything happening to Aiden. He's the only stability they have. I can only imagine how terrifying it would be to see your house covered in police tape; I'd never had to.

"I didn't tell them the whole story. They're nine—I don't want them to think about a murder happening on the front lawn of where we live. I don't need them to have that kind of trauma in their lives, it's enough they've already lost our mom. They know Greg's dead, but I sort of left it at that."

Putting my hand on Aiden's shoulder for support is all I can manage to do. Even though my own heart aches for them, I don't dare to speak over the lump in my throat.

He looks at me for the first time. "I assured them that I wasn't going anywhere, that nothing would ever split us up."

"They're just in shock."

"I hope so," he says. "We sat and I answered all their questions, and they're handling it well, considering. They seemed like their usual selves before I left. I hate that this is going to ruin their winter break."

"We'll find a way to make it fun," I assure him, already running through a mental list of things we can do before school starts again in January, forgetting for a moment that I won't be here.

He shakes his head as if clearing the troubling thoughts from it. "Anyway, if you still want to talk, we should before we get interrupted by everyone."

My breath hitches, but I still manage to choke out, "You're right."

Suddenly, the two of us standing in front of one another feels awkward, distant. Keeping my secrets has been about survival; they're stories that should probably be reserved for me and a future therapist. But I'm going to tell him anyway, which makes me realize just *how much* I trust Aiden. "Let's go sit on the couch. It's more comfortable, and it's a long story."

The last time we sat on the couch alone together, it ended up turning into the best make-out session of my entire life. We sit, and I turn my body sideways to face him, crossing my legs underneath me. His facial expression is neutral, and I can't tell what he's thinking, probably Get the fuck on with it, Thea, and stop being so dramatic.

"Do you remember when I told you about my dad, how he died? How he picked me up one day plastered and ended up killing himself and a six-year-old named Sabrina?"

If Aiden's surprised about how this is starting, he doesn't show it. I'm suddenly all too aware of how much *space* Aiden takes up on my couch, of how his body is turned toward me, how he's giving me his full and undivided attention. Ignoring the squeezing in my throat, I push on with the story.

"You know that Tony, her father, hates and blames me for what happened. But I didn't tell you to what extent. How his sorrow turned to anger, which turned to revenge. He's made it his life's mission to haunt me, to *destroy* me."

A deep breath calms me as the memories I've tried so hard to repress come flooding forward. My focus shifts to the wall behind Aiden, because if I look directly at him, I don't think I'll be able to continue.

"The accident happened in November of my junior year, and that was a really bad time for me. We were still living in Mayford, my hometown. I was mourning the loss of my father, who, despite everything, I loved and missed more than anything. I was thinking about what I could have done differently to prevent the death of my father and of Sabrina, playing the accident over and over in my head, torturing myself with the what-ifs. I was consumed with guilt and was an emotional wreck. Add that to my broken arm and other physical injuries from the accident, and I was not good company at the time. I wanted to be alone, and I was haunted by my father and Sabrina, an innocent little girl. I even slipped into the back of the church during her funeral, just to torture myself some more."

His strong but gentle hand grabs my face, pulling me out of my reverie, and turns me so that I'm looking deep into his eyes.

"Thea," Aiden starts. "It wasn't your fault. I've said it before—"

"Aiden, stop." I cut off his assurances and pull myself from his grasp. "Please. Just let me tell the whole story. No interruptions. Okay?"

He hesitates for a second but then reluctantly nods. Satisfied with his reply, I force the memories to come back to me.

"In the weeks following the accident, I'd walk. I never told anyone where I was going or how long I'd be out, because the point was to be alone. I was trying to clear my head, trying to mourn my father. Night or day, snowing or sunny, I was outside, not paying attention to my surroundings and hoping to clear my thoughts."

My vision blurs as I recall the next part, my heart beating faster, as if I'm reliving the experience again.

"Just over a year ago, after dinner, I decided to go for a walk despite the biting cold and inky darkness spreading through the air. My thoughts consumed me and I didn't notice that a truck had been following me since the moment I'd left my house. I didn't turn to look when it pulled up beside me and a door opened. I barely blinked when there were heavy footsteps crunching in the snow behind me. Only when I heard my name being called did I turn around. Only then did I realize that it was too late for me to stop living in the past and to start paying attention to the present."

My throat feels like it's closing, and just when I'm sure I'm going to pass out, a comforting hand lands on my leg, just above my knee. Aiden's hand tightens on my leg, and he doesn't need to speak out loud for me to know what he's saying. He's here with me. I'm safe. Silently borrowing his strength, I force the words out.

"There was a man, pointing a gun at my head. Shock took over, and I didn't recognize him at first. He held the gun on me with callous determination, his eyes dark and empty, like an open grave. Tony Derando, Sabrina's father. He said that I killed his daughter. I replied that I didn't, but I was sorry that she'd passed. That's when his expression changed."

The wall behind Aiden suddenly looks very interesting, and I keep my attention there.

I can't explain it. He was an empty shell of a man with no hope, with no desire to move on. It was like he didn't care about the future, didn't care about anything except right then, that moment. It was like he saw nothing except a way to relieve the anger, relieve the pain over losing the most important—the only important—thing in his life. His rage radiated off him, and even then I knew that he had a need to exact revenge, to hurt me.

At this point I zone out, the memories rushing back to me as if a floodgate has opened and the angry water is speeding out, almost overwhelming me with how clearly I remember everything. It's as if I'm reliving the moment my life changed forever as I share my story with Aiden.

"Tony was going to shoot me. Should I try to run, talk him down, or just accept my fate? He took the decision from me when he suddenly lifted his arm and smashed me over the head with the end of the gun, and that's the last thing I remember."

4

The first thing I noticed was soreness. The pounding in my head was hard to ignore, but the rest of my joints felt stiff, as if I had been thrown around. I was lying on the floor and hazily sat up, rubbing my head, my body pushing to stay conscious.

My feet were completely bare but I could've sworn I'd left the house with shoes on. The light-blue color of my cast wasn't obstructed by my winter jacket. Where *was* my jacket? It was cold, I hadn't left the house without it.

But I was no longer outside, I was in a small bathroom. Standing up, I assessed my surroundings. In the bathroom there was just a toilet and a sink; there were no mirrors or cabinets, and the walls were bare and windowless. There was an eerie chill in the air, which had nothing to do with the fact that I was just in jeans and a T-shirt.

The door wouldn't open. It wasn't locked because the knob turned, so there was probably some type of dead-bolt system added to the outside too. Heavy things seemed to be pushed in front of the door as well, since when I looked through the tiny slit between the door and the threshold, I was met with some type of sturdy, wooden furniture.

Tony had taken me, and I knew it was only a matter of time before he came to finish his plans with me. I had to get *out*. There were no windows, so my only hope was to escape through the door. I tried to escape for hours, sitting on the hard floor and kicking at the door until the heels of my feet bled. Desperation took hold. Even punching and clawing at the door and its hinges until my fingers were numb and my knuckles were raw and bloody did nothing. I was hopelessly trapped.

After the adrenaline and desperation of trying to escape faded, frustration at my own uselessness clawed at my chest. I wasn't strong enough to break the door down, and I wasn't smart enough to devise a plan. All I could do was think of all the ways Tony could hurt me—all the ways he would torture or kill me. All I could think about was how before he took me, he seemed to lack all compassion or humanity—he'd had the eyes of a desperate man with nothing to lose, nothing left to live for.

There was only one thing left to do—lay down on the floor and cry. I cried so hard that my stomach ached and I could barely breathe through the gasping. I cried until there were no more tears left for my body to expel. Laying there on the bathroom floor, staring at the white ceiling littered with pot lights, I was overtaken by a sense of emptiness.

I didn't bother to wipe the hot tears from my face, and exhaustion took over. I had used my anger and fear to try and escape to no avail, and crying had accomplished nothing except giving me a blotchy, puffy face. It was then that the lights cut out, enveloping me in a darkness that rivaled my growing despair, a darkness that matched the hole in my heart where hope had been. I lay there in the dark, tearstained and bloody, feeling hollow and drained, and allowed sleep to distract me from my new reality. Time didn't exist while I was trapped in the bathroom. I was told later that I was missing for three days—and it was arguably the scariest and worst three days of my life.

Tony never visited me, never brought me food. I didn't know where I was or what Tony wanted. I didn't know if he was planning on torturing me or killing me, or even just leaving me there to starve to death. I was weak, drained of energy, and survived by drinking water from the tap and from sheer force of will.

The lights of the bathroom flickered on, and it was obvious Tony was coming. It was so bright that I had to shield my eyes with my arm until they adjusted to the brightness again. The last thing I was prepared for was a confrontation, but when I heard heavy things being moved away from in front of the door, something in me snapped.

My survival instincts and my burning will to live gave me a rush of adrenaline. All I knew was that I wasn't about to let myself be a victim—I wasn't going out without a damn good fight. If I was going to die, I was going to do so knowing that I'd taken a chunk of Tony with me.

My breathing was loud in my ears and my heart beat hard against my rib cage. The blood in my veins sped up as Tony got closer to me. With the lights back on in the bathroom, I surveilled my options. There was no mirror that I could shatter and use as a weapon, no cabinets I could search or unhinge. As the last heavy object slid away, the part of my brain that was being blocked by hunger and fear took over, and my attention narrowed in on the toilet—specifically on the lid of the tank.

I remember reading or seeing somewhere that if you're ever home when there are intruders and have no weapons, the lid of the tank is a great option because it's thick and heavy. In the seconds between when the dead bolt slid open and the doorknob turned, I grabbed the lid, satisfied at feeling its weight, and turned toward the door just as it was pulled open. With all the strength my body could possibly muster—strength I didn't know I possessed—I swung my makeshift weapon without aim as hard as I could in a direction I prayed belonged to Tony's head.

With time simultaneously speeding up and slowing down, the tank lid connected with his skull, the momentum of the impact almost causing me to fall over. His body slammed against the wall and immediately slumped to the floor.

I didn't wait to see if he was unconscious or not. Tossing my weapon to the floor, I jumped over his body and ran out of the bathroom as fast as my weakened body could take me. Sprinting barefoot through the basement, adrenaline pushing me forward. Not registering the pain of my scraped heels, I focused only on the exit and my path to freedom.

I took the steps two at a time, my rising hope briefly deflating when I came into contact with a locked door. Registering movement from somewhere behind me, I frantically jiggled the doorknob and attempted to push the door open, but it stubbornly remained in place. In my haste and fear, I barely noticed the three dead bolts on the door.

As I looked down the staircase, the blood in my veins turned to heavy lead as I made eye contact with a maniacal gaze. Standing at the bottom of the staircase was a bloody, furious Tony.

There wasn't time to take in the damage I had caused, or the details of his facial expression. The second I saw him there, so close to me, so close to overpowering me, I turned back around and set all my attention on the door, ignoring the way my heart had jumped into my throat and the panic that was trying to take over my body.

Fumbling and feeling time slowly slipping away from me as heavy footsteps ascended the stairs, I slid the dead bolts open with shaking hands. Practically falling through the doorway as the door swung open, I slammed it shut behind me in a split-second decision, hoping to momentarily delay Tony and buy a couple more precious seconds.

As I collided with the front door, my hands automatically went straight to the dead bolts before turning the traditional lock and pushing the heavy door open to reveal my awaiting freedom.

Without pausing to look at where Tony was or how close he was to capturing me, I took off the second the door was open. My bare feet pounded against the hard concrete and carried me onto the road, into fresh air that I'd previously taken for granted.

The sun was setting, and there weren't any cars driving down his street. My first instinct was to run, to put as much distance between me and Tony as I possibly could. I barely registered the cold air or my overworked lungs or the new blood escaping from the soles of my feet and mixing with the light layer of snow on the ground. I kept thinking about how I was so close, *so close*, to being safe.

I must have run a couple of blocks before a car drove by, the driver slamming on their brakes at seeing a disheveled, shoeless girl running at a full sprint in the middle of the road. Was it Tony, coming to recapture me? No, it wasn't. An older woman with a soft face who was wearing a pink turtleneck stepped out of the car and rushed to my side to ask me what had happened and what my name was.

I blankly recited my name to her and she gasped and told me that she'd call the police right away. I didn't say or do anything else. All I kept thinking was one word, which played on a continuous loop in my head.

Over.

It was over. I was safe. I could go home. At the time, I didn't know how mistaken I was.

At the police station I told my story countless times. It was there that I first discovered my hatred for those beige chairs and the shrill sound of multiple phones ringing. The police searched Tony's house, his neighborhood, and other places that he might be. They put out an APB on him, but he was never found; it was like he'd disappeared off of the face of the earth, like he'd never existed.

They told me that they wouldn't stop searching for him, but for the time being I should go home, try to live normally, and give them a call if I noticed anything unusual. In other words, they sent me off with a pat on the back and good luck wishes.

I wasn't so confident that this fight was over. They hadn't seen Tony—they hadn't felt his anger, they hadn't seen the way his rage was practically controlling him. He wanted me for a reason; he wasn't just going to let me go off on my way, happily ever after.

Starting the second my mom brought me home from the police station, and for the weeks that followed, I was paranoid, walking on pins and needles in my own house. Every noise startled me, every stranger who looked at me made me uneasy. Someone who wanted to hurt me was out there, and he wouldn't let a little police APB or locked door stop him.

During those weeks the phone calls started. The person on the other end of the line would hang up immediately if I answered. I was getting way too many hang ups from a blocked number for it to just be coincidental—it had to be Tony. I screened my calls, only answering for my mother, but calls from the blocked caller didn't stop.

There was never a voice mail, but I could hear him on the other end of the line—waiting, planning, plotting—a promise that he'd never forget about me. I told the police, of course, and they tried tracking the calls, but he always hung up right away, even when the police urged me to engage him in conversation.

The death threats were unnerving when they started coming in. Notes in the mail directed to me told me how I deserved to die, and how he was going to get justice, no matter what the cost to him was, by making sure I was dead, just like his daughter, Sabrina. My mom took my key to the mailbox away when she found out, but I knew they were still coming, that she was reading them.

I couldn't sleep, I couldn't eat. I was a shell of a girl named Thea going through the motions while living in constant fear. I started learning jujitsu, and working out to build up strength and learn some self-defense, but I was always nervous; I could never be strong enough to beat him.

The last straw came when my friend dropped me off after school to find black spray paint all over the light-pink walls of my room. I stood still, shell-shocked, in my room, silently turning around and taking in the vandalism. Everything on the surface of my four walls was covered in death threats. Black spray paint over my white furniture, over my mirror, over my posters, anything that touched the wall was included in the canvas of spreading hate.

That was when I realized that Tony was beyond your run of

the mill revenge seeker. He was like a wild animal who knew he had his prey caught in his trap, and now he was just toying with his food for amusement. He was teasing me, taunting me, letting me know that I was under his mercy and he could get to me with ease, whenever he wanted. That was when I had my very first panic attack.

After I had calmed down enough, I went to my neighbor's house, where I called my mom and the police. Of course they couldn't find him. They couldn't even prove that it *had* been him, and that was when it was decided that the best thing to do was just to relocate me. They wanted me to pick up and move to a different state, leaving all my friends, my school, and my identity behind.

The federal agents became involved because of who Tony was, and they set everything up. Apparently, he wasn't your average father-turned-stalker, but an actual person with a criminal past. They gave me and my mom new identities, a new house, and a new car, and set her up at a new job. They continuously stressed how important it would be to keep my real identity and story a secret. If I slipped up, then Tony could find me. No social media, no posting things on the internet, and especially no telling people.

In January, I became Isabella Smith, one of the most common names in the United States. I dyed my hair blond and cut it into a short bob, wearing it straight every day instead of my natural long, brown curls. I wore thick-framed glasses that didn't have a prescription in them, and started a new life.

It was good for a while. I let my guard down, made friends, went to school events, and just lived a normal life. I got to enjoy about three months in peace, and started being hopeful about my future. Maybe Tony had given up on looking for me?

It soon became evident that he hadn't, as suddenly that new reality came crashing down on me as the same patterns as before started happening again. The calls to my new phone number, where all I heard was heavy breathing. Then he started leaving voice mails, telling me that he'd find me and make me pay, make me *suffer*.

I was reassured by Agent Dylan, the man assigned to my case, that Tony couldn't track my phone, but that didn't comfort me at all. If he could find my phone number, then he sure as hell could find my house. After that, I was constantly paranoid, and what little sleep I was getting virtually disappeared, making me reliant on sleeping pills.

Not long after that, I came home from school and could tell that something was off. Nothing in my house was out of place, nothing was there that would have alerted me that Tony was there. But somehow, I felt the shift in the atmosphere, felt the tension and dread snaking its way through my body. Grabbing the baseball bat I kept by new habit by the front door, I slowly crept up the stairs.

I tiptoed through the house, holding my breath at every creak the floor made as I got closer and closer to my room. When I finally peered into my room, nothing was out of place, no black spray paint decorated my white walls with death threats. I sighed in relief and slumped against the door frame, placing the bat down and laughing at my own paranoia.

But then I froze—I had celebrated too soon. Something caught my attention: an object sitting innocently on my bed that I had definitely not put there. I tiptoed over to it, not daring to draw a single breath, as if it would manifest into Tony himself and fulfill the promises he'd made about revenge.

Looking at the object that was taunting me, I recoiled in horror when realization sank in. Sitting innocently on my bed was a doll, with a very real, very sharp kitchen knife stabbed through its head. As if that wasn't creepy enough, the doll had been altered to look just like me—not Thea, but *Isabella.* And as if that didn't get the point that he knew what I looked like across, stapled to the doll was a picture of me, as Isabella. It had been taken a couple of days ago, as I was leaving school, and I wasn't aware that it had been taken. It looked like a surveillance picture, like Tony was following me and taking pictures of my whereabouts.

Tony knew where I was—he knew what Isabella looked like. He had been in my house, in my room, without anyone having the slightest clue. I dropped the doll on my bed and took a couple of steps backward, shocked by the revelation that Tony had found me, and was taking his time toying with me. Before I could decide what to do, there was a loud crash, and I instinctively ducked to the floor and threw my hands over my head as pieces of glass rained down on me.

I barely registered the glass creating tiny slices on my arms as a heavy object thumped onto the floor next to me. Once the glass stopped falling, I hesitantly looked at the object—a brick had been thrown through my window. As I rushed over to the window, I was met with the taillights of a truck speeding off into the distance.

Tony was here. He was outside, and he knew where I was.

I walked over the glass, not caring that I was only in socks, and picked up the brick. There was a note attached to it, Tony's crude writing spelling out: "You can run *Isabella,* but I will *always* find you."

I dropped the brick on the floor and sprinted out of my house, not stopping until a few blocks later when I got to a friend's house. I didn't explain anything, didn't justify why I had shown up bleeding, breathless, and shoeless at her front door. I asked her if I could stay there for a bit until my mom arrived, lamely muttering something about how I'd lost my house keys. I called my mom from the bathroom and she took care of the rest.

Like the previous time, there was no trace of Tony, no evidence of where he was or where he could've gone. After a few days in a hotel, during which I refused to sleep and was constantly paranoid, it was quickly arranged for us to be relocated again.

Like last time, my mother and I were given new identities in a new state, a new house, a new car, a new job, and a new school. In May of my junior year, I became Hailey Johnson, with straight, black hair and colored contacts that made my eyes blue. I thought maybe this time it would be different. Maybe as Hailey I could live comfortably and make new friends, get involved in school, and just live normally.

I didn't know then that because I was Hailey, people would die.

For a few weeks I was constantly paranoid. I refused to take my sleeping pills, which meant I was completely sleep deprived, which only made me more paranoid, and the vicious cycle continued.

After a few weeks of nothing out of the ordinary happening, I let my guard down. I started feeling like a regular, normal teenage girl with regular, normal teenage-girl problems. I even got a part-time job at a clothing store at the mall.

Being Hailey was working out so great. Everyone was super-nice, I made lots of friends and even went out on a couple of dates. My boss was cool and I loved my job. I got to work with my new best friend, Ashley, and on our Friday-night shifts, our boss would order take-out for everyone. Even the new jujitsu gym I'd joined was bigger and better equipped than the last two. I finally felt at peace, like I was finally somewhere I could call home.

When I made it three months without receiving any odd phone calls or death threats, I cried tears of joy for ten minutes straight, then celebrated by eating an entire Nutella cheesecake all by myself and not even regretting it. But like always, my happiness didn't last too long.

This time, the way Tony made his reappearance was different. It was like he didn't care about toying with me and teasing me anymore—he just wanted the job done, to fulfill his own twisted sense of justice. He skipped the phone calls and death threats and break-ins, and went straight to finding me.

A couple of days after I started my senior year as Hailey Johnson, I was completely unaware of how I would never get to be Hailey again, never get to see my friends again.

It was like any other day. I drove to work, walked into the mall and waved hi to Frank, one of the security guards I'd gotten to know, and started my regular weeknight shift. The mall wasn't too busy but I was still finding things to do to keep myself occupied. We were about to close, the mall shutting down in twenty minutes, when I took a quick break to eat my Nutella sandwich and text my friends.

Ashley stuck her head into the back room. "Hailey, there's a guy here looking for you."

"Is it Hunter? I told him I was still hungry and he likes to surprise me by bringing me food."

As I stood up, Ashley shook her head, her eyes shifting to look at something behind her, something on the other side of the door that I couldn't see, and I noticed how she was sweating despite the usual chill in the store.

"He . . . he told me to tell you that he's your father. He was very adamant about that."

I froze where I was. "Ash, you know my father is dead," I said slowly.

I'd been best friends with Ashley for months, practically since the first day I'd moved here. I hadn't told her how my dad died, but she knew he was gone, and by the way she was acting, she was uncomfortable with the man out there.

She nodded her head slightly but her jaw was tight, her movements stiff. Now I was positive something was wrong. All that was in the break room was a table and some chairs, a microwave, a small filing cabinet, and a bulletin board with some memos for the staff.

"Okay, I'll be right out," I said loud enough for the man I assumed was right behind Ashley to hear, the man who'd been hunting me for almost a year now.

Ashley, who had been working here for years and who'd gotten me this job, exaggeratedly looked back and forth between me and the small filing cabinet, telling me a story that I got immediately.

"I'll tell him you'll be right out," she said, disappearing back behind the door.

I couldn't help myself. I peeked out the staff door and the floor practically fell out from under me. It was him. He was tapping his foot and glaring angrily at everyone who crossed his path. I didn't even have to see his face to know who it was. I saw him every night in my nightmares. He'd found me. He just hadn't followed his usual pattern of teasing and torturing me first.

He was anxious for the kill.

There were a few other people in the store, all oblivious to the hostage situation taking place. I felt cornered even though Tony hadn't noticed me. I didn't know what to do. I couldn't run and risk Tony hurting people because of me. I couldn't fight him and risk failing and having him hurt people. I didn't want anyone, especially Ashley, to get hurt because of me. That group of preteens looking at leggings was not going to have their lives cut short because of me. That pregnant mother and her young daughter were not going to die because of me.

Swiftly moving to the filing cabinet, trying to figure out what Ashley was telling me, I opened the first drawer and found it stuffed with envelopes. I couldn't figure out what Ashley wanted me to find here.

My breathing got heavier and my head spun. Tony was going to kill me and I had nothing to use against him except my own two hands.

As I closed the drawer with some force, a rattling drew my attention, so I opened the drawer again and shifted around the mess of envelopes. My hand connected with something solid, and I pulled it out, feeling slightly comforted by its weight. It was an envelope opener, one of those knife-shaped ones, like older people use. It was not the sharpest, but I could use it to distract him enough to get away, maybe even aim for an eye.

I mumbled a thanks to Ashley as I stuck the opener into my combat boot, my pulse speeding up as I promised myself that I was not going to die that day.

I stood in front of the door, preparing to come face to face with the man who could end my existence the second he saw me. But before I gathered the strength to walk out the door and live my worst fear, the door swung open, taking me by surprise and making me jump backward out of the way. Ashley entered, with Tony shuffling in behind her. The door swung shut, cutting off my oxygen supply with it.

"Thea." A smile slowly spread across his face.

He shoved Ashley at me, and that was when I noticed the gun. I froze, not knowing what to do, my previous confidence draining from my body.

"Give me your phone," he said to Ashley, whose face paled as she handed it to him. Tony smashed it on the floor, crushing it with his foot for extra measure. Then he moved behind me and pressed the cold gun into my back.

Ashley looked at me, an apology written on her face, but it wasn't necessary. She shouldn't feel guilty about this. This was my mess, my fault.

"Scream, and I kill her," he said.

Then he raised his gun and smashed my best friend over the head, and her body went limp, her head bouncing on the floor from the impact, just like he had done to me all those months ago. I covered my mouth to stop the scream from escaping my lips, somehow knowing that he'd do worse if I drew attention to us.

My best friend was bleeding all over the floor, her head at an unnatural angle, her body splayed out like the murder victim she was on her way to becoming.

My cheeks were wet from salty tears as I realized that if she wasn't already dead from the impact, she'd probably die from the injury if it wasn't treated as soon as possible.

Tony pressed his gun into my side, his slimy voice instructing me, "We're going to walk through the mall and to my truck. If you draw attention to us, I'll kill anyone who tries to help. Then when

I find you again, I will take my time torturing you. Understand?"

As the tears streamed down my face, I nodded silently, still looking at my best friend, who would probably bleed out and die because of me. Prodded by the gun, I reluctantly turned away from the bloody sight on the floor and took a step toward the door to leave the break room.

"Wait," he said.

He smothered my mouth with his repulsive hand, pulling me in closer to him. Before I could even try to maneuver myself out of his hold, my eyes widened when I felt a hard sting on my outer thigh. I didn't process what had happened until I looked down. When I saw the blood, I felt a heat like nothing I'd ever imagined, and a hot pain radiated through my leg from the spot where Tony had stabbed me with a pocketknife.

He yanked the knife out with a twist and I screamed against his hand.

"That's to make sure you can't run from me this time," he whispered, his breath vile against my ear.

With his gun hand, the one not smothered against my mouth, he reached down to my wound and forcefully pushed his finger into it, making me squirm and cry in pain. I could feel the sting all the way up my spine.

"And that was for fun," he told me with a gleeful smile.

My eyes widened when he brought his bloody finger up to his face and put it in his mouth, savoring the taste of my pain and misery. He smiled a warped smile, his dark eyes lighting up at my obvious fear and disgust.

"Just remember: do something wrong and people die. Let's go." He removed his hand from my mouth and forced me to walk, the gun pressed inconspicuously into my back.

I didn't get a chance to look back at my best friend, who was bleeding out on the floor, or think of the pain in my leg. I just did what he said, stepping out of the back room and into my uncertain future.

The few people who had been in the store had left, leaving it empty, filled only with the pop music that was always on repeat. It was a good thing no one was in the store—I didn't want to risk Tony hurting anyone else. The man had savored the taste of my blood for goodness' sake! Who knew what else he would do?

We exited the store and walked toward the stairs. For some reason, the elevator music that filled the mall seemed blaringly loud—maybe because the mall wasn't as busy as it usually was. My sluggish brain refused to come up with an escape plan. But I refused to give up that easily, to let him torture me, kill me. I needed to find a way to get away from him without getting anyone else hurt.

Before we got to the stairs, Frank, the regular security guard, saw us. He was the nicest man. He had two kids a bit older than I was, and was friendly to everyone. He had people who loved and cared for him, and even though he was the security guard, I couldn't have him notice Tony and his gun. Frank would have tried to be a hero. Tony didn't care who he hurt. I forced myself to look away, praying that Frank wouldn't notice me or the bloody mess all over my jeans.

"Hey, Hailey!"

Tony's grip tightened on my arm and his gun pushed harder into my back, both hard enough to bruise.

"Hey, Frank."

We kept walking. Tony started to steer me in a different direction, away from Frank. We were almost at the stairs when Frank stopped us. "Hailey, there's blood all over your pants."

In a split second, Tony removed the gun from my back and shot Frank. Time slowed as my friend clutched his chest and fell down, blood spilling through the slits between his fingers.

Shaking off the shock, I acted quickly. Pulling the letter opener out of my combat boot, I plunged it into Tony's stomach. The impact forced him to drop the gun, but then he landed a punch to my face that caused me to stumble back. Nothing I'd learned from jujitsu and self-defense classes came to my mind—it was all gone like a child's balloon being ripped from their hands in a violent windstorm. I scrambled for the gun while Tony pulled the letter opener out of his gut. The cold steel was just in my grasp when Tony landed a kick to my ribs, and I toppled over onto the floor. He kicked me again and put his knee on top of me, letting his full weight pin my small frame.

"I'm going to enjoy making your death a slow one," he growled, clutching the bloody opener in his hand.

In this position, on my back and his knee on my stomach, a memory from practicing jujitsu surfaced of how to escape this position.

Tony raised his arm to stab me, and using his momentum against him, I brought my knee under his butt and bridged my hips at the same time, driving up toward the sky and causing him to lose his balance. He fell toward me but I put my forearms in front of my face so he wouldn't land on it. He was forced to put his hands down to stop himself from smashing his face on the concrete floor, and his bleeding stomach came to rest on my forearms.

Then, adrenaline pumping, I abandoned all proper form and technique, and before he could regain his balance, I drilled my fist into his wound, hearing him yell, and used my hips and legs to throw him off of me and roll him onto his side. I sat on my butt and kicked him with the heel of my foot, then stumbled to get up.

Before I could even think of reaching for the gun again, I was violently shoved, sending me tumbling, and knocking the air out of my lungs. My head banged against everything and my body was tossed around like it was a rag doll. The spinning stopped and I look around in a haze, barely registering anything I was seeing. Everything was sore and I started coughing, blood spilling out of my mouth and onto my hand.

I forced myself out of the haze and sat up, realizing that I was sitting at the bottom of the staircase. Tony had pushed me down the stairs.

I stood up, my adrenaline helping numb the pain my body should have been feeling. I looked at the top of the staircase and we made eye contact. I had a sudden flashback of the first time I escaped from his house. The two of us on opposite sides, staring each other down, separated by only a few steps. He was staring down at me with a rage and a hate so venomous you could ignite it.

He raised the gun and without a second thought, I sprinted through the mall, gunshots sounding off behind me.

I ran out of the mall where there was already a police presence, and they noticed me running toward them. With raised arms, I approached the ones that hadn't already stormed inside. I told them what had happened. I told them that Ashley was bleeding out in the back room of a store, that Frank was shot in the chest, and other people may have been shot as well.

I did not tell them my real name.

5

Strong arms encircle me, pulling me into a comforting embrace and out of the trance I'd entered.

I hadn't realized that I'd started crying—Aiden kept his promise and hadn't interrupted me. His face is unreadable.

I rub the tears from my face. "My injuries weren't too bad in comparison to those of the others—just a concussion, bruising, some stitches, and a couple of broken ribs—but I didn't care about any of that. After that I became Amelia Collins, and then I started at King City High a couple of weeks later. I was supposed to keep a low profile and not make friends, so that I wouldn't get attached when I inevitably have to leave, or watch them get hurt when Tony finds me like he always does."

Aiden opens his mouth to say something but I keep talking. "But then I met you and Char and Anna and everyone else, and you guys wormed your way into my heart. I've never had friends like this before, and believe me, it kills me to have kept this secret from you. But you understand now why I had to, right? Why I couldn't tell you about my real identity? The more people who know, the more chance there is that Tony finds me and hurts the people I love most."

I pull out of his comforting embrace, instantly missing his warmth. "Last time people *died* because of me. Tony shot people because of me. Ashley survived but Frank, and the others caught in the cross fire, didn't. I can't do anything to risk Tony finding me again, because it's not only my life that's in danger because of Tony, it's everyone's who's around me too.

"I know you opened up to me and told me things that you've never told anyone else. I know that you've been totally honest with me and trusted me to do the same. And I'm so sorry that I couldn't tell you about this, and that I've had to keep secrets from you. But just know that all this time, it's been the real me. I may have a different name, but I'm still the same person you know and opened up to. I just . . . I did it for my safety, for your safety, for everyone's safet—"

I'm cut off when Aiden surprises me by hugging me tightly to him, and I melt into his embrace.

"It's okay. I understand why you did what you did. You're so strong, Thea," he says, and his deep voice fills me with relief. "I'm sorry you had to go through all of that."

Aiden has single-handedly pushed off the giant weight resting on my chest. It feels so good to finally tell someone what I've been through—for someone to truly see me, the real me. To know that someone is here for me, unconditionally. Not because they have to be, but because they *want* to be. Because they *choose* to be.

Aiden lightly rubs my back, not even getting mad that I'm ruining his shirt with my tears. He moves slightly back so that he can see me, and moves his hand to gently force me to look up at him.

"None of it is your fault, Thea. You did not kill Sabrina. You did not kill or even hurt any of those people." He emphasizes each word, as if to really make me understand. "You do not deserve any of this, okay? You don't deserve to constantly run from Tony or to torture yourself with memories of your past, or to be so scared and plagued with nightmares that you have to take fucking sleeping pills to get some rest. You're a good person, Thea. Stop thinking that you are personally responsible for all the shitty things happening around you."

I just told him about my damaged past, about all the lies I've been telling, about all the people who were hurt because of me, and he's telling me that I'm a good person? He's not mad or repulsed by me. He's looking at me like I'm the bravest and strongest person he's ever met. I act without thinking; I can't help myself.

I draw my arms around Aiden's neck and bring my lips to his, pulling him in close to me. He's taken off guard but recovers quickly, kissing me back with an intensity and passion that rivals the hottest flame, the brightest star.

His hands tighten on my waist and like last time, he quickly lifts me so that I'm straddling him on the couch, my knees on either side of his body. His arms wrap tighter around me, pulling me close, deepening the kiss as fireworks erupt in my stomach.

It feels like everything I'd been through—all the times I'd had to move, all my brushes with death, and all those terrified, sleepless nights—have been worth it for this. For Aiden. He pulls back suddenly, cutting the kiss much shorter than I would like it to be.

"Wait," Aiden says, guilt and horror written all over his face. "The first day we met, the day you ran into me in the hallway and I dropped you onto the floor in front of your class. Your ribs were injured because you'd just been in a fight with Tony—you'd just been pushed down the stairs."

He's talking more to himself than to me, but I answer him anyway. "Well, technically, yes, but I told you I didn't blame you—"

"What the fuck is wrong with me? I am the shittiest person ever. I felt awful before when I found out about your ribs, but now that I know *why*. Fuck, Thea, I'm sor—"

"Aiden!" I cut him off. "If I didn't already have healing ribs and you did that, nothing would have even happened. If you did that to me now I wouldn't be hurt. I'd probably be pissed and thinking of a way to get you back, but I wouldn't be hurt. You didn't know."

His thumb gently strokes my cheek as he looks right through to my soul. "I'd never hurt you," he says softly. "And I'm sorry for the times I have, even if they were unintentional."

His words have a deeper meaning, and I know he's not just referring to my ribs.

My heart stutters at his honest words, at this guy who's being so open and vulnerable with me when to the rest of the world he keeps an impassive, tough, and confident façade. I remember how he always softens when he's looking at me. I pull myself back into him, burying my face in his neck and instantly realizing how good he smells. His arms tighten around me, making me feel like there has never been any place I need to be other than right here, in Aiden's strong arms. After Aiden's reaction to my past and his comforting me, I realize that there is no mistaking this emotion that I'm feeling, that I feel whenever Aiden so much as glances in my general direction.

I've fallen in love with Aiden Parker.

Shit.

6

Aiden and I spent the afternoon lounging around on the couch, watching TV and occasionally stealing earth-shattering kisses, and we are now in the kitchen. The day passed by so quickly—telling secrets does that, makes time move at lightning speed—but I feel lighter than I have in ages.

"Should I call you Thea or Amelia?" Aiden asks me as we're setting the table for when our friends get here.

This is the most open and vulnerable I've ever been with anyone, and it feels really good. Actually, it feels *fantastic* to know that someone knows the real me, and still likes me despite my fucked up past, present, and, let's be honest, future.

It helps that this person is Aiden. Now he knows my dark past, just like I know his, and I think we might be stronger for it, closer . . . not that we're a couple or anything.

"You've been calling me Thea since you found out."

"Because that's your name," he says. "But when you mumble to yourself, you refer to yourself as Amelia, not Thea."

I ball up a napkin and launch it at his head with a laugh, and he easily deflects it with an effortless wave of his hand.

"Hey, I'm not crazy, okay?"

"Says the girl who talks to herself."

"Plenty of normal people have conversations with themselves," I say.

"But they usually talk to themselves *in their heads*."

"To-mae-toe, to-mat-oe."

He hides a smirk from me, knowing he's won, but then I get serious about his question. "When I move, I get in the mindset that Thea doesn't exist anymore. I'm Hailey or Amelia or whatever other name I'm given. That's the way I was taught to think—it's safer."

He puts the last glass down and turns his full attention to me. "Would you prefer it if I called you Amelia?"

Looking at him there, his tall frame taking up space in my kitchen, a sense of comfort flows through me, melting any worries I may have had. I think honestly about his question and about what I *want*, not about what I think I need to do.

I haven't been called my real name in so long; it's nice to be reminded of who I am—of Thea Kennedy. Plus, hearing the way my name sounds in Aiden's perfect, deep voice, just seems right.

I smile shyly, as if this admission somehow makes me even more vulnerable. "I'd like it if you called me Thea—only when we're alone, of course. And only if you can manage not to slip up in front of everyone."

His eyes light up briefly before he masks it, as if I've given him the answer he was secretly hoping for, almost like this small act is verification that I trust him with something huge. And clearly I do. I trust Aiden without hesitation, with my life—which is what it quite literally comes down to.

"Your secret's safe with me."

"I know." I get serious again. "Really, Aiden, thank you. For always being there for me. I know I'm a handful sometimes, and I know I've caused a lot of drama between us and Kaitlyn and the Silvers. But I do recognize everything you do for me—for everyone—and you never get a thank you. So thank you. For keeping my secret, for being so understanding, for making me not feel so alone—"

He cuts me off when he closes the space between us with two big steps, grabs my face in his hands and forces me to look up at him.

"Don't thank me for that. I'm here for you. Always."

My heart hammers in my chest and I'm unable to string together the words needed to make a coherent sentence with him so close, looking at me like I'm all he's ever needed.

He leans in toward me, his lips close to mine but never quite making it. Because the doorbell rings. And we pull apart.

I scream internally. *Great timing everyone. You couldn't have waited a couple of minutes?*

The doorbell rings a couple more times, our friends either freezing their asses off in the cold December air or anxious to see Aiden.

Aiden suddenly seems so far from me. I gesture at the hallway. "I think that's for you."

The doorbell rings some more.

"I guess I should get it." Aiden chuckles and gives me one last look before moving to the door.

He opens it, and he's instantly tackled by Annalisa, the force catching him off guard and causing him to take a few steps back.

"I knew you didn't do anything. How dare you scare us like that being all mysterious and brooding and not giving us any answers?" She releases him from her tight hug to scold him. "I mean, seriously? 'Go home and stop worrying, everyone?' Do you even know us? Is it ever possible to stop worrying about you?"

If you didn't know Aiden, you'd think he was annoyed by Annalisa's scolding, but we can all tell he's loving her pestering.

"Next time I'm arrested I'll remember not to order you to go home." He smirks.

Annalisa gasps before she fixes a death glare on Aiden, made even more intimidating by her signature black smoky eye and red lipstick. "There better not be a next time, Aiden Parker."

Everyone laughs as the rest of the group hugs Aiden and expresses their gratitude that he's not in jail anymore.

Noah's the last one through the door. He smiles at Aiden and raises his arms as if to hug him. "*Bestie!*"

He moves toward Aiden, but then at the last minute pushes him aside and engulfs me in a bear hug.

"I missed you so much," he says as I laugh and return his hug.

"I always miss you, Noah."

Aiden shakes his head as he closes the front door.

Noah releases me and turns to Aiden. "Oh, Aiden. Didn't see you there. Back from betraying your best friend, I see?"

We all look at Noah with confusion.

"What are you talking about, man?" Mason asks, and we all follow him into the kitchen, where he, Julian, and Chase put down the pizza boxes they were holding.

"I mean, I thought we were all bros. We were supposed to be sitting in jail together. Not sitting there watching you get arrested," Noah says.

We laugh as Noah and Aiden hug. Noah's making jokes; of course, humor is his only setting.

"Honestly, out of any of us, I would've thought Noah would be the first one to get arrested," Julian admits as we all sit around the table and grab a slice of pizza.

"What? Why me?"

"Come on, Noah," Mason says, "you're the most likely out of all of us to do something stupid and get arrested."

"What? I am a perfect, law-abiding citizen! I'm a good boy when the cops are involved."

"Oh really?" Mason challenges. "What about that time you got pulled over for speeding and the cops asked if you'd had anything to drink, and you thought you'd be funny and reply 'Just the blood of my enemies who are currently stuffed in my trunk, if that counts.'"

We burst out laughing, Charlotte almost spitting out the water she was drinking.

Noah raises his hands innocently, a pizza slice in each one. "In my defense, I thought he'd know I was joking! Not ask me to get out of the car and do a search of it!"

I smile affectionately at Noah as we share stories about the stupid things he's done.

My kitchen seemed so big and empty just a few moments ago, but not so much anymore. Looking around the table, eating pizza with everyone, laughing and joking and having a good time, I can't help but feel like this is where I belong, especially after having just relived the past couple of places I'd lived, or even the crazy events of the last twenty-four hours. None of the previous towns have truly felt like home, not the way King City does.

Julian, Chase, and Mason argue over who gets the last piece of pizza, and Annalisa decides that she, in fact, is the most deserving of the piece. Noah's doing an impersonation that makes Charlotte laugh so hard she's gasping for air, and Aiden's looking at me with a smile that reaches his eyes and fills me with such joy. My stomach twists when I think about how I'll be leaving soon, that I'm keeping that part to myself, selfishly wanting to feel safe and normal for a few more days.

After all the pizza has been devoured and jokes about Aiden's time in jail gotten out of the way, the conversation progresses to a more serious matter: why Greg was bruised and bloody, found dead in front of Aiden's front door, with Aiden's lost cell phone at the crime scene.

Julian rubs the back of his neck. "The only information we have is that Greg's time of death was around six o'clock. We don't know anything else about what happened yesterday night."

Annalisa's phone vibrates on the table for what must be the fifth time since we started eating, and like every time before, she looks at the caller ID, scowls, then ignores the call. If it wasn't for the hard set of her jaw, I'm sure someone would've asked her about it.

"What was the timeline they established for you, Aiden? Do you remember anything suspicious?" She sets the phone down on her lap under the table.

"Nothing. I dropped off the twins at their friend Tyler's, got to Mason's around four thirty, we left to pick up the pizza, and got to Amelia's around seven. Just a normal night," Aiden says.

"Until you got arrested," Chase adds.

Annalisa's phone vibrates, and again, she ignores the call, but whoever the caller was leaves a sour expression on her face.

"Anna? Maybe you should just get the phone. It seems

important," Charlotte suggests, pulling the open ends of her knit sweater together.

Annalisa huffs and turns her phone off. "This caller hasn't been important to me since he ran off when my mom died and chose heroin over his own sister."

We look at her in stunned silence. She's talking about her older brother—or half brother—Luke. It was just a few days ago when Luke approached Annalisa at the Tracks, begging to talk to her for a moment, wanting back into her life. That had left her raw, him showing up, clean for the first time in years, wanting to be a part of her life. She's kept quiet about it, and after yelling that he had killed her mother and storming off, she hasn't mentioned him since, and we haven't pushed.

"Do you want to talk about it?" Mason asks gently as Julian pulls out his own vibrating phone.

Julian looks at the caller ID and sighs, a look of resignation on his face paired with a clenching of his jaw. He holds up his phone to show Annalisa who's calling, and her kohl-lined eyes narrow into slits.

She grabs the phone from Julian and answers it, not giving the caller the chance to speak. Her voice is hard and threatening. "Leave me the fuck alone."

She immediately hangs up, stopping herself seconds before slamming her boyfriend's phone onto the table.

Noah bites his lip as if to stop himself from talking, trying to take a cue from the rest of us, who remain deathly quiet, and fails. "I'm sorry, Anna. We've been trying to ignore the fact that you're very pissed off at someone, but it's hard. Like, you're angrier than my mom when she's just home from work and I forgot to take the chicken out of the freezer like she asked me to do hours before."

The only indication Annalisa gives to show that she finds

Noah amusing is that she doesn't roll her eyes as forcefully as she normally would.

"It's Luke," she says.

We look at her expectantly, having already pieced that information together ourselves. When she doesn't elaborate, Julian continues for her.

"He's been calling her all day. We haven't really heard from him since that night at the Tracks."

"And you're not going to answer? What if it's an emergency?" Chase squirms in his seat under Annalisa's intense stare.

"The only reason I haven't blocked his number yet is in case I need blood or an organ or something. But even then, we don't have the same father, so maybe we won't even be a match," Annalisa deadpans, no hint of joking in her voice.

Poor Annalisa. Other than Luke, the only family she really has are the people sitting in front of her right now. I can relate to that. My mother is absent the majority of the time and even when she is around, I still feel like we're miles away. The people crowding my kitchen table right now are the ones I feel I can call when I need help; the ones I can depend on.

I've never asked Aiden about Annalisa's past because like her, I also have things I'd rather keep a secret, things that I don't want anyone knowing. I understand secrets and messy pasts, and this is one that Annalisa should have the right to tell me and Charlotte about or not, since we're the only people at the table who don't really know her story.

"I mean, who does he think he is? Just calling me up like nothing ever happened?" Annalisa rants.

"He's sober now, Anna. Maybe he wants to make amends," Mason says softly.

Annalisa looks at Mason like she's trying to use her brain to make his head explode. "You're supposed to be on my side, Mason! Why are you sticking up for him?"

Mason shrinks into himself but holds his ground anyway. "You've been holding on to this extreme hatred and anger toward your brother for so long. It can't be good for you. Don't you just want to get rid of that and move on? Be happy?"

"I am happy. You guys right here are all I need. I don't need or want anyone else."

"Maybe you should just hear him out. See what he has to say," Aiden suggests. "If you decide you don't want anything to do with him, at least you won't spend the rest of your life regretting the what-ifs, and wondering what it was he had to say."

Family is the most important thing to Aiden. I don't think he could even fathom the idea of never speaking to his brothers again. His advice sounds pretty reasonable to me, and the others nod their heads in agreement, not wanting to push Annalisa into something she doesn't want but knowing that it might be best for her in the long run.

Annalisa squares her shoulders. "I will not speak to the man who killed my mother."

Julian puts a comforting hand on Annalisa's thigh. "Babe, heroin killed your mother," he says gently.

Annalisa's mother overdosed on heroin when Annalisa was sixteen, and then her older brother deserted her, leaving her to deal with everything by herself. So that day all that time ago, when Kaitlyn suggested that Annalisa drop out because she'll end up just like her mom, Kaitlyn was suggesting . . . a shiver runs down my spine. Kaitlyn is lower than low.

Annalisa sneers. "And who gave her the heroin? Luke. It all

comes back to Luke, and I will not forgive him for ruining my life."

"You know I'm there for you, always. And I'll always be on your side, but maybe Aiden's right. Just hear Luke out, and then once he says what he needs to say, maybe you'll never hear from him again, until you decide you want to," Julian advises, tucking a piece of hair behind Annalisa's ear.

Annalisa moves her head away from Julian's touch, and his hand falls to his lap. She frowns at the wall in front of her, choosing to ignore her boyfriend's reasoning.

"Julian?" Aiden asks, looking up from his phone. "What was the number Luke used to call you from?"

Julian reads off the number from his phone, Aiden following along while looking at his phone.

"Well, I think I know why Luke has been calling all morning," Aiden says, his facial expression cold and hard.

Annalisa sits up straight. "Did Luke message you?"

"I just got this message from that same number," Aiden answers, then reads the text out loud: "'*Heard what happened. Need to talk to you ASAP. I have information about Greg.*'"

Aiden's phone vibrates again, and he reads the next message: "'*Let's all meet somewhere public. Sweetie's Ice Cream Parlor. Half an hour.*'"

He sets the phone down and looks at us expectantly.

"If Luke has information, we need to go," I say before anyone has the chance to turn the meeting down.

"Do you think he actually has answers?" Annalisa blurts out, her words laced with disbelief. "He's a manipulative asshole, this whole thing could just be an excuse to talk to us."

"We'll never know if we don't go," Mason says.

"You guys don't have to come, but I need to go," Aiden says, grabbing his plate and putting it in the sink.

I stand up automatically. "I'm coming with you."

Aiden looks at me, and for a second I'm positive he'll demand that I stay home, but he doesn't. I bring my plate to the sink and stand in front of him, on the opposite side of the kitchen island, and he gives me a slight nod.

Mason gets up. "I'm coming too."

Noah follows his lead, a smile on his face. "I can never turn down ice cream, even if it is freezing outside. Count me in!"

"Looks like we're all going then," Chase says, and we look at Annalisa to see her decision.

She looks around the table at all of us, finally sighing. "He's my dirtbag brother. If this turns out to be a waste of time, I better be there to hit him."

Hopefully, it's not a waste of time, and he'll have some information that gives Aiden some closure.

7

Moments after we make the decision to meet up with Luke, we clean up my kitchen and head straight out the door for Sweetie's Ice Cream Parlor, hopping into three cars so not everyone has to drive.

No one mentions anything about which car I'll be riding in. I guess it's just known that I'll be with Aiden, and even I just sort of gravitate toward him. Aiden's always had a pull on everyone, always drawn the attention of everyone in a room without even trying. But the way I feel about him is stronger; I feel pulled toward him, like magnets.

Aiden also expects that I'll ride in his car. He leans on the passenger-side door of his Challenger as I lock my front door, waiting for me, and opens the door for me once I come down the steps. But I don't miss the way Mason frowns at us as Aiden closes my door for me. Bundled up in my scarf and mittens, I press the button to turn on my seat warmer. It's just the two of us.

"Are you nervous?" I ask.

"Why would I be nervous?"

"Because we're meeting Luke, who may help us piece together why your stepfather was murdered on your front porch?"

"Shouldn't you be the nervous one?" Aiden answers.

"Why would I be nervous?"

He stops at a red light and looks at me, his expression serious. "Because you haven't seen him since that day at the Tracks, when he saved you from Dave and you decided not to tell anyone about that part of the attack. Not even Anna."

My face heats up from his correct assumption about what happened that night. "What—I—how?—No. How did you know it was Luke who saved me? Did Dave tell you when you found out what happened and went all Rambo on his face?"

"It wasn't that hard to connect the dots, Thea."

Pleasant shivers run down my spine at hearing him say my real name. The light turns green and the car speeds up again.

"I couldn't tell you how I really met Luke. Then you'd have found out about Dave and his friend, who held me while Dave punched me, and I didn't want you to do the exact thing that you ended up doing."

"Dammit, Thea!" He hits the steering wheel. "You expect me to find out that the bastard was too cowardly to fight me so he targeted and cornered *my girl*, and then not make sure that he was shitting his own teeth for weeks? I *absolutely* had to go fight him and anyone else who was involved." He stops at a red light. "I'd do it again too."

Feeling bold and high off of his words, I quickly unbuckle my seat belt and kneel on the seat, put my hand on his strong jaw, and kiss him deeply and passionately, my heart beating erratically in my chest, threatening to explode.

He kisses me back, his hands feeling right at home on my waist. But all too soon I'm pulling away and sitting back in my seat, a stupid smile on my face as I buckle up again, and Aiden takes off when the light turns green.

"Just try not to get into any more fights on my behalf, okay?"

"I make no promises," Aiden says.

I huff out loud, but deep down, his words thrill me, and I can't fight the smile tugging at my lips.

» «

At Sweetie's we find a booth in the back for some privacy and sit down. Only Aiden doesn't have an ice-cream cone or cup in his hands, which, according to Noah, is a big no-no. Apparently, you can never say no to ice cream, even in highly tense situations, using the cones he's holding in each hand as evidence. I offer Aiden some of mine, but he shakes his head.

The booth is a little tight but we all fit. The red seat padding is well worn, with a few random patches covering older tears, but it's still comfortable. Considering it's winter, Sweetie's is pretty busy, and the loud chatter around us fills in the silence as we eat our ice cream.

Julian's the first to spot Luke, but he doesn't call out to him. Annalisa's brother looks a little worse for wear, sporting a black eye and a gash in his lip, his clothing covering any other injuries he might have. He heads straight over to us in a no-nonsense kind of way, managing to seem confident even though it looks like he's limping. He grabs a chair from an empty table and sits at the end of our table instead of in the booth with us. Aiden's the closest to him on one side, and at the other end of the booth closest to Luke is Chase, with Annalisa sitting directly in the middle of the booth, right across from her brother.

"Hi," Luke says, presumably to all of us, but never once looking away from his sister.

Something akin to sympathy crosses Annalisa's face, but it's gone almost as fast as it was there. She crosses her arms and glares into the distance.

"We're here. Tell us what you know." Aiden cuts right to the point.

Luke looks longingly at Annalisa for a couple of seconds before tearing his gaze from her and looking at Aiden.

"I'm sure you've noticed the shiner I'm sporting?" Luke says with a noncommittal gesture at his face.

"I'm guessing it happened last night," Aiden states more than asks.

"Afternoon, actually. But you should've seen the other guy." Luke's voice squeaks in what approaches a laugh.

"Around the same time Greg's injuries also occurred?" Julian asks.

Aiden leans over the table. "Cut the bullshit, Luke. Why are we here?"

Luke sighs and slumps back in his chair. "As you all know, I'm clean now. I'm trying to get my life back together, but it's hard. The friendships I've burned, opportunities I've ruined, relationships I threw away . . ." He looks at Annalisa, who looks away quickly, as if embarrassed to have been caught looking back at him.

He clears his throat. "I just—I want things to go back to the way they were before I got messed up with heroin, the way it should've been if I'd avoided falling in with the wrong crowd."

Annalisa fidgets in her seat, no doubt trying to keep the promise she made before we left—that she wouldn't explode on her brother. She's one of the most stubborn and headstrong people I know. She's determined to remain mad at her brother, so his emotional confession is probably driving her crazy. Julian grabs her hand and she noticeably calms down.

"But my life hasn't been back on track like I want it to be," Luke solemnly continues. "I slipped up. As part of my recovery, I committed to staying sober. No drugs, no prescription medication, and no alcohol. But yesterday, I was just sitting in my self-loathing, thinking of all the ways I fucked my life up, all the steps I could've taken to avoid Mom's death, to avoid losing my sister, the only person who matters in my life right now . . ." He takes a deep breath. "I went to one of my old bars, had a couple of drinks—"

Luke shifts in his seat. "A couple of drinks in, some of my old 'buddies' told me that our old dealer was out of jail, thinking that I'd want to pick up some heroin. But the thought of that dealer had the opposite effect. I didn't want any part of it, I didn't want anything to do with him. In fact, I *hated* him. He got me hooked on the stuff; he ruined my life. He was the little devil on my shoulder, encouraging me to choose the drug over my family, over everything."

I'm holding my breath. Beside me, Aiden tenses. Is he following my train of thought?

Luke runs his hand through his hair and winces, holding his arm close to his chest. "I didn't really think—I knew I had to go confront him. I left the bar and walked around his old neighborhood, not really thinking about anything except my hatred of him."

Oh God, please don't say what I think you're going to say. A large and comforting hand lands on my thigh, and it reminds me to breathe. I put my hand on top of Aiden's without looking at him, entwining my fingers in the spaces between his.

"Eventually, I found him; he was already a little doped up. He smiled and said he'd known it would only be a matter of time until one of his most faithful customers sought him out. I didn't think, I was just so drunk and angry, I threw a punch. We fought, and I don't really remember what happened after that."

"What are you saying, Luke? Why are you telling us this?" Annalisa blurts out, angrily wiping a stray tear from her eye.

He rubs the back of his neck with a little difficulty, looking solemn and regretful.

"I need you to know my side of the story, Anna. I wanted you to know how much I love you and how sorry I am for screwing up."

Annalisa rears her head back as if Luke had delivered an invisible blow.

He takes a deep breath. "I don't know if I did it, I don't know how he ended up at Aiden's house, or even how I woke up at home this morning. But I know how angry and drunk I was, and everything lines up. If I get arrested and thrown in jail for murdering Greg, I wanted you to know that I didn't stop trying to see you. I'll never stop wanting to be back in your life. But if I'm arrested, I don't know if I'll even be able to contact you, and I didn't want you to think it was because I stopped caring."

No one moves. No one breathes. We're all just trying to process what Luke just admitted to.

He killed Aiden's stepfather.

"Well, gang, I guess that mystery is solved. Back to the mystery machine?" Noah imitates Fred from *Scooby-Doo* as he loudly finishes off the rest of his ice cream.

"Noah," Charlotte hisses beside him when everyone shoots him a look. "Now isn't the time."

"Just trying to break the tension." He shrugs.

Aiden ignores Noah, his attention still focused on the man who basically just confessed to murdering his stepfather. "Where were you when you found him? How did he end up in front of my house? With my old cell phone?"

"I honestly don't remember where I found him or how he got to your house. I'm pretty sure I didn't find him at your house or even on your street. I don't even think I killed him! But your cell phone . . ."

"You had his cell phone, didn't you?" Mason realizes what Luke is saying, not trying to hide the accusatory tone in his voice.

"Well, yes, but—"

"What were you planning on doing with it? Keep it to frame Aiden like you did for Greg's murder?" Chase narrows his eyes at him, and I squeeze Aiden's hand, which is still on my thigh.

"What? No!" Luke defends himself a little too loudly, and the other people in the parlor glare at us in annoyance.

They probably think we're just stupid, annoying teenagers getting into a heated discussion about something of little importance, like what the proper text abbreviations are, when we're really discussing the intricate details of a homicide.

If only they knew.

Luke lowers his voice. "Look, I found it at the Tracks when the police crashed the party and everyone scattered."

"You had my phone for almost three weeks, and it didn't occur to you to give it back?" Aiden says.

Luke opens his mouth as if to protest, but Aiden beats him to it. "Don't you dare say you didn't know whose phone it was. Yes, it was locked, but my background picture is of the twins, and I know you know what they look like."

"Yeah, okay, I knew it was yours. I never got around to returning it. I wanted to use it as an excuse to talk to you, to try to convince you to get Anna to talk to me. I must've dropped it when I got in the fight with Greg."

Annalisa scoffs and crosses her arms. "That's a stupid plan and it wouldn't have worked anyway."

Luke looks directly at her, then speaks only to his sister. "Lise, everything I do, it's with the single purpose of getting you back in my life. But I don't think I can fix this fuckup this time. I've been arrested before, my DNA and my prints are in the system. It's only a matter of time until they link me to Greg; I'm probably the last person seen with him anyway. But I'll never stop worrying about you, never forget about how much I screwed you over, no matter how long I'm in jail. You're my sister and I love you, and no amount of hatred or resentment you hold toward me can change that."

I'm not even his sister and still his words pull at my heartstrings. A few more tears escape from Annalisa's eyes before she swipes at them violently, her eye makeup smudging slightly.

"This is stupid. We're done here," she states, trying to get up and leave but failing since she's in the middle of the booth, surrounded by people on both sides.

She swipes some more tears. "Who's the dumbass who designed a booth? Did they not think about how much harder they make it for people to storm off?!"

She stands up on the seat and places her combat boot–clad foot directly on the table despite our protests. She ignores us, stepping right up onto the table and walking on it, jumping off just to the left of Luke without looking at him, ignoring the looks of outrage and disgust being sent to us by the other patrons.

"Anna!" Julian calls after her as she storms out of the parlor and into the cold winter air.

"Guys, do you mind?" Julian looks at Noah, Charlotte, and Chase on his right, who all slide out of the booth so he can chase after his girlfriend. The three of them slide back into the booth once Julian's left Sweetie's, and we all look at each other, as if silently asking, So now what?

"Don't you think you should turn yourself in instead of waiting for the cops to find you and arrest you?" Mason asks.

Luke shakes his head. "Have you ever been in prison before? I'm going to enjoy my time out here for as long as I can. Even if I didn't do it, it's not looking too good for me."

There's an awkward pause. What more is there to say?

"Is there anything else you needed from us, Luke?" Aiden's face is still neutral and unreadable, his hand still in mine.

Luke slumps a bit in his chair. "Yeah, I guess that's all. I just wanted to talk to Anna before I got twenty-five to life."

He gets up and leaves dejectedly without another word or glance back at us, walking out the door with his head down.

The group of us sit at the table in stunned silence. Who would've thought the first few days of our Christmas vacation would be so full of drama? I don't think any of us saw that coming. Not even me, and drama is kind of my thing.

"*Now* can we head back to the Mystery Machine?" Noah asks, trying to break the tension per usual.

"Do you think he did it?" I'm pointedly ignoring Noah.

"The police said that the primary location was Aiden's house, which means Greg died there. They didn't say anything about it looking like a fight took place, just that Greg *looked* like he'd been in a fight," Mason answers thoughtfully.

"The evidence against Luke doesn't look too good either. Plus, he basically confessed to it," Chase reasons.

"But he doesn't even remember what happened," Charlotte points out.

"That doesn't mean he didn't do it. How many times have I gotten black-out drunk and not remembered how I got home, or why I woke up naked and covered in barbeque sauce and Cheerios?" Chase counters.

That boy seriously needs to cut back on the alcohol consumption.

"What do you think, Aiden?" I ask, squeezing the hand that still feels heavenly in mine.

"Honestly, I don't care," he says almost breathlessly, as if relieved to finally admit it. "Greg's dead. Out of my life and out of the twins' lives. I don't care who did it, Luke or anyone else. They probably did me a favor, since I probably would've killed Greg if and when he came near the twins."

"You don't mean that, man," Mason objects.

"Oh, yes, I fucking do," Aiden confesses without a hint of doubt. "I'm glad he's dead. And right now all I want to do is go to enjoy my time with the twins without having to look over my shoulder."

I don't doubt that Aiden's glad Greg's dead; he doesn't have to worry about him anymore. Hell, my life would be a lot easier if Tony dropped dead, but clearly I'm not that lucky.

"What are we sitting around on our asses for then? Let's go!" Noah exclaims, looking at Charlotte and Chase expectantly so they can get up and let him out.

As we move out of the booth, I try pulling my hand out of Aiden's, but he just tightens his grip and looks at me with such a heart-melting intensity that I'm sure he feels my pulse speed up. I blush and look away, catching Charlotte's eye in the process as we walk out of the parlor. I haven't told her that Aiden and I kissed, not the first time or any of the other times after that.

She looks back and forth between our entwined hands and my face, a gigantic smile growing on her face, shooting me a look that says, Oh, you are so explaining everything after. At least she didn't jump up and down squealing and clapping her hands.

If Noah and Chase notice, they don't say anything. They're in a heated debate over whether pineapple belongs on a pizza or not. But Mason—his gaze lingers on our hands, and for some reason my heart squeezes. Now's not the time to dwell on that, though. Right now I just want to enjoy the sensation of my hand engulfed in Aiden's.

The wind is biting and I bundle my scarf close to my chest. The streetlights illuminate the parking lot clearly, as well as the huffs of our breath. Groups of people are gathered in the parking lot of the arcade across the street, and we can hear their animated conversations from here. From the other side of the parking lot, there's a screech of tires and doors opening and slamming.

I look at Charlotte as we walk toward the cars. "I'll call Anna after she's had some time to collect her thoughts and see how she is," I say.

Aiden suddenly pulls me behind him with our attached hands and simultaneously steps in front of me, at the same time a malicious and familiar voice yells, "There you are!"

I peek out from behind Aiden's tense back. Mason steps in front of Charlotte, and since Noah and Chase were walking in front of us, they're the first ones greeted by Ryan and his friends. But Ryan isn't even looking at them. His venomous gaze is locked solely on Aiden, the hate in his eyes plain to see.

"*You're a fucking murderer!*" Ryan yells.

Before I even notice Ryan lunge, Aiden gently but firmly pushes me farther behind him and simultaneously steps forward toward the action. At the same time, Chase and Noah, being the closest to Ryan, grab him on either side, stopping him from advancing any farther.

Noah and Chase push him back, and Ryan fixes his jacket. Dave and another Silver who they're always with, Ian, I think his name is, stand beside him. I can't help but notice the remnants of a black eye Dave's sporting haven't completely healed yet. A small, victorious smile spreads involuntarily on my face. Is that from Aiden? I hope so.

My smile disappears, however, when Kaitlyn emerges from Ryan's Mustang and hangs back a bit behind them, a scowl etched on her face. She looks tired and drawn, as if she hasn't been sleeping properly.

"Calm down, Simms. I had nothing to do with Greg's death," Aiden explains evenly.

"Like hell you didn't!" Ryan counters, looking less and less composed. "I know you were arrested! I know where his body was found. I don't know how many officers you had to blow to get released, but I know you did it!"

I scoff out loud, and I'm pretty sure I'm not the only one either.

"Aiden is a thousand times smarter than you, Ryan." I can't help but interject, ignoring the warning glare Aiden's shooting me and taking a few steps closer to Ryan. "Do you think if he was going to murder your father he'd be stupid enough to get caught? To leave the body in front of his own house as if showing off a prize?"

"Well, Parker's whore, let me explain something to you." Ryan takes a step closer to me, and I sense more than see Aiden also moving toward me. But I don't care, all my attention is focused on squaring off with Ryan.

"Parker is trash," he continues. "He's a product of his filthy, trailer trash whore of a mother. He keeps company with you fuckwits because scum is attracted to other scum. It's practically his destiny to get shanked and die in prison because that's all he's good for anyway. Those bastard brothers of his are better off jumping off a roof than continuing to live with him. They're probably little incest babies anyw—"

Red. All I see is red. My mind shuts off and instinct takes over as I raise my fist and punch him with all I have, harder than during training, harder than when I practice on the punching bag, hard enough to cut him off midsentence and make his head snap to the side and throw him off balance.

"Fuck!" I hiss as I pull my hand to my chest. I forgot how much it hurts to throw that kind of a punch, especially when the target is a human face.

Before anyone even has time to process what happened, strong hands are on my shoulders, practically throwing me back into a hard body with open arms, as if they were waiting to catch me. The arms wrap around me, both familiar and comforting, but they're not the arms that I basically know by heart, that belong to the man who takes my breath away.

Aiden now stands in the place I was, and in the second it took him to pull me out of the way, Ryan straightens up and swings without looking at the target, aiming lower since he expects it to be little ol' me, not the tall wall of muscle that is Aiden.

Aiden catches his wrist in his left hand with ease, automatically returning the favor and knocking Ryan straight to the ground, where he curses and moans.

I shrug off whoever is holding me and look back to see that it was Mason. Stay out of trouble, his eyes seem to say. It's like he doesn't even know me.

I get that Ryan's primary emotion is anger, but I also know he must be in pain. I understand that he's hurting—I really do. I lost a father, too, one that was great to me, even if he had his problems, and one I loved. But now Ryan's lashing out at the people I care about, and that is not acceptable, even if he's in pain and thinks it's all our fault.

Aiden strides over to where Ryan's laid out, fully conscious but clearly in pain. He crouches down and rests his forearms on his thighs.

"You can talk shit about me or fight me all you want," he says, his voice low and menacing. "But you leave my friends and family alone. And you *especially* don't talk about my brothers *or* lay a hand on my girl."

He looks at Dave at that last part, too, as if proving his statement that no one messes with his girl—with me.

They both get to their feet, Ryan spitting blood out as he does. Kaitlyn comes to his side and wraps her arm around his waist but he pushes her off him and wipes his lip with the back of his hand.

"Listen, Ryan," Aiden says, his arms at his side but still tensed and ready for a fight. "Greg was a shitty person, but he's still your father, and I'm sorry he's gone. But I had nothing to do with his death. The truth is, he was the last thing connecting us. With all of this happening, your mom's no longer my guardian. We can all move on with our lives and drop whatever juvenile rivalry we have. Channel your hate into something productive. We don't *ever* have to see each other again."

My heart swells with pride at Aiden trying to be the bigger person, even if he didn't say it in the nicest way, and even if he did just try to rearrange Ryan's face with his fist.

Ryan spits again. "Fuck you, Parker."

Kaitlyn must not like the scowl on my face, because her icy, blue eyes narrow at me and she says, "Have something to say?"

"It's funny how obsessed with Aiden you all are. Like, I get it, he's great. But seriously, this is getting very tiring and I'm done with wasting time on dealing with this stupid bullshit." I walk over to Aiden and take his hand confidently in mine. "Let's just go."

I don't give anyone time to protest—I drag Aiden with me, hoping that the rest of our friends are behind us. A few seconds later, Charlotte falls into step with me, Noah and Chase right behind her, and Mason just a few steps behind them.

"Amelia's house," Aiden says as we all get into our respective cars.

Julian's truck is gone, so he's presumably off somewhere consoling his girlfriend, so Charlotte gets in the back of Aiden's Challenger, while Noah and Chase go with Mason.

"Always have to get right in the middle of a fight, don't you, Amelia?" Aiden sighs as he pulls out of the parking lot.

I turn on my butt warmer and sigh, looking at my hand, which I'm still cradling. I really hope Ryan's face didn't break it.

"If drama didn't find a way to insert itself into my life, it wouldn't really be my life," I answer.

As Sweetie's recedes in the distance, I watch Ryan's Mustang pull out and head in the opposite direction. Maybe we'll be given a break, and this branch of drama can be cut down and out of our lives forever. Maybe we can actually spend the rest of my time here just us friends, completely drama free.

>> <<

When we get to my house, I get out of the car and pull down the seat to let Charlotte out too. Mason's SUV stops beside Aiden's in the driveway and we all meet up on the porch. So far, Aiden hasn't yelled at me like he normally would for getting in the middle of a fight—or for technically initiating it. Other than that comment in the car, he's remained pretty quiet.

Charlotte has basically hailed me as her hero. "I wish I had the balls to punch someone right in the face!" she gushes. "Did you see how useless I was hiding behind Mason?"

She pauses, considering what she said. "Okay, maybe I'd never punch someone, but at least I wish I wasn't so scared of confrontation. Like, my locker neighbor keeps spraying this god-awful cologne every time I'm there, and I'm pretty sure I'm allergic to it. But will I ever say anything to him? Nooooo. Because that would involve confrontation."

She frowns, and I feel like she's talking more to herself now than to us. I unlock the front door and we all pile in, out of the chilly winter air. I check the garage and find my mom's car missing. I shoot her a quick text, asking when she'll be home, but don't expect a reply anytime soon. She probably went to her new boyfriend's house—the one I'm not allowed to know anything about—instead of coming home.

"Who's your locker neighbor, Char?" Noah asks as we take off our shoes and jackets, and head into the living room to sit. "Is it Lakerman?"

Charlotte sits cross-legged on the floor, facing the couch, and Chase sits beside her. Noah sits on the smaller couch, and Mason and I sit on the bigger couch. Aiden heads into the other room, presumably to call and check on the twins.

"Yeah, Peter Lakerman. Every time he sprays it, my neck and chest break out in hives," she explains, subconsciously rubbing her collarbone.

"After the Christmas break when school starts again, I'll talk to him," Noah promises.

Charlotte's blue eyes widen with alarm. "Oh, no! It's fine, really. You don't need to say anything."

"Charlie, you're breaking out in hives. Clearly it's not okay," Chase emphasizes, giving Noah a look laced with some jealous undertones. Chase is in love with Charlotte. I'm assuming it bothers him to know that she never stands up for herself, even if it is just asking her locker neighbor to spray the cologne after she leaves so she won't break out in hives. Is he jealous that Noah stepped in to play hero before he got the chance? Noah doesn't even feel the same way Chase does about Charlotte, he's just being Noah.

"Lakerman is cool. I'll just tell him you're allergic and to switch colognes, or at least spray after you get your books and are long gone," Noah explains, smiling like he just solved a Rubik's Cube in under thirty seconds.

"But you don't have to go through the trouble," Charlotte says timidly.

Noah frowns and looks at Charlotte like she just told him the earth was flat.

"We're friends. It would be trouble if I *didn't* say anything," he confidently asserts, making Charlotte blush slightly.

"I wish you would've told me." Chase frowns. "I could've done something to help."

Chase would've helped Charlotte right away if he'd known what was going on—he *is* in love with her, after all. I'm sure he's not happy that Noah gets to be her knight in shining armor before he got the chance.

Aiden walks back into the room and my eyes are automatically drawn to him.

"It's okay, Chase, really," Charlotte says as Aiden crosses the room and sits beside me on the couch. "You know I don't like being the center of any kind of drama."

"Speaking of drama," Noah starts. "What the hell, Amelia?"

"At least you didn't miss out on any of the drama this time, Noah," Mason teases.

"I didn't set out to start anything this time!" I defend myself, but as I think about it, I add, "Not that I did the other times."

"What happened to all that hippie-dippie make love, not war stuff you always preach? All that 'I don't want anyone else getting hurt so let's stop fighting and sit around braiding people's hair' bullshit?" Noah asks with a smirk.

"I don't want anyone getting hurt on *my behalf*. Yes, I want the cycle of violence to end, but he started saying all that stuff about Jason and Jackson and I don't know . . . I lost my shit."

Now I have a better understanding of why the Boys automatically want to punch people when they find out their friends have been hurt; you just don't let people disrespect the people important to you like that.

"You threw the first punch! I was so not expecting that!" Chase exclaims.

"Yeah. It was hot." Mason winks, and Aiden stiffens beside me.

"Don't get used to it," I mumble. "My hand is still throbbing."

"It hasn't stopped hurting yet? Why didn't you tell me?" Aiden demands, gently taking my right hand in his two larger ones and analyzing it.

"I don't know. I figured it would stop hurting after a while. I've punched people in the face before—remember at Noah's Halloween party?"

"I think we all remember Noah's Halloween party," Mason says.

"Some spots are a little fuzzy for me, but I know what you mean," Noah says, rubbing the back of his head where he got stitches. "I hate those damn concussions."

"Didn't your hand hurt that time?" Chase asks me. "I'm pretty sure you hit the guy at the party harder than you hit Ryan today, since you knocked him on his ass."

I try not to seem too proud of that, but come on! I think it was pretty badass if you think about it.

"I guess it did hurt," I answer. "The guy at Noah's party was drunk and caught off guard, but I've never hit anyone as hard as I hit Ryan today."

Geez, I'm such a hypocrite. I go around telling Aiden and the Boys not to go off and hit a guy because he pissed them off, and here I am, doing the exact same thing. Not that I regret it.

"Can you open and close your fist for me?" Aiden asks, still gently holding my hand in his.

I try to do as he asks and study his handsome face while he focuses on playing doctor. Even Aiden took the high road today. Ryan was saying really awful things about his family, about his brothers, and he didn't beat him to a bloody pulp. Mind you, he still did knock him on his ass, but I think it was well deserved. He could've kept going—he would've won the fight—but he chose to walk away, to acknowledge that Ryan was hurting and lashing out, and to try and bring an end to all the unnecessary hate and drama.

He turns my hand over, and I can't help but smile as I watch Aiden—who's normally so tough and intimidating—handle my hand with the utmost delicacy and care.

"You can't straighten your middle finger?" he asks.

I try and then shake my head no.

"Your finger is swelling too—you might have broken something or dislocated your finger. We'll have to go for X-rays," he states with authority.

I try to pull my hand away but he doesn't let me, not done with feeling around it.

"Aiden, please. My hand is fine. You punch people all the time and have never broken your hand. Your knuckles are usually all bloody!" I exclaim, nodding at my blood-free knuckles.

He pauses from analyzing my hand to raise a smug eyebrow at me. "I know how to throw a punch, though."

"I do too," I mutter. "Or at least I thought I did."

I sulk as he releases my hand and proceeds to google X-ray clinics, clearly having already decided that I am, indeed, in need of medical attention. God. That would be so embarrassing. Ryan didn't even have to do anything and he still wins if his stupid face broke my stupid hand.

"Aiden, you should go spend time with your brothers. I know they were looking forward to a movie marathon when you got back to Julian's," Mason tells him, looking at him from over my head since I'm sitting between them on the couch. "I'll take Amelia for X-rays after I drop everyone off."

I stubbornly cross my arms. "If I want to get X-rays—which I don't, by the way—I'm perfectly capable of driving myself," I interject, knowing full well that I'm about to be ignored.

"It's fine," Aiden answers, locked in a stare-off with Mason. "I want to take her."

Honestly, I don't even know why I bother.

"Really, Aiden. I can take her," Mason asserts, his broad shoulders set in determination.

I'm torn between trying to figure out if Mason looks like he's squaring off with Aiden, or if he's just trying to be a good friend. I don't think Aiden can decide either.

"I'll take her. I still need to lecture her about starting a fight, putting herself in harm's way, etcetera, etcetera." Aiden waves his hand in a noncommittal gesture. "And I just know she's looking forward to that."

Shit. I totally thought I was off the hook.

"I'm not a child, Aiden," I huff, wishing it was socially acceptable to throw a tantrum—you know, to prove my point that I'm not a child.

Aiden takes his eyes off Mason to look at me. "Yeah, but you get in some kind of trouble, I lecture you about always putting yourself in harm's way… it's what we do."

I can't help but laugh at that. It's easy to forget that Aiden actually has a sense of humor when he spends most of his time being all intimidating.

"Wow, so does everyone have a *thing* with Amelia except me?" Noah huffs, but everyone ignores him.

"I can do that for you," Mason says to Aiden, not ready to back down. "We won't even realize you're not there."

Aiden doesn't seem to like that, and I interject just before he's about to reply.

"Aiden, it's fine. If I'm going to be forced to have a stupid X-ray, and clearly no one is letting me go alone, Mason can just take me. You go spend time with your brothers, especially after everything that happened. It's my own stupid fault I threw the punch wrong," I say.

Aiden looks taken aback that I just chose Mason over him, if that's how you want to look at it. But he recovers quickly, throwing up a wall of stoic impassiveness and clearing any hurt emotions from his face.

"I guess you're right," he says, but now I feel like I betrayed him in some way. I just want him to spend time with his brothers instead of wasting it all with me in a stuffy doctor's office.

"Perfect. Then I'll take her," Mason says, his eyes dancing in victory, while Aiden's calculating eyes narrow at him. "And you guys can all come over tomorrow. My mom's making empanadas."

"Hell, yeah! Natalia's the best!" Noah exclaims as we all stand. "Hey, Amelia, do you like empanadas? That could be our thing."

"That can't be your thing if we're all there," Chase says, standing up from the floor and helping Charlotte up as well.

"Fine. We'll find something else, Amelia, don't worry." Noah says, then addresses the group as a whole as he puts on his jacket. "We'll confer in the group chat about the plans for tomorrow."

We all pause and tilt our heads at him.

"Confer? Really, Noah?" Chase asks while he puts his shoes on.

"What? It's my word of the day! I'm trying to broaden my horizons, you know?" Noah smiles, before letting it drop. "Wait, I used it correctly, right?"

"Yes, you used it right," Mason answers. "Now broaden your

horizons all the way to the truck. Amelia's hand looks like it's getting worse."

I frown and look at my hand. Yup, the swelling definitely went up. Fucking Ryan.

Everyone steps out onto the porch and I lock the door. I turn around to say that I'm ready to go, when suddenly Aiden pulls me into him. Before I can think, his hands are on the back of my head, and he lowers his mouth to mine, surprising me with a kiss. *What?!*

I recover quickly and kiss him back, the fire from his lips igniting my veins, spreading through my body all the way to my toes. I will never get tired of kissing Aiden. He pulls away and smiles a beautiful, genuinely happy smile at me, and all I can do is blush back at him. I can just imagine the shocked looks on our friends' faces—I'm almost too scared to look.

Aiden isn't ready to release me yet, so I just risk a sideways glance at everyone. Yup, we might have just broken our friends from the sudden shock. Charlotte looks like she practically dislocated her jaw from how far it dropped. Well, I guess we just officially came out as a couple to our friends.

"I'll call you later," he breathes.

He gives Mason a pointed look before kissing the top of my head and leaving to get in his car. I stand there staring after him, feeling just as shocked as everyone else, but infinitely more embarrassed. What was that about? And why did he look at Mason like that? Was that him engaging in some kind of jealous, primal man-staking-a-claim thing?

Mason is suddenly very interested in the ground, and a lot less happy than before. Yeah, it totally was. Geez, Aiden, be a little more discreet next time. Maybe bang your chest and carry me up a building?

"*It's about damn time!*" Noah calls after him, recovering the fastest. "I swear, the sexual tension was so strong it could probably bench press more than me, Mason, Julian, and Chase combined."

I laugh with everyone else, even though my face is probably as red as a tomato. Aiden looks back at us and smiles before getting into his car and revving the engine.

Before anyone can grill me, I run down the steps and to the passenger side of Mason's Range Rover. "Shotgun!"

After everyone piles in, we barely close all the doors before Charlotte shares her delight.

"Sooo. . . . Is no one going to talk about what just happened out there!" she exclaims, her whole face lighting up like a kid who was just told they could eat an entire chocolate cake for dinner.

"*Aiden and Amelia, sittin' in a tree,*" Noah starts, and Charlotte joins in to sing, "*K-i-s-s-i-n-g!*"

"Oh God," I mumble, wishing the seat would swallow me whole.

"Was that the first time he kissed you?" Charlotte presses. "Because it so didn't look like it was your first kiss. Damn it, Amelia, if you guys kissed before and you didn't tell me I'll be so pissed!"

Mason's focused on driving, but I know him well enough to tell that he's uncomfortable. I wish we didn't have to talk about this in front of the guys.

"I'll explain everything *later*, Char," I emphasize, hoping that she'll understand and drop it.

I love Charlotte; she's my best friend and one of the smartest people I know. But if there's one word to best describe her, it's *oblivious.*

She's talking a mile a minute. "But I just need to know

everything! I'm so happy for you! Oh man, I can't wait for Anna to find out, she'll be so excited! Wait, she'll definitely be excited, but then she'll for sure be pissed because you never told her. Do you think she'll hit you? She might hit you."

Mason's hands tighten on the steering wheel, his knuckles going white.

I turn around in my seat and look at Charlotte, sitting in the back between Chase and Noah.

"I'll tell you and Anna together, *after*." I try really hard to put an emphasis on it without making it obvious, and exaggeratedly move my eyes back and forth from her and Mason.

Her eyes widen, finally getting the hint, and she nods. Unfortunately, Chase and Noah don't.

"But we still want to know!" Chase exclaims, and Noah nods in agreement.

Before I can think of a reply, Mason turns up the radio, the music blasting so loud through the speakers the car practically shakes. Yeah, guess that'll effectively end all conversation.

After we drop everyone off, Mason lowers the radio, and we sit in an awkward silence as he drives.

"How's your hand?" he asks, glancing at my right hand in my lap.

I give my hand a dirty look. "Who cares, I'm mad at it."

"You're mad at it?" he repeats.

"Yeah. That was my supercool, stand up to the man moment, and it will forever be marred by the fact I broke my hand."

Mason laughs, and the air around us starts to feel lighter. "Cheer up. You don't know if it's broken."

I hold up my hand for him to see—my middle finger is swollen and actually looks a little crooked.

He looks at it and grimaces. "Ohh. Why don't we just stay positive?"

I laugh humorlessly. "God, I'm so embarrassing. Everyone's gonna be all 'Hey, how'd you break your hand?' And I'm gonna have to be like 'Well, actually, I was tryna be all tough and punch someone. But jokes on me because his face broke my hand!'"

"Hey," Mason says, "if you didn't break your hand throwing a punch, you wouldn't really be Amelia Collins. You like to keep things interesting. Never a dull moment with you."

I'm technically not really Amelia Collins, but I get what he means. My life is just one constant shit show after the other.

"Yeah, I guess." I sigh. "It might just be karma for punching a guy whose dad just died."

"Aiden punched him and everything's working out just fine for him," Mason mumbles.

My head snaps over to look at him, but he's not even looking at me, focusing on driving.

"I wish Anna could've seen it." I change the topic. "She would've been so proud. How many times has she wanted to punch him? Like, a million. Actually, she probably would've done it first."

"Yeah. She probably wouldn't have broken her hand either."

I scowl at him and he laughs, the old, effortlessly charming Mason back as his chocolate-brown eyes light up with mischief.

"I'm sorry, I'm sorry." He smiles. "Too early for jokes?"

"At least wait until *after* we leave the doctor's," I reply, not mad at him in the least.

"Deal." He laughs.

We eventually check into urgent care, since it's almost midnight and everything else is closed. They give me an ice pack for my finger and we sit in the waiting room in chairs that are infuriatingly similar to the ones in the police station waiting room. Do all waiting rooms have furniture from Shitty Chairs Are Us? At least it's much quieter here than at the station, and the air isn't as suffocating, but it still smells like disinfectant.

"Hey, that was cool of your dad to do what he did for Aiden and the twins," I tell Mason as we wait.

"Yeah, my dad's great. I'll deny it if you repeat this because I need my street cred, but I wouldn't mind ending up just like him."

"He is good looking, so you're halfway there," I joke.

"Oh, so you think I'm good looking?"

My smile mirrors his. "No, you're not listening, I said your *dad's* good looking."

He barks out a surprised laugh and I think back to what his dad did for Aiden. "But seriously, that *was* awesome for your dad to suggest becoming their legal guardian. I guess that technically makes them your foster brothers."

Mason shakes his head. "I've known Aiden for years. We've been through some shit. I don't need a piece of paper to tell me he's my brother."

That statement makes my heart swell. I wish someone felt like that about me. Mason shuffles his feet and shifts uncomfortably in his chair. I can tell he wants to ask me about Aiden, but I'm not ready to talk about it—it's easier to talk around it. "What did your mom say about it all?"

"Oh, she thinks it's a fantastic idea. If anything, she's upset I didn't say anything earlier," he admits sheepishly. Mason gets the hint and keeps the conversation in safe, let's not address the elephant in the room territory. "Did you tell your mom about any of this stuff going on?"

I laugh humorlessly. "My mom and I don't have that kind of

close relationship. We don't really tell each other things unless it's absolutely necessary. If anything, we usually hide stuff from each other."

Mason frowns. "Why do you say that? I'm sure she doesn't hide stuff from you."

I think about his statement. "She has this new, secret boyfriend I have yet to meet, or even know anything about. She's always giggling at his texts and coming home late when I know she doesn't have a flight."

"Secret boyfriend, huh? Is he a secret agent or fugitive or something?"

"No. I'm sure he's just a regular, run of the mill, boring man. He's just a secret from me."

"Why is that?"

I sigh and honestly consider it. "I don't know. I think she thinks I'm not ready to see her with someone who isn't my dad. I want her to be happy, and I already know their marriage was crumbling before he died. I don't think it'd be a big deal if I met him, or even just knew his name."

Mason purses his lips in thought. "Maybe she just doesn't know how she feels about him yet. She wouldn't want to introduce someone she isn't one hundred percent certain about to her daughter."

"Maybe."

It feels good to talk this through with Mason, and I'm really glad he's here with me. We are friends, and I don't want him to forget that even if I know how I feel about Aiden now, and how Aiden feels about me.

"Are you really close with your mom then?" I ask.

"Yeah, I guess I'm a mamma's boy, but don't tell anyone." He laughs, but his smile falters. "I just feel bad for her sometimes. My dad really wants this promotion at his marketing firm, so his work is getting busier and more demanding. He's spending later nights, more time locked in the office on the phone. I'm proud of him and his accomplishments—he's already pretty up there in the company—but I hate that my mom's alone a lot. He's even supposed to go on a business trip next week, and I just wish they didn't send him on one over Christmas break, you know?"

"Are they doing something after he comes back?" I ask.

"The weekend after school starts again my mom is going to surprise him with a romantic getaway. So guess who has a free house to throw a party?"

"Please, Mason. I'm sure we're going to see you, like, every day over the break. I think we'll be too sick of you to spend the next weekend with you *again*."

"'Sick of' and 'Mason' have never been uttered in the same sentence before, unless the words 'not being with' are in the middle." He winks, making me laugh and I lightly hit him with the back of my good hand.

"I miss just hanging out with you, k-bear." His tone is serious and thoughtful. "It's nice to talk things through with you."

"I said it before, and I'll say it again: I'm fantastic," I joke, and he rolls his eyes at me, still smiling.

"I think all the blood's rushing from your head to your hand." He nods at my swollen finger.

"Probably, but it doesn't make my statement any less true," I tease. "I like talking to you, too, Mason. That's why we're bestest friends."

An unknown emotion passes over his face briefly before he masks it, smiling at me, but not genuinely.

“Yeah,” he says. “Bestest friends.”

It takes about an hour, but we finally see the doctor, and after looking at my X-rays, she tells me I dislocated the middle knuckle of my middle finger and it has to be realigned. It takes her about one-point-three seconds to pop it back in. I have to keep my middle finger taped to my pointer finger for about four weeks, visual evidence of my complete failure. But in my defense, I can’t feel *that* bad about dislocating my finger from punching Ryan. The doctor said it happens to lots of people who punch hard objects, even if she did add that it was usually walls or inanimate objects. Still, I’m counting that as a win. My status in the cool kids club hasn’t been revoked just yet.

8

Urgent care was shockingly fast and by the time Mason drops me off, it's almost two in the morning. Sticking my head into my mom's dark room, I announce that I'm home from hanging out with my friends and slip off before she wakes up enough to question me. I'm too tired to tell her about my finger right this minute. I'll explain later, when I've come up with a good enough lie. After sending Aiden a text, quickly brushing my teeth and slipping into my pajamas, I take my sleeping pill and crawl into bed, sinking into the warmth and softness of my sheets.

Aiden calls me not even two minutes after my head hits the pillow. I tell him what happened with my finger, and he seems more amused than anything.

"Guess that means I have to teach you how to throw a proper punch when you're feeling better," he says, his voice laced with amusement.

"I know how to throw a punch, Aiden," I complain. "Ryan must have, like, a metal plate in his jaw or something."

"I can assure you that he doesn't." I can almost hear the smirk in his voice over the phone. "But when you're better I *will* teach you. It'll make me feel better."

"Make *you* feel better?" I ask incredulously. "How will it make you feel better? I'm the one who's gotta change the tape on my fingers every twenty-four to forty-eight hours."

"Well, if you're going to keep going around punching people despite my protests, I'd rather you not hurt yourself every single time."

"God, I'm never going to live this down, am I?"

He chuckles, a beautiful deep melody to my ears. "Give it a couple of days. It'll pass."

"How are the twins?" I ask, turning onto my back and staring up at the ceiling.

"They're having lots of fun here at Julian's, but poor Bubba's started hiding when he hears their voices—they're having too much fun terrorizing the poor dog when all he wants to do is sleep." He chuckles. "They're excited about Christmas but wondering how Santa will know that they're going to be staying at Mason's over the break instead of at home. I assured them that Santa knows everything and guaranteed them that they'll still get their presents no matter where we are."

"Have you heard from Anna?" I ask. "My calls are going straight to voice mail."

"Yeah, Julian said she's fine—she just unplugged for a while to relax. But they're coming to Mason's tomorrow."

"I'm glad Anna feels better," I reply, then, after a pause, softly add, "And I'm glad Greg is out of your life. You shouldn't have to spend it always looking over your shoulder."

It sucks, I should know. Aiden always understands the deeper meanings. "I know," he says quietly. "It'll get better, Thea. I won't let him hurt you."

I turn my head to look at my closet, the door wide open, and stare at the shoe box with my memories and reminders inside, recalling the conversation my mom had with Agent Dylan. The connection on the phone crackles with our silence.

No, Aiden. I won't let him hurt *you.*

» «

On Sunday morning when my mom walks into the kitchen, her eyes go straight to the tape on my fingers.

"What happened?" She moves to grab my hand, but I pull it away.

"I'm fine, I dislocated my finger. It'll be back to normal in a couple of weeks."

She narrows her brown eyes at me, her face serious. "And how did that happen?"

I shrug. How would she react if I told her I punched a guy? That's definitely not keeping my head down and staying out of trouble like I'm supposed to be doing.

"You don't know?" she deadpans, propping her hand on her waist.

I have to stop myself from getting defensive since that's a sure sign of guilt. "You know me, I'm superclumsy. I was being silly with Char and Anna and ended up banging my hand on the table."

Nothing about her disbelieving facial expression changes except a raised eyebrow. She's totally not buying it. "You banged it on a table?"

"Yes, Mother. What do you think I did? Punch a guy?" I lace my voice with as much sarcasm as I can, even though that's *exactly* what I did.

She studies me for a moment longer before turning around and pulling a box of cereal out of the pantry. "If I know my daughter, that's exactly what she did."

I freeze. Is she spying on me again?

"Ha-ha," I say dryly.

She grabs a bowl and pours herself some cereal. "You need to be more careful, though. Stop adding to your list of injuries."

"Yes, Mom," I say in a flat tone, just to stop the impending lecture.

"And while you're at it, stop sneaking boys in."

My head snaps up to look at her. She's not even looking at me, her back turned to me as she rummages through the fridge.

"What?"

She grabs the milk and turns back to me. "This is the first time I've properly seen you since Friday night, so don't think I forgot to yell at you for letting that boy stay over on Friday."

Shit. After her reprimanding text I thought she'd drop it. I thought I'd gotten away with that. I open my mouth and close it, no sound coming out.

"He wasn't in my room!" It's all I can say.

She pours the milk into her cereal and places it back in the fridge. "I know, I checked your room. But seriously, Amelia? This is why we need to move. You *really* think it's smart to let this boy sleep over? You don't even know him."

"His name is Aiden, Mom. And I do know him." My voice creeps up. I'm trying really hard to stay calm and talk to my mom like an adult and not throw a tantrum like I really want to. "I was helping a friend. I'm allowed to have those."

She sits down at the table in front of me. "You can have a friend. You cannot have a boy sleeping in my house without my permission."

"Would you have given me permission if I had asked?"

She glances up from her cereal and sends me a look that says, Really?

"And that's why I didn't ask," I mumble, pushing around the remnants of the cereal in my own bowl. "He couldn't go home."

"Why not? He didn't even sleep in your room, so what was the purpose of the sleepover? Why couldn't he go home?"

Great. Now I've done it. She already doesn't like Aiden, and here I am giving her more ammo against him. I can just imagine how that conversation would go: Well, Mom, he was arrested for killing his stepdad and his house is a crime scene. Yeah, that would earn him all the brownie points with my mom.

"He just couldn't," I mutter, standing up from the table to escape more questions. "Next time I'll tell him to park around the block, okay?"

"Amelia!" she exclaims, a frown on her face. "That wasn't the lesson you should be taking away from this. Don't be a smart-ass."

I inhale deeply as I try to keep my frustration from escaping. "And what should the lesson be, Mom? That I'm destined to live alone? That I'm not allowed to talk to anyone? That I'm supposed to be miserable until I die? If that's the case, why don't you just ship me to Bum-Chuck-Nowhere in the middle of the Arctic, where I'll be the only person around for ten thousand miles?"

"You're being dramatic, Amelia."

I push through the lump in my throat. "I'm trying really hard to not hate my life, Mom. If I'm not allowed to live my life then I might as well just let Tony find me."

"Amelia!" She's been relatively calm throughout this conversation, but that made her mad. She takes a breath. "I know it's been hard on you Amelia . . . Thea," she adds on quietly. "But we're doing all of this to keep you safe. I love you and I want you to be happy, but most importantly I want you *safe*. If that means making some sacrifices then that's what we'll do."

I look away from her. "You don't understand. You got to have your high school experience. You get to leave and go anywhere and be anyone you want. You even get to have a boyfriend. I just don't want to live my life by going through the motions."

She's quiet for a moment as she looks out the sliding door. "When you become a parent, you don't ever think this is something you'll have to deal with. I'm doing my best, Amelia."

I hesitate, the anger draining from my body even though I really want to stay mad. I think back to how she's making us leave, tearing me away from my friends, while she'll still be able to take flights to visit *her* boyfriend.

"Well, your best sucks." I turn to run out of the room before she can say anything else, not even caring that I rudely left my half-eaten bowl of cereal on the table for her to clean up.

» «

"This is seriously the best empanada I've ever had," I tell Natalia, Mason's mom, as I stuff my face with seconds.

She laughs as she puts down a tray of other finger foods on the couch sectional in front of us. All of our friends are sitting in Mason's basement on a large, black, U-shaped couch that accommodates us all nicely. There's a flat screen TV mounted to the wall in front of us tuned to the news, though no one's really paying attention to the guy running for governor who is making a speech. It's really just background noise.

"I'm glad you're all enjoying it," she says, brushing her dark hair out of her face. "I always tell Mason to invite you all over more often."

Mason loads his plate with the new food she just brought in, talking around a full mouth. "And I told you that I don't wanna share your food."

She playfully swats the back of his head, distracting him long enough for Noah and Chase to grab the last two chicken wings he was reaching for.

"Not cool, guys!" Mason directs his comment at the two food thieves, who just smile as they stuff their faces.

"Relax, I have more," Brian announces as he comes down the stairs with a tray of hot chicken wings, not even getting to set them down before everyone's grabbing them off the tray.

Brian shakes his head and sits at the end of the couch. "Wow, you'd think you guys haven't seen food in weeks."

"Don't look at us," Annalisa says, gesturing to me and Charlotte. "We've just learned to adapt. If we're not fast enough, they finish all the food."

"Mmm-hmm," Mason agrees with a mouth full of food, and Natalia swats him again.

"Manners," she scolds, but she's smiling anyway. "Do you boys want something before it's all gone?" she asks Jason and Jackson, who are sitting in the entertainment section of Mason's basement, a foot away from the television, playing a video game.

"No," they shout back in unison.

"No, thank you." Aiden reprimands them, and the boys repeat the phrase robotically.

"Sorry." Aiden looks back at Natalia a bit sheepishly. "I bought them that video game as an early Christmas present and they've become obsessed."

"It's not a problem," she says with a genuine smile.

Noah clears his throat. "Uh, I didn't want to tell you because I thought it would make things worse"—he shifts under everyone's gaze—"but social media's blowing up with people wanting to know if you killed Greg or not."

Aiden exhales sharply and runs a hand through his hair. "Yeah, I know. Are you guys getting bombarded with questions?"

Everyone makes a noncommittal sound, trying to not make Aiden feel bad but basically confirming his question.

"I've just been telling everyone to go fuck themselves," Julian asserts with a crooked smile.

Aiden breathes out a chuckle, but it's obvious to everyone that it's forced. For all his toughness and confidence, knowing that his situation is affecting the people around him bothers him.

Brian sits up straighter. "I have an idea. It's winter break, you guys don't have school. Why don't you all take these two weeks to go away? It doesn't even have to be far. Just get out of town to take your mind off of it and let this all cool down."

We look at each other. Can we all just skip town and have fun together? Drama free?

Noah's the first to speak. "If my mom doesn't kill me I am *so in*!"

What seems like a collective sigh of relief escapes us as everyone jumps in, admitting that it's a good idea. Even Aiden admits it would be good to get away from everything and let the twins have fun, if it doesn't ruin everything with the social workers checking in with Brian.

Can I go, though? Even if I *could* convince my mom to let me go, I'd be around everyone 24/7. I'd have to be myself, sleeping pills and closet baseball bats and all. As I glance at Aiden, who looks like his mind is running a mile a minute, a swirl of guilt wraps around my heart and squeezes. I'll be leaving everyone in just a few weeks. This is my last chance to be with them all, and I don't think I can pass that up.

Brian claps his hands together once, a huge smile on his face. "Great. Any idea where you'd want to go? Break officially starts tomorrow, so you might be hard-pressed finding a place."

"Torywood Springs." Aiden speaks up before anyone can suggest anything else. "It's a shore town about five hours away. It'll be too cold to swim, but . . ."

"Actually, I think a friend from work has a vacation house there," Brian says. "She's in Australia right now, so she's not using it. Let me make a phone call—she'll probably even let you stay there for free."

"Wow, that'd be great. Thanks, Dad," Mason says as Brian stands up.

"It's not a problem. You kids deserve a break from all of this. I'll go make a call, and if your parents are all okay with it, you can probably leave as early as tomorrow."

Brian exits the room, leaving everyone, including his wife, staring after him in admiration. He's such a great man to have on our side, and it's moments like these that make me miss my own father.

The oven timer goes off and Natalia runs back up the stairs, leaving everyone to talk excitedly about the trip. Charlotte's even making a list of stuff we'll need to bring and calculating how much supplies will cost.

"Actually," I jump in, "I still have all the money Aiden gave me from winning the race against Ryan. We can use that for food and activities and stuff if we get the house for free."

"What?" Aiden leans in, speaking in a low voice. "That money is for you to do whatever you want with."

I meet his steady gaze. "What I want is to spend it on all of us."

He studies me for a second longer before nodding and leaning back. This can be like a good-bye gift to them; maybe it'll ease the guilt that's gnawing at my chest, especially since I still haven't figured out how I'm going to tell them that I can never see or hear from them again.

"I still can't believe you gave her four thousand dollars! You never give me anything." Noah glares at Aiden, then adds in a low tone, "Clearly you gotta be a pretty girl with a nice ass to get anything around here."

My cheeks turn red but I still burst out laughing with everyone else, while Aiden shoots Noah a glare.

"You have a great ass, Noah," Annalisa says matter-of-factly while munching on a potato wedge, making Julian look at her quizzically.

"Plus," adds Mason, "last week Aiden got you an oil change and fixed your exhaust for free."

"Four grand still would've been nice . . . at least a couple of burgers thrown my way," Noah mutters while playing with the straw of his now-empty soda.

Charlotte looks up from the list that she's making. "Hey, he's technically buying you all kinds of food now for this trip. You can make all the burgers you want when we get there. Hey, do you think I got everything?" She tosses her list to me and I skim it over.

"Probably." I nod admiringly and hand it back. Thank goodness for her organizational skills, because I didn't even think about bringing half of the stuff she put on that list. Who thinks about bringing toilet paper? That stuff always just appears in my bathroom.

"Great news," Brian says as he appears back in the basement. "Michelle said the house is all yours. You can meet the cleaning lady there tomorrow at three and she'll let you in and show you where the spare keys are. It's six bedrooms too."

Everyone starts talking at once, and even the twins pop in to ask us if Santa will know that they're there, and we assure them he will. I catch Aiden's eye and smile when I notice the heaviness around his eyes has eased. Now there's no doubt in my mind that I have to go, and all that's left to do is somehow convince my mom.

» «

It's only eight by the time I walk in the house, and I find my mom on the couch in the family room, with a glass of wine and a book. We haven't spoken since our fight this morning, and I hadn't been planning on breaking my silent treatment anytime soon, but I guess now I need to.

"Can we talk?" I ask her, timidly walking into the room and stopping a few feet away from her.

She sits up and takes off her reading glasses. "Of course."

I take a steady breath for confidence. What will I do if she says no? I don't even know, but I do know that failure isn't an option. "We want to go away for the two weeks of Christmas break. Torywood Springs—it's not far from here. We have a house for free and it's right on the beach and we have money for food and stuff and it's break anyway and I'm all caught up on courses." The words rush out together before I can stop myself.

She frowns. "Who's we?"

I shift nervously. "Me, Aiden—"

"No."

I'm taken aback. "What? Mom! You didn't even let me finish!"

"You're not going away to some random place with Aiden."

I huff in annoyance, my tone clipped. "If you had let me *finish*, then you'd know that it's not just me and Aiden. It's me, Aiden, Anna, Chase, Julian, Char, Noah, Mason, and Aiden's brothers, Jason and Jackson."

She tilts her head slightly. "And where are you going?"

That's not a straight up no. Hope builds up in my chest. "Mason's dad's friend has a beach house. She's not there right now so we can use it for break. It's only five hours away."

One of her eyebrows draws up. "Mason's dad set this all up?"

Mentally high-fiving myself for mentioning another adult's involvement, I steam ahead. "Yeah. We're all so stressed about"—I pause and pick my words carefully—"school. So Brian suggested we have some fun, and he set up the house for us."

She takes a sip of her wine, studying me intensely. "I don't know if this is a good idea. You're not supposed to be getting close to people and now you want to *live* with them for two weeks?"

The hopefulness that was bubbling through me deflates. "We're leaving anyway, might as well let me spend the little time I have left with them before I never see them again. Plus, it's a completely random town, Tony won't know I'm there."

She sighs and grows serious, setting her wine glass down. "I've been thinking about our conversation this morning. I really *am* trying my best here, Amelia. I know it must be hard for you to go through all of this, and I know that I'm hard on you. I want you to live your life but I just want you to be safe . . ." She trails off, thinking, and I don't dare breathe. "You'll need to check in every morning and night."

"Ahh!" I squeal, not really believing that she's agreeing. I wasn't even completely sure that I wouldn't have to sneak off.

"And you still have to be responsible. No getting drunk and posting on social media," she continues, a small smile growing on her face.

I nod vigorously. "Yes, yes. Same rules, etcetera, etcetera. Thanks, Mom!"

I wrap my arms around her, and for the first time in what feels like forever, feel like our relationship isn't past saving, that she really truly does want me to be happy, and is willing to compromise so that I don't feel like I'm living out a jail sentence. For the first time in a long time, I feel like my mom *gets it.*

9

On Monday morning I wake up pretty early, excited about our trip. I do a quick workout then text Aiden, asking if he and the twins want to come by a bit earlier for pancakes. After I shower and get dressed, I smile at Aiden's reply.

> Trying to buy the twins' happiness through fluffy, sugar-loaded clouds of joy? I always knew you were smart. Be there in 15

Just as I finish mixing the batter, the loud purr of an engine alerts me to Aiden's arrival. Smiling, I rush to let them in before anyone rings the doorbell and wakes up my mom.

There are two adorable, mini-Aidens standing on my porch. They have some telling features that mark them apart, but I have difficulty remembering which features belong to which child. The difference between them and Aiden is striking. They're so young and carefree, whereas you can tell that Aiden's been forced to grow up, and has carried more than one type of burden for too long.

"Boys, where are your manners?" Aiden scolds them as he walks in and catches them throwing their shoes and jackets on the floor.

I close the door behind Aiden and tell the boys it's okay, watching their faces turn bright red in the most adorable way.

Aiden wraps his arms around me and gives me a quick, chaste kiss that still manages to fry my brain and leave me smiling at him like an airhead.

"*Ewwww!*" The twins grimace at the same time.

Aiden chuckles and lets go of me. "Come on, boys. Go wash your hands so we can have breakfast."

I point out the bathroom and as they walk away, the boy I now undoubtedly know is Jason mumbles to his brother, "Well, now we know why Aiden's in such a good mood all the time." I muffle a laugh but Aiden just smiles unabashedly.

After breakfast, Aiden grabs my giant, slightly overstuffed duffel bag from upstairs and shoves it in the trunk of the Challenger. I make coffee for my mom as a piece offering for when she wakes up, and we jump in the car, heading to the designated meeting spot.

We pull into Noah's driveway, the first ones there. Charlotte opens the door for us, red faced and clearly embarrassed. I wonder what's wrong with her. She closes the door behind us and as we walk in, I discover why she looked like that. She met Noah's mom, Judy Adams.

"Noah, really. I'm just trying to help!" a motherly voice exclaims from the kitchen.

The three of us sit on the couch in the living room where we see Chase, who's desperately trying not to laugh.

"Mom! You can't just do that!" Noah argues, clearly annoyed.

"What's going on?" I whisper to Charlotte when Noah's agitated voice answers the question for me.

"You can't just barge in my room and throw, like, a dozen different boxes of condoms at me!"

I slap my hands over my mouth so that a surprised laugh doesn't escape. What did we just walk into?

"STDs are a thing, Noah! You're going on vacation with your friends, you need to be safe," Judy explains, and I'm so glad we got here in time for the entertainment.

"*God*, Mom! What is your deal? You're so embarrassing!" Noah groans.

"I'm not ignorant, Noah. I know what goes on—"

"*Jesus, Mom!*" He cuts her off. "I don't need my mommy buying me condoms! And eight boxes? Really? I'm going away for twelve days."

"Well, I didn't know which brand or size you—"

"*This conversation is over!* Canceled! I am officially canceling this conversation," he states with finality.

My hands are still over my mouth, trapping the giggles just begging to escape. He storms out of the kitchen and into the living room so we can see him for the first time. He looks like he can't decide whether to be extremely grossed out or super-annoyed and angry.

"Monkeys!" he exclaims, and the twins run and jump on him, tackling him to the ground. They fall to the floor in a laughing heap.

Judy walks into the room a few seconds later. "Oh, it's so nice to see you, Aiden. I didn't hear you come in."

She's a tiny woman. She must be a whole foot shorter than

Noah. She has the same smiling, pale-green eyes as him, and the same bright, white smile. Her straight brown hair is cut just above her shoulders, and I'm struck that *this* is the woman Noah always describes. She doesn't look scary in the least.

After Aiden says hi to her I introduce myself and we talk for a bit. She's honestly one of the nicest women I've ever met, and it's clear that Noah gets at least some of his sense of humor from her. When the doorbell rings again, I'm the one who goes to answer it. Julian, Mason, and Annalisa walk in, and before I can say anything, Annalisa hits me with the back of her hand.

"What the hell?!" she exclaims, narrowing her eyes at me.

"Ow!" I flinch away from her, even though the hit wasn't hard.

"You and Aiden have been swapping spit this whole time and no one felt the need to tell me?!"

My face heats up. "It wasn't this *whole* time, Anna."

"If it makes you feel better, they didn't tell anyone," Noah offers, and I shoot him a look. *Not helping, Noah.*

After I promise that I'll tell her everything once we get to the beach house, we say good-bye to Judy and head out the door, ready to embark on a five-hour drive to a place that will be our escape from all the drama.

Last night, Annalisa, Julian, Mason, and Charlotte went shopping for the trip, so most of the supplies are already loaded in the back of Julian's pickup truck. We decided we'd all get the food together once we got there. Julian, Noah, and Aiden are the volunteer drivers, so everyone divides up into the three cars, and I end up riding shotgun in Aiden's car, with the twins in the back.

About an hour and a half into our drive, Aiden shuts off the radio when another one of those annoying political ads runs. We play some road-trip games for a bit, but after a while the twins drift off. Aiden assures me it's better they sleep for the five-hour drive than ask us if we're there yet every five minutes.

We're almost at the two hour mark when I realize I've screwed up.

"What's wrong?" Aiden asks when he sees me frantically turning my purse inside out.

I look at him, prepared to lie, but then I remember I don't have to. "I forgot my sleeping pills." I sigh and throw my stuff back into my purse.

His gray eyes shift from the road to me. "Are you sure?"

"Yes, I'm sure. I took one last night then put the bottle on my nightstand so that I'd remember to pack it when I woke up this morning." I sigh again, annoyed at my own dumbness. "Guess I'm not sleeping for two weeks."

Aiden's head tilts slightly, and I can tell that beautiful brain of his is trying to work out a solution. "Can you get them there? Or somewhere along the way?"

I lay my head back against the headrest in defeat. "Not the ones I like. I need a prescription, and I don't have one."

"Okay."

Very calmly, he signals to the right and pulls onto the gravel shoulder of the deserted country road, the two cars behind us following suit.

"What are you doing?" I ask as he takes off his seat belt and turns around to wake his brothers up.

"Fixing it."

"What do you—"

"Are we finally there?!" I'm interrupted by Jason, who's just woken up.

"Not yet, buddy," Aiden tells him, getting out of the car and moving his seat up so Jason and Jackson can get out of the back. "Get your stuff and your brother, you guys are going to ride in Noah's car the rest of the way."

"Why?" Jackson asks, rubbing the sleep from his eyes.

"I forgot to do something at home. Either you guys spend an extra four hours in the car with us, on top of the remaining three, or you go ride with Uncle Noah."

Jackson and Jason look at each other for a moment before practically jumping over each other trying to get out of the car.

"That's what I thought." Aiden chuckles and closes the car door behind them.

I undo my seat belt and get out of the car, turning to see Aiden walk to the back of the car.

"Aiden, we don't need to turn back, really. It's okay." I don't want him to think of me as some burden, making him waste all that extra gas and time because my dumb ass couldn't even remember to grab the most essential part of my nightly routine.

Aiden shoots me a look that says, Don't be ridiculous, which is one part disbelief, and one part annoyance. He opens the trunk and hands his brothers their bags, then closes it again.

"What's going on?" Julian asks as he and Noah walk toward us, everyone else waiting patiently in their respective cars but looking at us curiously.

Noah notices that the twins are holding their bags. "What did you monkeys do? You annoyed Aiden so bad that he's decided to leave you here, didn't you?"

"We only annoyed him for the first hour!" Jason defends himself.

Noah shakes his head, almost disapprovingly. "Only an hour? Clearly I haven't taught you well enough."

"I have to take care of some stuff back home," Aiden clarifies, choosing to ignore Noah. "Can you take the twins? I'm going to go back and Amelia volunteered to keep me company. We'll be there later tonight, don't worry."

He's covering for me so I don't need to explain or lie about why I need sleeping pills in the first place. Also, he's saving me from looking like a complete dumbass for forgetting something so important to me.

"Aiden, I—" He quiets me with one look and I stop my protests.

Noah and Julian exchange glances.

"Sure, they can ride with me," Noah says, eyebrows drawn together. "But can't whatever it is you have to do wait until after the trip?"

"No," Aiden replies, his body relaxed, as if he has nothing to hide, but his broad shoulders are set as if daring anyone to challenge him. "Some stupid police release forms or something, I don't know. I just got a call, it needs to be settled now."

"Okay, then, but you're forfeiting your right to have first dibs on a room, you know that, right? Once we get there it's an every-person-for-themself race to pick a room," Noah adds, only half joking; I've seen the guy push a twelve-year-old out of the way for the best seat in a movie theater.

He opens the door to his truck so the twins can get in beside Charlotte.

"I trust Char to beat you all up in order to get the best room for us," I say loudly enough for her to hear.

"Already got my elbow pads out and itching to use them!" she yells out the window, even though I know she has zero intention of racing for a room.

Noah closes the door once the twins are in and comes back over to us.

"Make sure they help you bring all the stuff inside, not just go straight to playing," Aiden tells Noah and Julian, gesturing to the twins with a nod.

"You got it."

"Guess we'll see you in a few hours," Julian says, and they start to turn back to their cars.

"Wait!" I say, remembering something at the last minute.

Aiden glares at me, thinking I'm going to undo all his work, but instead I run back to the passenger side of Aiden's car and pull an envelope from my purse.

"This is some of the money from the race. You're going to be hungry and we probably won't be back in time to go grocery shopping with you, so here. Just get whatever."

Noah holds out his hand to take the envelope and I'm about to hand it to him when I think better of it and hand it to Julian.

Noah scowls adorably and Julian laughs. "No problem. Text the group chat when you're on your way back."

"We will," I say, and we all head back to our respective cars.

Once we get in the car, I put my seat belt on and then turn to very obviously glare at Aiden. He puts his seat belt on, starts the car, and executes a smooth U-turn, all while ignoring my heated glare, which I know he can feel.

He sighs in defeat. "Why are you looking at me like that?"

"Because this is so unnecessary! I didn't want you to turn all the way back just for me. I'm a big girl, I can deal with my own consequences."

"Thea, I know why you need pills to help you sleep. I'm not going to sit back and watch you torture yourself over memories and worries when there's something I can do about it."

My heart pounds in my chest with the weight of his words.

"But it's still so out of the way. We're going to be in the car for another seven hours. I feel bad."

"Don't," he says, looking back at me, his steely gray eyes set with determination. "I *want* to do this for you. Let me."

He wants to do this for me. For *me*.

"Plus," he adds, a flirty smile spreading across his handsome face, "I get an extra four hours alone with you. I don't think I pulled the short straw here."

Again and again I'm reminded why it's Aiden that I fell for. He's not frustrated, bothered, or annoyed at all about having to turn around for me. He does things for me all the time without even being asked. Like the incident with Ethan Moore or when my car was vandalized—he just takes care of the people he cares about, no complaints or holding it over anyone's head. And I am so, so blessed to be one of those people.

I reach out and squeeze the hand that's on the shifter, before quickly letting go. "Thanks."

He looks at me, his eyes dancing with unsaid emotion. "Anything for you."

10

The neighborhood is quiet, lazy even, by the time we get back to my house around two o'clock. The drive was nice, just some quiet, uninterrupted alone time with Aiden. We got to talk about the trivial things that we've never really had time for before because of all the drama. Like I learned his favorite color is navy blue. Who would've thought? Totally thought it would've been black or slate or some variation of black. But I guess navy blue is kind of close.

I also learned that he sticks to a strict workout regimen and never misses a day. Like Monday is apparently international chest day or something, so he does chest and abs. Then Tuesday he does back and abs, and it continues throughout the week until all body parts are taken care of. That explains why he looks so good. Boy works hard for it.

When Aiden pulls into my driveway, I hop out of the car and promise I'll be back real quick. As soon as I unlock and open the door, my ears are overwhelmed with superloud, romantic

Spanish music. I imagine my mom singing into inanimate objects or dancing around doing some barely passable salsa moves. I really don't want to know what she does during her alone time.

Closing the door, I freeze when I hear a distinctly male laugh. *Please, no.* Tell me he hasn't found me. He's got my mom tied up somewhere and ready to use as bait. *Not today, buddy. Not on my watch.*

With my heart pounding in my ears and adrenaline coursing through my veins, I carefully open the closet door. Reaching slowly and quietly for the baseball bat we keep there, I'm about to grab it when my mom laughs like a thirteen-year-old girl at her crush's first house party.

The tension leaves my muscles as I realize how dumb I am. It's just her new boyfriend. *Geez, Amelia. Freak out much?*

Not wanting to interrupt them and have an awkward meet the family moment, I quietly make my way up the stairs, careful to avoid being seen from the kitchen. I'm glad my mom has someone new to make her happy in the midst of all this drama. She's never given me any details about him, but I can tell he makes her happy, which is all I really care about.

I'm almost up the stairs when the radio is lowered a bit, and I freeze as I make out the voices. There's something eerily familiar about that voice. I know it from somewhere. A commercial? Maybe he's a lawyer or real estate agent with ads on TV?

With the gnawing feeling in my stomach feeding my need to figure out who this mystery man is, I make it to the top of the stairs and hide in the dark shadows, peering down at the front foyer.

"I'm so glad we have the house to ourselves these next few days before our flight to Hawaii for the week," my mom says giddily.

Right then, my mom and the mystery man come into view in the front foyer. No. it can't be. I stop myself from gasping out loud and giving away my hiding spot. How can this be? Does she even know who he *truly* is? Even I feel betrayed in a sense.

My mom laughs and I zone back in on their conversation. Oh shit, they're heading for the stairs! I scramble soundlessly into my room, the music from the kitchen obscuring the creaky floor.

I make it into my room and shuffle quietly into my en suite bathroom. I stand frozen in there, practically holding my breath, waiting as I hear my mother's ecstatic giggles and some gross kissing sounds make their way through the hallway. Her bedroom door closes and I breathe again.

Before Aiden comes looking to see what's taking so long, I grab the pills from my nightstand and quickly head back downstairs, grateful that the music is still playing and hides my steps. Locking the door again once I'm outside, I practically fly to Aiden's car, ready to get the hell away from here.

"Got them," I say, buckling up, only relieved once we turn the corner and my house is out of sight.

I'm a bit shaken, but I think I've managed to hide it from Aiden's intuitiveness. I always thought my mom wasn't telling me details about her new boyfriend because she didn't know how I'd react to her being with someone other than my dad. I thought she was trying to protect my feelings, or was possibly just embarrassed by me.

Aiden asks me something but I'm not paying attention, so I just mumble back a generic response. I thought my mom let me go away this week because she was finally starting to understand me. Did she just want to get rid of me?

Aiden says something else. I reply with a generic "Yeah, sure."

"Thea!" Aiden demands my attention.

"Hmm?" I reply, looking at him for the first time since I got back in the car.

"Are you okay?" he asks, genuinely concerned.

"Yeah," I answer, my voice coming out a little too high. I clear my throat. "Why?"

"Because I asked you whose car was parked in front of your house, and you replied 'Pizza's fine with me.'"

I close my eyes and do a mental facepalm. *Really, Amelia? That was your idea of a generic response?*

"Sorry. Just tired from the drive, I guess. And apparently hungry," I reason, hoping he buys it. I am kind of hungry.

"We'll stop for pizza. But first tell me what's wrong," Aiden gently demands.

"My mother is a homewrecker."

Aiden brakes a little too hard at the stop sign. "Of all the things I expected you to say, that definitely did not top my list."

The car moves smoothly forward again, and I turn in my seat to face Aiden. "Believe me, I never thought that was a statement I'd ever utter."

"What are you talking about? You were only in there a minute or two. What happened?"

I explain briefly, telling him everything from the gross kissing noises and schoolgirl giggling, all the way to my escape, purposely leaving out any names.

"How do you know he's married?" he asks me, trying to make sense of it.

"Because I know this man, Aiden."

"Who was it?" he asks, not to be prying and nosy, but to try and help me work through and wrap my head around what's happening.

I can't tell him, can I?

"Thea, what are you not telling me?" Aiden responds to my silence.

"She was with Brian Evans," I whisper. "As in Mason's dad."

To Aiden's credit, he doesn't jerk the car into oncoming traffic when hearing this new revelation, but his head does whip over to look at me briefly, eyes wide.

"Brian Evans. Our friend *Mason's* dad?" he repeats.

"The very same."

"Oh fuck."

"Does he have an identical twin brother?" I ask hopefully, already knowing the answer before Aiden shakes his head.

"Do you think he suggested this trip so it'll be easier for him to sneak around on Natalia?"

Aiden's fingers shift on the steering wheel. I don't even know how he's processing this, especially after all Brian's done for him these last few days. Plus, Brian is one of the father figures in his life; does this change how he sees him?

"I don't know. I hope not," Aiden says. "That wasn't his car outside your house. He told us he was going on a business trip this week anyway, which from the sounds of it, is really a trip to Hawaii with your mom."

Everything Mason said about his father working extra hard and taking business trips was bullshit. He was here. Figuratively screwing his wife and *literally* screwing my mom. Oh God, poor Natalia. And poor Mason. Should I tell him? Does he know? I don't want to destroy his family or his view of his father.

I can't believe it. My mind's running a mile a minute with this new information. My mom and Mason's dad. I know the Evans men know how to charm the pants (literally) off a girl, but that particular Evans is *married.* Does my mom even know that Brian is married? She must know. Why else would she have kept him a secret from me? No. She was just hiding the fact that she's messing around with a *married* man, who happens to be the father of one of my best friends, and that she's the other woman in this situation.

Was she cheating on my dad when he was alive? I knew their marriage wasn't the best at the end, but did she cheat on him before it was even over? Was one of the reasons they were fighting in the first place *because* she was cheating on him? It's like I don't even know my own mother.

"Do I tell Mason? Do I confront my mom? What do I do, Aiden?"

I honestly don't know what the right thing to do here is. I don't want to have to deal with this kind of drama; I wish someone would just give me the right answer.

"I think Mason would want to know," he says, eyes focused on the road, but I can tell he's thinking through all the options.

"But he'll hate me. He'll hate my mom. It'll ruin his family." I frown.

I don't want to hurt Mason and I can't stand the thought of him hating me. He would be learning that everything he's been told is a lie; that there weren't any long nights or business trips. He'd learn that his father *chose* not to spend Christmas with his family because he'd rather spend it in Hawaii with his mistress.

Aiden looks at me thoughtfully. "Would you want to know, if you were him? Would you be mad if you found out some other way, and then found out your best friend knew the whole time, and didn't tell you?"

Why does he have to present logical facts? Why can't he just say, I'm sure it'll go away by itself, Thea, no need to worry, like I want him to?

"I'm already keeping a bunch of other secrets from him and lying to all my friends, one more can't hurt, right?" I ask hopelessly, because I already know the answer.

"It's not the same and you know it."

I sigh heavily. "Of all days for me to screw up, it *had* to be today? I just *had* to go back to get my sleeping pills and walk in on an affair. Typical, Amelia."

The corner of Aiden's mouth turns up in amusement. "Oh, don't place all the blame on Amelia. Thea seems to like drama just as much, keeps her life interesting."

I playfully hit him with the back of my good hand, but he still manages to make me smile. I know that Mason has the right to know, but what if I'm not the one who tells him?

"Technically, this is all your fault. I didn't want to come back, but you just had to play the knight in shining armor. I could've been blissfully sitting on the patio sipping some fruity cocktail, ignorant to the problems of the world, but noooo, you wanted to turn back." I cross my arms.

He raises an amused eyebrow. "Are you honestly blaming me right now?"

"Yes," I say confidently. "And the only way you can make it up to me is if you tell Mason for me?" The statement ends up coming out as a hopeful question, a silent prayer that he'll take the responsibility for me. I just can't stand to see Mason's reaction. Will he be angry? Sad? Heartbroken? Will he even believe me?

"Thea," he starts softly. "You know if I could take your pain and problems from you, I would. In a heartbeat."

He runs his hand through his hair, and despite the sincerity and sweetness of his statement, I can feel a big fat "but" coming.

"But," he continues, "I think you should be the one to tell him. I'll sit there with you when you do it and support you any way I can, but it'll mean more coming from you. I didn't even see anything, Thea. You need to tell him what you saw with your own eyes."

Damn him. He makes perfect sense. I don't even know how I could logically argue with him.

I sigh for what must be the twentieth time in the last ten minutes. "Fine, I'll tell him. But if he doesn't believe me or throws a table at me, it's not my fault."

"Mason wouldn't throw a table at you. He might try, but he's not nearly strong enough. I mean, maybe Julian, but then again—"

"Aiden!" I exclaim. Why is he making light of this situation and trying to make me laugh? Why is it working?

"Relax, Thea. Mason trusts you—he'll believe you and won't throw a table at you. Plus, you know I'd never let that table get close enough to hurt you."

A smile creeps onto my face, my heart a permanent pile of mush whenever he's around. "Okay, I'll tell him. But *after* we get back home. I don't want to ruin the vacation for him."

"That seems reasonable to me," Aiden agrees.

I might possibly be hurling Mason into a messed up, stressful, complicated family life. A couple of weeks having fun with friends with no worries or problems won't kill him.

"How are you doing with this new information?" Aiden asks.

"I'm fine. It's not my family that's going to be torn apart. I guess I just feel bad for Mason."

I really am fine. I should be mad at my mom for sending me

away not because she understands me but because she wanted more alone time with her *married* boyfriend. I should be mad at her for knowingly being a mistress, but she's supposed to be the adult here. She should know what's right and wrong and not rely on her teenage daughter to teach her how not to be a scheming bitch.

Okay, maybe I'm a little mad at my mom, but that's probably normal. I did just find out she's a homewrecker.

11

We pull into the driveway of the beach house a bit after seven o'clock since we stopped a couple of times to eat. My first impression of the house is that it's beautiful. Not so big that we'll never see each other, but not so small that we'll invade each other's personal space. Aiden grabs our bags from the trunk and we walk onto the porch, waiting for someone to open the door for us.

"Finally, you're here!" Noah says when he opens the door. "We figured you guys decided to pull over and f— Ow!"

Aiden cuts Noah off when he shoves my duffel bag into his chest, forcing him to grab it.

We step into the small foyer and close the door behind us, and I'm greeted by a spacious, brightly lit open area, with couches and a television, where the twins and Julian are playing a video game. Just to the side of the living area is the kitchen and an eating area right beside it. A porch runs from one side of the living room all the way to the end of the eating area, visible through all the windows and clear sliding doors.

Mason's standing in the kitchen, and my stomach instantly starts hurting when he waves at me. I avert my gaze, but before he can comment on my rudeness, Annalisa and Charlotte appear at the top of the stairs, which are to the right of the foyer.

"Amelia! Finally! Come look at the view from our room!" Charlotte exclaims, and I don't waste any time following her up the stairs—anything to avoid Mason, even if it's putting off the inevitable. You'd think I'd be better at hiding secrets, but this is different—it's not about me, and it's really going to hurt him, destroy him even. I don't know if I'll be able to face him at all over these next two weeks.

Noah follows us with my bag since he refused to let me carry it when I offered, and Aiden stays behind to say hi to his brothers.

"There are three rooms downstairs. Noah is in one, Aiden is in the other, and Julian and I are in the bigger one," Annalisa explains when we get to the top of the stairs. "This room here is Mason and Chase's, the one down at the end of the hall is Jackson and Jason's, and this one is yours and Char's."

"How did Noah and Aiden score rooms by themselves and everyone else has to share?" I ask, more out of curiosity than anything.

"We figured Aiden should get a room to himself since he just got out of jail and deserves a nice room. You know, since the bunks in prison are terrible," Noah jokes and I laugh despite knowing I probably shouldn't.

"And how did you get a room?" I reply with a smile.

"We put Mason's, Noah's, and Chase's names in a hat and the name we pulled out is who got the room to himself," Charlotte answers.

"And I didn't rig it, despite what Mason says!" Noah defends himself loudly enough that Mason can hear from the kitchen.

"You sit on a throne of lies!" Mason calls back.

"He's just jealous he's not incredibly good looking, funny, smart, talented, *and* lucky like I am," Noah rationalizes, opening the door to the room Charlotte and I will be sharing.

My eyes are immediately drawn to the queen-sized bed, for no other reason than because Chase is lying down on it, flipping through one of Charlotte's magazines like he has all the time in the world.

"Oh, hey, Amelia," he says casually. Annalisa and Charlotte just shrug.

The room is nothing luxurious, but apparently we got the nicest one because we got the balcony. Noah puts my bag on top of the dresser and sits down beside Chase, while Annalisa, Charlotte, and I cross the room and head for the balcony. I slide open the balcony door and see the grass of the backyard, which eventually turns into sand, then ocean. It's so peaceful.

"Char, did you end up knocking people out for this room after all?" I tease her, wondering how we landed the balcony and gorgeous view.

"They let us have it since you're paying for all our food and stuff," Charlotte answers as we step back into the room and close the door.

"Plus, we figured that you two would be least likely to jump off the balcony in a drunken stupor," Annalisa says, giving Chase a sharp look.

"*Once!* It happened once and I landed in the pool!" Chase defends himself, adding in a mumble, "They never let me live that down."

I've only ever seen Chase drunk once, when he showed up at

Charlotte's resolved to declare his love for her before I stopped him, but clearly this guy does some pretty dumb things when he's had too much to drink. Drunk Chase stories just get weirder and weirder every time I hear them.

"Technically, it's Aiden's money," I clarify. "He should get first choice of rooms."

Annalisa scoffs. "Please, have you met the man? He wouldn't let us give him the better room instead of you."

I hide my blush behind my hair.

"Speaking of," Charlotte continues for Annalisa, "you promised us details. You and Aiden. Kissing. For who knows how long now?! Spill."

"Yas, give us all the deets!" Noah squeals, trying his best to imitate Charlotte. All that does is earn him three glares; only Chase finds it hilarious.

"Okay, out now you two. Go make us some hamburgers or something if you're bored," Annalisa commands, opening the door wider and pointing into the hallway.

They don't move, but Chase looks at Noah. "You hungry?"

Noah smiles. "I could eat."

They get up and head out the door, arguing about which type of meat to barbeque.

"I want cheese on my burger!" I call after them as Annalisa shuts the door.

She and Charlotte turn on me, their eyes focused on me like they're stranded on a desert island and I'm the last ounce of life saving water. Suddenly, I wish Noah and Chase were still here.

"Are you going to tell us the details or are we going to have to force them out of you?" Annalisa threatens.

"Put your throwing knives away. Sit down and I'll tell you." I sigh, mentally preparing myself for Charlotte's squeals of delight and Annalisa's line of interrogation.

We get comfy on the bed, sitting in a circle facing each other with our legs crossed.

"When did you guys become official?" Charlotte asks, eyes lighting up with excitement.

"We're not official. We haven't officially had that awkward what are we conversation. We technically haven't even been on a real date."

I know that Aiden and I have a deep connection—I know all his dark secrets and he knows mine—but I can't really tell them that. Plus, we really *didn't* have that what are we conversation that no one ever looks forward to, and I'd rather we didn't. I still haven't figured out how to tell him I'm leaving in a few weeks. I've been trying not to think about it but he has to understand. Right?

"When was your first kiss? It looks to me like he has a full access pass to kiss you whenever he wants." Charlotte smiles, genuinely happy for me.

I tell them about our first kiss. I tell them how I avoided him for weeks after that because I was scared. I don't tell them about my confession to Aiden about my past, but I tell them that after he got arrested, we cleared the air and since then we've just had a connection.

"I'm so happy you and Aiden found each other! If there's anyone who can put him in his place, it's you. We've seen it multiple times." Annalisa laughs.

"I'm happy for you too! Totally not trying to think about how you two can go on supercute double dates and I'll get ditched and sit at home like a single loser," Charlotte says, I think only half joking.

"It's okay, Char. I don't see Aiden and me going on a date and ditching you anytime soon," I reply.

Really though, I won't be able to ditch Charlotte to go on a date, since I'll be leaving town before that can happen. But I guess that means that I technically am ditching Charlotte, except for forever instead of one night.

"That just means Char is next on the boyfriend list," Annalisa jokes. "You got your choice of Mason, Noah, or Chase. Slim pickings, I know. But I'm sure you can turn any of them into respectable boyfriends in no time."

We laugh along with Annalisa, even though I know Chase would love nothing more than to be Charlotte's boyfriend.

"Maybe I'll try my luck with some locals here." Charlotte laughs, twirling a piece of hair with her finger. "A nice winter-break fling."

"There's actually supposed to be some kind of carnival going on here in a few days. The cleaning lady was telling us when we got the key. It's supposed to be a big deal, even the mayor is going! We have to go! It sounds like it'll be a lot of fun," Annalisa declares, adding that the twins would love it too.

Before we can agree, Chase and Noah holler to us from downstairs, telling us that 'Their meat is ready,' and laughing at the dirty double meaning. We roll our eyes, thinking about how we have two weeks of this. Lucky us.

12

Even though we're at a beach house, it's not the warmest weather. It's a lot nicer than back home, but it's not really swimming weather. Plus, it's a bit drizzly. But despite that, we decide to explore the town the next day.

"So who's coming into town with us?" Annalisa asks from the kitchen, which is open to the living room.

"I'm coming," I answer, pulling on a sweater and grabbing an umbrella.

"I don't feel too good today, guys. I think I'll just stay here," Charlotte says, plopping down on the couch beside the twins, who are playing a video game against Julian and Noah.

"Are you sure, Charlie?" Chase asks with concern. "Do you want me to stay here with you?"

"No, go have fun. I'll just sleep it off," she replies, pulling her sweater closer around herself and leaning back on the couch, getting comfortable.

"Mason and I are coming. Boys, go get ready," Aiden says, looking at his brothers and waiting for them to get up.

"I want to stay here and keep playing," Jason says, Jackson nodding in agreement as neither boy takes their eyes off the action on the television screen.

Aiden sighs. "I just got you that game a couple of days ago. You guys are going to finish it already."

"But we can't go! We've almost beat Julian and Noah for the first time. If we leave now we won't have this kind of lead again!" Jackson argues.

"Plus," Jason adds, "it's way too cold outside."

"As a responsible, intellectual adult, I have to agree with the monkeys. Way too cold outside for my liking," Noah states matter-of-factly, still not taking his eyes off the screen.

"It's not *too* cold. But I'd rather stay here," Jackson says, sitting up a bit taller and shooting a quick sideways glance at Charlotte.

"It's, like, negative gazillion degrees outside," Noah counters.

"Hey, at least it's not negative pertrillion degrees," Jackson replies.

"Gazillion is a bigger number than pertrillion, so your argument isn't even valid," Noah, the responsible, intellectual adult, scoffs.

Jackson sticks his tongue out at Noah, who returns the gesture with just as much ferocity.

"Why don't we let the children stay and argue and we'll go?" Mason suggests. "I think Jason and Jackson are responsible enough to babysit Noah while we're gone."

Noah sticks his tongue out at Mason in reply, clearly favoring the insult.

"Now we can finish the video game!" Jason exclaims, happy the situation worked out in his favor.

"Sorry, boys, but Julian's coming with us," Annalisa states with finality.

They pause the game on the screen for the first time.

"Really, dude?" Jason asks in disbelief.

"Sorry, guys." Julian shrugs, puts down his controller, and stands up.

"You're picking a girl over us?" Jason asks bewildered. "What happened to 'bros before hoes'? 'Dicks before chicks'? 'Misters before sisters'? 'Balls before d—'"

"Jason!" Aiden interrupts, not amused. "You just called Anna a ho."

Annalisa raises an amused eyebrow at Jason, not the slightest bit offended.

"I-I didn't mean it like that," Jason stutters, probably a little scared of Annalisa, like everyone is. "I just meant—"

"We know what you meant." Julian laughs as he pulls on a sweater. "But when you get older, you'll understand."

Noah makes a whip noise in response, and Annalisa lobs a pillow at his head. "*Return of the Zombie Aliens Part Three and a Half* will just have to wait, guys."

"Charlotte can take Julian's place since she's staying here anyway! Right, Charlotte?"

Three sets of hopeful eyes turn to Charlotte at Jason's suggestion.

She sits up and shrugs. "I don't know how good I'd be. I've never played Alien Vampires Comeback or whatever, before."

"It's Return *of the* Zombie Aliens *Part Three and a Half*," Jason emphasizes, trying to play it cool since he knows she'll be on Noah's team, increasing his own chance of winning.

"It's easy, I'll teach you," Noah says, moving so that he's sitting beside Charlotte on the couch, and going over what each control means.

Barely a few seconds pass before Jason looks over his shoulder at us. "You guys can go now."

We look at each other, astonished at being so curtly dismissed.

"Well, then, no ice cream for you," Annalisa says as we turn to leave.

We all silently laugh at the shock and regret that fills his face as his eyes widen, realizing his grave miscalculation in choosing to stay at the house.

"Are you sure you don't want me to stay here with you, Charlie?" Chase asks again, warily eyeing the shrinking space between Noah and Charlotte.

"I'm fine here. Go have fun!"

She doesn't even turn back to look at him when she responds, busy listening to Noah's instructions, and I can almost hear Chase's heart deflating a bit.

» «

After Aiden tells his brothers to be good and to listen to Charlotte, we take two cars into the heart of the town, where all the activity is. I waited to see which car Mason was getting in, then immediately ran to the other one. It's so hard to be in such a small space with him without feeling like I'm breaking out in hives. After parking, we walk through the little downtown area filled with cute, well-maintained storefronts. The majority of the stores have an overhang covering the sidewalk, which shelters us from the drizzle. I smile like a love-struck schoolgirl when Aiden intertwines his fingers with the fingers on my good hand.

He smiles at me, looking genuinely happy. It's a good look on him, much better than being constantly closed off and all stoic.

Looking up at his chiseled face when he's not paying attention to me, I smile when he laughs at something Chase says. I clench my teeth to stop my chin from quivering. He deserves to be happy more than anyone; I just wish he'd found it with someone more reliable. Someone who isn't planning on jumping ship in a few weeks.

I pretend to be interested in something Annalisa points out, but I'm just counting the bricks on the wall behind her to forget about the stinging in my eyes. I know I have to tell Aiden I'm leaving. I just don't know when or how. I don't want to hurt him. I don't want him to be mad at me, or disappointed, or feel like I was just playing with his emotions this whole time, especially since I knew full well I was leaving before we kissed for the first time. Between what I know about Mason and what I know I have to tell Aiden, I'm surprised my body hasn't turned into one giant hive.

The feeling of my hand in his is ever-present in my mind, and something instinctive and primal in my gut tells me that I know I don't want to give this up. I'm brought out of my thoughts when Aiden's grip tightens painfully.

"What's wrong?" I ask him as we walk a bit behind the others.

I follow his gaze to one of many campaign posters plastered all over the town. VOTE MAYOR KESSLER FOR GOVERNOR, they all read.

The others notice what we're looking at and stop to look at the posters too.

"Guess this guy must really want it," Julian comments. "His commercial has been running so much I practically have it memorized. 'I'm a family man, fighting for the rights of your children, our future,' yada, yada, yada."

Annalisa shakes her head. "All politicians are full of shit. He says he cares about low income families, single mothers, etcetera, but he's probably never even stepped foot in a house that cost less than seven figures."

"Who cares? Why are we staring at his campaign posters anyway? Let's eat," Mason says, leading the group onward.

"Is everything okay?" I ask Aiden softly.

He looks at the poster with his eyebrows drawn together, as if trying to put pieces of a puzzle together in his head. He finally shakes it, as if to clear it.

"Yeah. Let's go," he says, back to his old, confident self.

"Aiden! K-bear! What do you think?" Mason calls to us as we reach the group.

"About what?" I reply, not meeting his eyes for fear I'll see his dad's face.

"About going roller skating in that place over there?" He points at a building advertising indoor Rollerblading, laser tag, and an arcade.

Roller skating means lots of activity and moving around, not sitting in a small room and sweating when I feel Mason's presence *right there*, and thinking about how I'm going to ruin his home life. It also means I can keep holding Aiden's hand—if I concentrate on the now, and not the later, I can convince myself it's okay to let go and have some fun.

"I say let's go."

When we walk to the old building, I pay for everyone with the cash Aiden won, and everyone suits up. Aiden and I are the last people to get our roller skates, so everyone is already on the rink. Multicolored lights are flashing and the whole place smells like old shoes—it's both comforting and nauseating at the same time.

"I don't want this to count as our first official date," Aiden says out of nowhere as we're putting our skates on.

"Oh, we're dating?" I tease him.

He smirks up at me as he ties his laces. "I certainly hope so."

My smile probably takes up half my face, and I focus on tying my skates so he doesn't see me blush. He knows exactly what buttons to push to make me react how he wants. Asshole.

"Why don't you want this to count as our first official date? It's like a triple date. We've got three couples," I joke, looking over at Mason and Chase who are arguing over something dumb with Julian and Annalisa.

Aiden sits up and laughs, a sound that I will never, ever get tired of hearing.

"We both know Chase only has eyes for one particular girl. And Mason isn't nearly as pretty as her," he jokes, referring to Charlotte, who's still oblivious to Chase's feelings.

I shake my head in mock pity. "Poor Mason. He never even stood a chance."

We laugh as he helps me stand up. I stumble a bit on the unsteadiness of the wheels, but he keeps me balanced. I end up incredibly close to him, his hands on my waist, mine on his broad shoulders. Suddenly, our joking demeanor is replaced with something much more serious, something that makes my pulse race and heart stammer.

"When we go on our first real date, I want it to just be the two of us. Without everyone watching our every move."

Mason is, sure enough, watching Aiden and me like a lion stalking its prey. Aiden's grip on my waist tightens.

"Somewhere no one knows us," he continues, his voice lowering. "Where we can just be Aiden and Thea."

Aiden and Thea. Warmth radiates through my chest. I can't even describe how much I like the sound of that.

"We've been alone plenty of times. Gone out just the two of us all the time," I reply, but it comes out sounding as nervous as I feel, so very aware of his proximity.

"But now I know you're Thea," he replies simply.

A smile spreads across my face. "Just the two of us, huh?"

I like the sound of that. We've been at the beach house for less than twenty-four hours and we've already been interrupted more times than I can count on two hands.

He nods, a small smile aimed at me. "Somewhere I can kiss you whenever I want. Without an audience."

He's so close to me. All I have to do is reach up on my tippy-toes for my lips to meet his.

"You could kiss me now," I breathe, captivated by all that is Aiden.

"I could. But maybe I'll save it for later." He pulls away from me with a smirk, mischief lighting up his eyes as he moves away from me.

I'm suddenly reminded of just how old Aiden's forced to act, and how rare it is that he gets to just let go and act his age. Mature, responsible Aiden is sexy, but carefree, fun-loving Aiden is too.

I was going to tell him I had no problem with him kissing me now and *again* later, but if he's going to play the whole self-restraint game, I can too.

≫ ≪

Aiden says he's never been roller skating before, but like everything else, he's naturally great at it. It takes me a bit but I get the hang of it pretty quickly, especially with Aiden's help. I'm tempted to pretend I still can't skate by myself if only to make Aiden keep playing the knight in shining armor and holding on to me, but my pride won't let me.

There are some other kids our age in here who we end up making friends with, but at two o'clock on a Tuesday, it's mostly dead—which is great for us. The others introduced themselves as Erin, Vee, Lilly, and Oliver. Erin and Lilly must be sisters, since they look almost identical with dark hair and chestnut eyes, and Oliver is Lilly's boyfriend. He's got wide shoulders and likes to overuse the word *man*. Vee is stunning, though, and the way she keeps looking over at Aiden makes my fingernails bite into the palms of my hand. Her face is perfectly symmetrical and unblemished, and her brown hair falls over her shoulders in effortless waves.

"Okay, okay. Me next!" Erin exclaims, getting in position between Julian and Chase at one end of the rink. "You better be sure to catch me, hot stuff!" she yells at Mason, who's positioned at the other end of the rink.

"You got it!" he shouts back with a flirty grin.

Julian and Chase each grab one of her hands and skate forward while she keeps her legs still. Once they gain some speed, they fling her forward, and she flies across the rink at top speed, laughing and shrieking the whole way.

Mason's arms are out, ready to catch her before she slams into the boards, but she's still gaining speed by the time she gets there. To Mason's credit, he does his best, but Erin crashes into him, and they go down in a tangle of laughs and screams.

"You guys okay?" Julian calls to them, trying not to laugh with the rest of us.

"We're fine," Mason replies, helping Erin up. "Her knee just missed my *precious jewels*. That would not have been okay."

"Aw, really? I was aiming for them." Erin smirks, and Mason gives her a playful shove.

"Can I go next?" I ask hopefully. "Unless Vee wants to go?"

"Why don't we both go?" Vee suggests.

In the short time we've gotten to know her, it's clear she's a pretty wild one. In fact, I'm pretty sure she's drunk at the moment, but I'm not judging. It's her winter break, too, and she can spend it however she wants as long as she's not driving. She's a pretty loud person, someone who commands the attention of the room, but hands down one of the friendliest people I've ever met when she's not making googly eyes at Aiden.

"How would that work?" Lilly asks, slightly less drunk than her friend.

"It'll be a competition. Oli and Erin will toss me, and Julian and Chase can toss Amelia beside me at the same time. You have to throw her at the Kessler campaign sign on the boards, and the first girl to pass the cola advertisement on the boards wins!"

I look at the boys to gauge their opinion, and clearly their competitive side has already switched on. They're ready to win.

"I'm game if you guys are," Oliver says to the boys, a friendly challenge in his voice.

"Oh, you are so on," Annalisa replies, a fire in her eyes.

"Is it okay with you, Amelia?" Aiden asks, eyeing my taped up finger.

I look over at Erin, Oli, and Vee, who are already talking strategy.

"Let's win this thing." I smile and skate over to my team.

Obviously, Lilly would not be strong enough to catch Vee as

she whips toward her, so it somehow ends up being Mason who will catch her, and Aiden who will catch me. I'm definitely not complaining about the new arrangement, since it means Aiden putting his hands all over me, and no one in their right mind would complain about that.

From outside the rink Lilly and Annalisa are refereeing. It's just a friendly little competition, but clearly everyone here is interested in winning.

"Remember, you have to let go of your girl by the campaign sign!" Lilly reminds us as we get ready to start. "In three, two, one, *go*!"

Julian and Chase skate forward and pull me along with all they've got, the wind against my face feeling refreshing and freeing. I laugh, having way too much fun with this compared to the seriousness on Annalisa's face when she told us we better win.

We reach the campaign sign and they let go of my arms, throwing me clear across the rink. Vee is right beside me, having just been thrown herself, and we laugh as the boys cheer for us to pass the finish line.

I'm going so fast and laughing so hard I have no idea who passes the finish board first, but suddenly I crash into Aiden, who manages to keep us from falling until the last second, when his roller skates cause him to lose his balance.

I already heard the crash, laughs, and swears from when Mason and Vee hit the ground, and I'm sure we were just as amusing as they were falling. We fall, and Aiden twists so that I land on top of him. Despite his body being 99 percent pure muscle, it only hurts a little bit, probably lessened by the fact that I'm having so much fun.

Lying on the floor with his hands around my waist, we look at each other and can't contain our laughter. I feel like a child who wants to clap her hands and chant, Again, again!

Our laughter dies down when the butterflies in my chest make an appearance, like they do whenever I'm this close to Aiden. His gray eyes flicker to my lips, and like granting an unspoken wish, he lifts his head to kiss me. Like every time our lips touch, the fire that ignites within me spreads, and everything else melts away. He kisses me slowly and deeply, like there is nowhere else in the world he needs to go, nothing else that matters. He pulls away, frankly entirely too early for my liking, and looks at me with a smirk, a spark alight in his eyes.

"Told you I'd save it for later."

I laugh and push myself off of him, helping him up in the process, but not before catching the look on Mason's face as he watches us. A look that manages to leave me feeling cold despite the fact that I'm sweating from all the exerted energy.

The rest of the time goes by in a blur, and I don't remember ever laughing so hard, even as I'm busy trying to ignore Vee making eyes at Aiden and avoiding making eye contact with Mason. By the time we're ready to leave, we've invited our new friends to come back to the house with us to hang out, but they all say no. Erin, however, gives Mason her number, and promises to come by later. I'm not a mind reader, but even I know what that means, at least if the suggestive way she runs her hand down his chest and the sultry look she gives him is anything to go by. He smiles and promises he'll see her later, then catches me looking and hastily shoves his phone back in his pocket and stares down at the floor.

"Ready to go? I'm thinking we pick up sushi for dinner," Aiden says as he comes back from returning our roller skates.

"Sounds good to me," I tell him, taking his offered hand and walking out into the fresh air together, the rest of our friends trailing behind us.

13

We've only been here for three days and we're already getting sick of only eating various types of barbequed meat for lunch and dinner. Since tomorrow is Christmas Day and the guys have been so good about taking turns being grill master, Annalisa, Charlotte, and I have shooed them out of the kitchen, where we're making our "family" dinner. Tomorrow will be a traditional, big Christmas lunch—Julian even managed to get a whole turkey from the market and googled stuffing recipes—but we're still making a big Christmas Eve dinner.

"Quick! Someone take a picture! Anna's *voluntarily* helping in the kitchen!" Julian jokes.

Annalisa responds by lobbing a wooden spoon at her boyfriend, which he easily deflects with a laugh.

The house is beautiful, but the only problem is that it's open concept, so there are no walls dividing the kitchen and TV area. This is a problem because it's raining outside and the guys are bored, which means annoying us is their only form of entertainment.

"Go video call your parents," I tell them. "You all promised you'd wish them Merry Christmas on both Christmas Eve and Day."

"We all did that already," Julian says.

"Then go play outside or something," Annalisa orders them as she gets another spoon, having lost hers.

Noah sits down beside Julian at the kitchen island and steals a cucumber from the salad we just finished preparing.

"It's raining outside." He reaches to steal another cucumber but Charlotte swats his hand away, and he gives her a kicked puppy look.

She huffs but ends up falling for it, giving him another cucumber slice before moving the salad to the counter.

"When has the rain ever stopped you from doing something?" she asks him.

He tilts his head, contemplating the question. "Well, never. But dinner's almost ready, and my mother would have a conniption if she found out I ruined Christmas Eve dinner by showing up soaking wet." Judy is a woman to be reckoned with.

We tell them to make themselves useful and set the table if they insist on bothering us, which they do with the utmost dedication. Eventually, we're sitting around the table eating, and the guys are too busy stuffing their faces to annoy us any longer.

Jason looks at me, sauce all over his face. "I already knew you made good pancakes, but your pasta is amazing!"

"I'm glad you like it, Jason." I smile at him, then laugh when Aiden throws him a napkin and tells him to try not to miss his mouth anymore.

"This cucumber salad is really great too. What dressing is this, Char?" I ask, scooping a second serving onto my plate.

"Actually, Mason mixed a bunch of stuff for the dressing and wouldn't tell me what it was," she tells me, and the blood drains from my face. I've been an expert at avoiding speaking directly to Mason since we got here.

"It's a secret," he replies. "My mom taught me. But maybe I'll show you, k-bear, since you clearly like it so much."

His mom taught him? Natalia? The sweet, innocent woman who was nothing but nice to me when I met her? Is it hot in here? Why am I sweating?

"Actually, you know, I think too many cucumbers give me a stomachache, so it's probably best I don't know the recipe. Hey, is that a bunny outside? I swear I just saw one jump by on the back porch." All my words jumble together and when everyone turns to look for the fictional bunny, I pull on the collar of my shirt a few times to air myself out, dropping my hand and smiling casually when everyone turns back to look at me.

"Uh, I guess we missed it. Are you sure you don't want the recipe?" Mason asks slowly.

"Yup. Hey, Jason and Jackson, why don't you tell everyone about the level you beat on Intense Alien Vampires today?" I say, and the twins take the bait and the spotlight off of me immediately.

"It's Return *of the* Zombie Aliens *Part Three and a Half*." Jason sighs exasperatedly. We're never going to get the name right. "But it was so cool! We used the trick you told us about, Noah, and . . ."

I tune out after that. Aiden nudges me and tilts his head in a silent question. *I know, Aiden, I know. I'm a mess.* I just send him a tight smile and stare at my plate for the rest of dinner, not at all hungry for that second serving of salad on my plate like I was a few minutes ago.

»«

Everyone helps clean up after dinner and Aiden takes out the stockings he brought—ten in total, one for each of us—and lets the twins hang them up above the electric fireplace. They then set out some cookies and promise to put the milk for Santa out before bed. Afterward, Aiden and I somehow get lucky and manage to get some uninterrupted alone time.

We're sitting cross-legged on his bed, facing each other, eating Nutella sandwiches for a late-night snack and playing a very intense game of would you rather.

"Okay, would you rather lick Nutella off Noah's toes or streak at the next school football game?"

"That's easy," he answers. "Streaking."

I take a bite of my heavenly sandwich and instantly disagree with his choice. "Really? Over Nutella?"

He gives me a sexy smirk, which causes heat to rush to my face. "I've got nothing to be ashamed of."

I wouldn't know, but when he looks at me like that . . .

I clear my throat. "I'd still choose the Nutella. It's the most rational decision."

"Tell you what: Why don't we call Noah over here and slather some Nutella on his toes? If you lick it all off, I'll streak at the next game."

"You would never."

"Not normally, but I always keep my promises. So if you do yours, you know I'll do mine."

I eye my Nutella sandwich, then think about Noah's toes.

"Fine. You're right. I'd rather streak."

"So we both choose being naked. Clearly it's the better choice."

Aiden. Naked. I think my senses would go into overload.

"We're talking hypothetically, though."

Aiden knows exactly where my mind has gone, and naturally, has to tease me about it. "Does the thought of me naked make you nervous, Thea?"

Hell, yes. "Of course not."

He looks at me skeptically, and I don't blame him; I didn't even believe me.

"I think you're lying."

Obviously. "Am not!"

Ever since we arrived at the beach house, it's been apparent to everyone that Aiden hasn't been as burdened as before. His spirits are lighter, and he's in a playful mood more often than not. Knowing that he's letting his guard down is one of the most heartwarming things. I can't help but get butterflies every time I look at him goofing off, being a teenager, letting loose. He's still Aiden, scary as ever and not someone you'd want to piss off, but he smiles quicker here, laughs more freely.

To me, he says, "Should we call your bluff?"

"But it's not a bl—"

Jesus Christ.

Aiden has just casually pulled off his shirt, and is now sitting here in all his muscly, godlike glory, totally letting my reaction inflate his ego.

"You sure you're not uncomfortable with me being naked?"

Forcing my eyes away from his abs, I make some kind of noise in agreement. He smiles at me, a mischievous gleam in his usually stormy eyes.

"So you wouldn't mind if I just . . ."

Instead of finishing his statement, he stands up, and slowly undoes the top button of his jeans. My eyes bulge out of my head. Dear God, is he *actually going to get naked?!*

He answers my silent question by slowly lowering his zipper, keeping eye contact with me the entire time. I sit silent. Frozen.

What is happening?!

He hooks his thumbs into his jeans and black boxers, raising an eyebrow at me. He wouldn't. Just as he's about to throw down his pants and Calvin Kleins in one fluid motion, I throw my hands over my face. "Okay, okay! You win! Stop getting naked!"

He laughs and sits back on the bed, not bothering to zip up his jeans or put his shirt back on. Not that I'm complaining, but it's kind of hard to think with him being all effortlessly gorgeous.

"If you were uncomfortable, you should've just said something," he teases, sitting closer than he was originally.

I finish my sandwich. "If I just started getting naked, would you not get uncomfortable?"

He blinks at me. "You literally just described the opposite of what I would consider a problem. But if you want to find out, you can always just start getting naked."

I laugh and play hit him, but he catches my wrist and pulls me closer to him. I react the way any rational girl in my position would—I kiss him.

No matter how many times we do it, my body always reacts like it's the first time. Butterflies, electricity, heart in overdrive. We end up tangled in each other, with Aiden lying on top of me. He pulls away and hovers over me on his elbows, my hands in his hair.

"You know I was just joking before," he says, his voice low and honest. "I would never force you to do anything before you're ready. I'm not in any rush."

I answer him by pulling him toward me and kissing him with all I've got.

Right when things are starting to get heated, the door bursts open. "Hey, guys, we're going to—*Oh God! Get a room, Jesus!*" Noah throws his hands over his eyes, acting as if the sight of us together has physically burned his corneas.

Aiden gives a very agitated sigh and grudgingly rolls off of me. "We did, Noah."

Since we hadn't yelled at Noah to leave, he peeks through his fingers and calms down when he realizes that I'm fully clothed.

"You should start knocking before barging into rooms," I tell him, not really mad, more just perturbed my time with Aiden was cut short.

"You guys should start locking doors when you're planning on getting it on."

"We weren't—"

"Doesn't matter! Don't want to know the details. Like, ever," Noah interrupts me. "Just came to tell you that the twins have passed out in bed and the adults have decided to play a drinking game, if you want to join."

"They're asleep already?" Aiden asks. "They're usually too excited to go to bed since they can't wait for morning to open presents."

"Yeah, I think they're just really tired, there's a lot going on here. We promised them we'd set the milk out for Santa before bed, though. Are you guys in for some Christmas Eve drinking fun?"

Aiden's not really a big drinker. In fact, I don't think I've ever seen him drink alcohol. He responds by pulling on his shirt and telling Noah we'll meet him in the family room.

"Are you sure? I can always just tell everyone you guys were too busy fuc—"

I cut him off by lobbing a pillow at his head à la Annalisa, and he laughs, shutting the door as he leaves and makes his way back to the group.

» «

The drinking game we settled on was king's cup. Basically, we sit in a circle with our drinks and a deck of cards in the middle, and take turns flipping over the top card. Every card is assigned a meaning, the end goal being that someone has to drink.

For example, two means you, so if I flip over a two, I get to choose someone to drink. Three means me, so whoever pulls a three has to drink. Seven means heaven, so the last person in the circle to raise their hands in the air has to drink, and so on until we finish the deck, shuffle, and repeat.

Aiden plays with us, and despite him not being much of a drinker, the alcohol is barely affecting him as far as I can tell. But four full decks and an endless number of empty beer bottles later, the rest of us are all pretty much smashed, Mason, Chase, Julian, and Charlotte the worst of us. It's a good thing Aiden got the twins' presents sorted out, along with the stockings, before we started, or else it'd have been a very disappointing Christmas for Jackson and Jason.

Mason and Chase are drunk because instead of taking regular sized drinks when it's their turn, they basically take two giant gulps or chug half their beer. Julian because he was a really good Question Master the first game and kept screwing everyone over, (if you pull a Queen you become Question Master until someone else pulls a Queen, and if anyone answers any questions you ask during that period, they have to drink), so for the rest of the night, everyone has been targeting him as retribution. And Charlotte's plastered because she's a lightweight.

"Whose turn was it again?" Noah slurs as I sit back down on the floor with a couple of beers for whoever's empty.

No one answers, not to be rude, but because we all remember that he's the current Question Master.

Instead, Mason flips over the top card. It's an eight, which means he gets to make up a rule that lasts throughout the entire deck, and every time you break it, you need to drink.

"If you say 'no swearing' again, I will dump my entire beer on your head," Annalisa threatens.

The no swearing rule in the second game is pretty much the reason most of us are a bit more than tipsy.

"Now, now, Anna. You can't coerce the rule maker." Mason smiles drunkenly. "Okay, if you pull a card with a suit of hearts, you need to kiss the closest person of the opposite sex on your . . . left!"

Mason is the closest person of the opposite sex on my left. No matter how hard I tried, fate put me right beside him.

"I don't want Noah planting his lips on my girl!" Julian announces, throwing a heavy arm around Annalisa.

"Why? Scared she'll realize she's madly in love with me and dump you?" Noah retorts.

"More like I don't want her catching whatever you've got," Julian counters.

"Relax, it doesn't have to be on the lips," Mason clarifies, and everyone settles down.

We continue playing for a couple of rounds and then Chase

pulls a six of hearts. I know the exact moment he realizes what that means, because his entire face lights up bright red; the closest girl to his left is Charlotte.

"Ooo, Chase and Char! You know what that means!" Mason smiles, excited that he gets to witness his rule in action.

Chase looks completely stunned, and Charlotte giggles then raises her bottle.

"Cheers!" she says to me and Annalisa, because six means chicks.

We take a drink of our beers, and when Charlotte's done, she puts her bottle down, puts her hands on Chase's face, and *kisses him right on the lips.* I think she stunned everyone, but she probably *broke* Chase. I wonder if she stopped his heart completely. From the angle I'm sitting at, I can't even tell if he's kissing her back or not. She pulls away quickly and tucks a strand of hair behind her ear.

"Okay, it's your turn to go, Aiden," she says like she didn't just kiss her best friend who's secretly in love with her.

Chase, however, is in a complete daze, a slight smile on his face as he looks off blankly in the distance.

"You know you didn't have to kiss him on the lips, right, Char?" Noah clarifies, his eyes shifting back and forth between her and a still shell-shocked Chase. She blinks at him, lids heavy.

"Oh." She shrugs and giggles at nothing in particular.

Okay, maybe she should stop drinking. I'm the one sharing a room and bathroom with her.

Aiden, Noah, Annalisa, and Julian pull cards as the game continues. On my turn, I pull a five of hearts.

Five means guys, so the Boys raise their bottles in a salute and take a drink.

"Suit of hearts means I get a kiss, Amelia," Mason gloats, almost smugly. "I want one like Char gave Chase."

Mason smiles, and I ignore the feeling of guilt that appears every time I look at him. Clearly a drunk Mason is not a more charming Mason.

Before I can even react, Aiden abruptly stands up from his spot across from me and purposely walks around and sits down between me and Mason. He throws a quick glare at Mason when he starts to object, shutting him up immediately, then turns to look at me.

"Guess I'm the closest guy on your left," he states.

Putting his hand possessively but gently on the back of my head, he tangles it in my hair and pulls me to him, kissing me deeply. My first thought is *Damn that was sexy*, but then the butterflies realize who's kissing me and decide to throw a party in my stomach.

I pull away from him, ignoring all the whistling and cheers from our drunk friends, and look at him quizzically. What was that all about? Aiden smiles at me, looking mighty proud of himself, and gives Mason a quick, pointed look.

Realization slams into me like an eighteen-wheeler. He just used me to make some kind of point in his macho-man standoff against Mason.

Mason's looking down at his bottle and not paying attention to the rest of the game. Sometimes, like at times like these, I think he likes me as more than a friend, and other times, like when we just joke around or when he flirts with other girls in front of me, I think he knows we're platonic. So it would be incredibly awkward if I just confronted him off of a suspicion, and he looks at me all, WTF, k-bear, you know we're just best friends.

And then there's Aiden. I don't really know how I feel about him pulling this possessive kind of stuff. I'm not going to lie, it's kind of hot, but then again, he didn't need to use me to get to Mason, if that was even his intention. I could've kissed him on the cheek, like Noah just did with Annalisa.

Is this just "drunk" Aiden being superjealous? He doesn't look drunk, though. After one more full deck of cards, we decide to call it a night.

I think Chase carried Charlotte up the stairs and helped her get in bed. Aiden helped Annalisa get Julian to their room, and everyone else kind of stumbled off to bed as well.

I decide to clean up before going to bed—I don't want the twins to discover our giant party among all their presents. I'm not really tired anyway, and it's not recommended to mix sleeping pills with alcohol, so I figure by the time I'm done cleaning up, plus the alcohol, I'll be tired enough to fall asleep without the pills.

After clearing away all the bottles from the family room, and putting away all the snacks, I tackle the kitchen. Currently, I'm trying to get Noah's shirt down from the top of the fridge. I have no idea how or why it ended up there, but at some point during the night Noah pulled it off, and then it ended up on top of the fridge.

I'm not the tallest person around and I don't think I'm too short, but even on my tippy-toes and stretching as far as I can, I still can't reach his stupid shirt. I'm past the point of going to grab a chair: this is personal now. I glance at the counter. Maybe I can jump onto it and launch off to grab the shirt? Or maybe open a cupboard door and monkey climb the shelves?

"Need some help?"

I twirl around and see Mason standing behind me, clearly deciding now is the time to practice sneaking up on people like a freaking ninja.

He looks at my face and laughs at my reaction, eyes bright. "Didn't mean to scare you."

I brush my hair off my face, avoiding looking right at him. I still can't face him, not completely. "It's fine. I thought everyone went off to bed."

"I was, but I heard you makin' so much noise I had to see what was going on. Sounded like you were skippin' rope or havin' a dance party with no music."

I look back at the top of the fridge, Noah's shirt at the very back, taunting me. Mason follows my gaze, a smile breaking out when he realizes the current situation.

"You know, you could've just gotten a chair—"

"I don't need a chair! I can do it myself." I narrow my eyes at the stupid white shirt, mocking me for my shortness.

"Wow. Good to know drunk k-bear is competitive."

With squared shoulders, I focus my full attention on the shirt. When I jump for it again, big hands land on my waist, lifting me up higher so I can reach the back of the fridge. I snatch the shirt and Mason lowers me back to the floor.

"Yes! Stupid shirt. I win!" I feel like whipping it onto the floor like it's a football and I just scored a touchdown.

"Technically, I win, because without me you wouldn't've gotten the shirt," Mason slurs with a smile, still buzzed from the game.

"Whatever. I've still got the shirt in my hand." I turn around to *literally* rub my prize in his face.

He laughs, and it's then I realize his hands are still on my waist as they tighten, pulling me closer to him, unconsciously, I think. There's a sudden palpable shift in the room. It was light, airy, and fun, but now it's serious, almost suffocating me with the intensity. My eyes widen as I end up chest to chest with Mason, who's looking down at me and smiling like I'm the most interesting girl in the world.

I clear my throat and try taking a step back. "Um, might wanna let go now, Mason."

He looks at me as if in a daze. "What?"

"She said let go," a harsh voice says from behind us, cutting through the room with undeniable authority.

At the sound of Aiden's deep voice, Mason shakes his head and drops his hands like I've physically burned him.

"Oh, umm, sorry. Dazed off there for a bit." He laughs forcibly, almost awkwardly.

"It's okay." I smile at him reassuringly as Aiden crosses the room in a few big strides.

Once he reaches me, he grabs my hand, possessively intertwining his fingers with mine, his eyes shooting daggers at Mason.

"We'll all help finish cleaning up tomorrow morning. Let's get some sleep."

Before I can even reply, he tugs me toward his room, throwing a "good night" to Mason over his shoulder, as if an afterthought.

He leads me into his room and closes the door behind me, the muscles in his back tense.

"What was that about?" I ask him.

He turns to look at me, his face blank, but his still tense back giving him away. "I don't know what you're talking about."

"The whole possessive caveman act back there? And during king's cup?"

Aiden never acts all jealous and possessive like this. Sometimes I know he is, but it's usually cute and endearing, not all must horde the shiny object so no one else can see it possessive.

He rolls his eyes. "I am not a caveman."

"You know what I mean. What's going on with you?" I realize I'm still clutching Noah's shirt, and toss it haphazardly somewhere on the floor, the previous significance of it having completely vanished.

"Nothing's going on with me." He's careful to keep his face neutral, his eyes devoid of any discernable emotion. He's good at doing that, but he usually doesn't guard his emotions with me. I don't like the distant way this makes me feel.

I sit cross-legged on his bed, and he leans against the door, arms tight across his chest, almost in defense.

"You've been acting like this around Mason a lot," I state matter-of-factly.

He studies me, opens his mouth, but then hesitates.

"Just tell me." I decide for him.

"Mason's basically in love with you, Thea."

What? Of everything he could've said, I didn't expect that.

"What are you talking about?"

He uncrosses his arms and strides across the room to sit facing me on the bed.

"It's incredibly obvious to everyone except you," he says gently.

I blink at him. "But literally two days ago, he brought Erin back to his room and did God knows what with her."

"Because he knows you're with me. He can't help how he feels, though."

I've had suspicions, but with Aiden confirming it now, I don't know how to feel. Should I say something to Mason? That's just awkward. Should I ignore it and act like I always have with him? I don't want things to change with us; he's, like, my best friend. And how can I possibly say something to him when I still can't look him straight in the eye without guilt gnawing at my stomach?

"Is that why you get all jealous around him?"

"I don't get *jealous* around him." He defends himself quickly.

I feel a corner of my lip curve up in a smile. "You totally do."

He runs a frustrated hand through his hair. "I just . . . I've never felt like this before. It's weird seeing my best friend trying to put moves on *my girl.*"

Oh my God. Is Aiden Parker insecure? I didn't think that was an emotion he even felt. And over me? Of all things? My pulse racing, I crawl into his lap, and his arms automatically go around my waist as he gazes down at me.

"It's you for me, Aiden."

He lowers his head and kisses me like he's suffocating and I'm the air he needs to survive, his arms tightening, pulling me closer to him until I don't know where he starts and I end. We end up tangled in his sheets, his kisses on my neck doing things to my nerve ends I have only dreamed about.

When he comes to kiss my lips again, I can't help what happens next: I yawn right in his face. My eyes widen in embarrassment, the mood totally killed. But instead of rolling off of me in disgust, Aiden laughs.

"Guess we should get some sleep," he says, moving so fluidly that he ends up under me, with his hard chest as my pillow.

"Aren't you gonna kick me out so you can get some sleep?" I tease.

He kisses my forehead so sweetly that my heart nearly explodes. "No, I'm comfortable just like this."

Whether it's the alcohol, the late hour, the new revelation, or Aiden's reassuring presence, I fall into a peaceful sleep as soon as he wraps a strong arm around my waist and pulls me close.

14

I wake up the next morning expecting to find Aiden's heavy but comforting arm wrapped around my waist, but the bed is empty. Trying to ignore the sense of longing as I sit up, I rub the sleep from my eyes. It's only six o'clock, and Aiden isn't in the room at all. I wonder if the twins are up and ready to open their presents.

When I slide out of bed, the early morning chill hits me all at once, and I slip into a sweater Aiden left on the edge of his bed. Snuggling into it, I resist the urge to smell it like a total psychopath, but it totally has the alluring smell that's distinctly Aiden.

When I get out of his en suite bathroom, he walks into the room at the same time, a tray in one hand and a present in the other. "Hey, Merry Christmas."

I sit cross-legged on his bed as he closes the door and smile at him, eyeing the items in his hands.

"Merry Christmas," I reply. "Did *Santa* come last night?"

He sits cross-legged on the bed in front of me and sets the tray between us. "Yes. The milk has been drunk and the cookies have been eaten. Even the carrots Jason and Jackson left out for the reindeer are gone. All the stockings are filled with chocolates, face masks, nail polish, and other sparkly stuff for the girls, lots of food for the guys. I think Noah got coal."

I bite back a laugh. "How about your brothers? What did Santa leave them?"

"Jason and Jackson got a video game each, and I'm kind of annoyed at Santa for indulging their video game addiction."

My heart warms at his humor. This is how Aiden should always be. Relaxed; happy. I gesture at the tray sitting between us. "What do you have there?"

"Since we all agreed to wake up at the ungodly hour of seven to exchange Secret Santa presents, I figured waking everyone up would go over better if we had some hot chocolate and coffee already made."

I laugh as I take my mug of hot chocolate off the tray and take a sip.

"This is so weird. You're a grinch the other 364 days of the year, but you're nice on Christmas."

"I am not a grinch." He looks into his coffee and adds quietly, "Plus, the twins love waking up on Christmas morning and drinking hot chocolate with those little marshmallows."

I try not to swoon, but I'm sure it's written all over my face. "You're such a good big brother."

He ignores my incredibly correct statement and drinks his coffee. "That's my favorite sweater, you know." He nods at the sweater I'm wearing.

I smile cheekily at him. "Good thing it's on your favorite person."

He raises an amused eyebrow and grins knowingly. "I wouldn't let Noah borrow my sweaters."

I fake indignation and play hit him, and we both laugh.

"Are you going to tell me what's in that box or are you going to let me die of curiosity?"

He laughs and moves the tray off the bed, replacing it with the small box wrapped in Christmas paper.

"I know we all agreed to do Secret Santa instead of everyone getting everyone a present, but I still wanted to get you something even though I didn't pick your name."

My heart skips a few beats and I discreetly pinch myself to stop from crying. It takes everything I have to stop myself from tackling him and kissing him until New Year's. I rest my mug on the floor and gently take the surprisingly well-wrapped present in my hands.

I raise my eyes to his, only to find him already studying me. "You didn't have to get me anything."

"Just open it."

It's a flat, red box, just a bit bigger than my hand, and I eye his stoic face before opening the lid.

It's a necklace, but not a normal, dainty, diamond kind of necklace. The chain is a regular, long, plain chain, and hanging from it is an object. It's long and skinny and looks wooden, with some ornate golden designs at the top and bottom, and some numbers burned into it. It looks vintage, and it's truly beautiful.

"It's beautiful, Aiden. Definitely one of a kind. Thank you."

I hold it up to examine it, and it has some weight to it, but not so much that it would bother me.

"May I?" He holds out his hand and I place the necklace in it.

"See these two things right here?" He points to the top of the wooden part where some gold decoration sticks out slightly. "You have to press them at the same time."

He does, and there's a very slight click.

"That was the blade unlocking."

Blade?!

He pulls on the new silver thing sticking out of the long side of the wood, and like he said, a blade swings out. I blink at him. Aiden seriously got me a pocketknife disguised as a beautiful necklace. I laugh. It's a carefree, honest laugh that has Aiden looking confused.

"Why are you laughing?" he frowns.

"This is probably the most useful and thoughtful gift I've ever gotten. I love it."

He smiles, looking slightly relieved but hiding it well.

"With everything going on, I wanted to make sure you're always safe and never left helpless, especially since I can't always be around. I know you're not helpless and can kick some ass, but I thought it would be better if you had something on you at all times."

Taking the necklace back from him, I close the blade. It's not a large blade and it's not like I could kill anyone with it, but I could do some serious damage if Tony snuck up on me.

"I honestly love it. It's such an 'Aiden' gift." I laugh.

This is just like Aiden, always looking out for the people he cares about and wanting them to be safe. I'm so lucky to have him in my life, even if it's just for a short while. I'll get to wear this necklace when I'm in whatever town I'm shipped off to, and always remember this moment with Aiden. I'll always be able to remember *him* and how he made me feel like I was floating.

"I was going to get you a Taser disguised as lipstick," he tells me, "but knowing how clumsy you are, I figured that might lead to some pretty bad accidents. At least with this you have to consciously unlock the blade first."

"I would not accidentally tase myself!"

"Better safe than sorry," he teases.

I run my hand along the handle of the pocketknife. "What do these numbers engraved in the handle mean?"

He shifts and sheepishly rubs the back of his neck with his hand.

"They're the coordinates of the school," he admits.

"The school?"

"Yeah, where we first met."

I think my jaw hits the floor as I stare at him.

Now I *know* he's uncomfortable, because he starts rambling. "I figured there wouldn't be any harm in the coordinates. If anyone who shouldn't know what those numbers mean gets too close to you, it'd be too late for them anyway. And I wanted the necklace to remind you of me, of all your friends, since that's where we all met and—"

I'm really glad he put his coffee down, because I save him from his rambling by doing what I wanted to do earlier and tackle him, kissing him with everything I have. He kisses me back just as passionately, pulling me close to him until I can barely catch my breath.

"Oh wait!" I pull back from him. "Stay right here, don't move!"

I put the necklace on his dresser and race out of his room, leaving him looking thoroughly confused.

I pass by Charlotte, Noah, the twins, and Annalisa in the kitchen, drinking the coffee and hot chocolate Aiden had made.

"Merry Christmas!" I say to them as I head toward the stairs.

They repeat the greeting back to me as they notice where I'm coming from.

"Pulling a walk of shame this morning, huh?" Noah says with a smirk.

"It's not a shame if it's from Aiden's room," I shoot back as I head up the stairs.

There's a small envelope with Aiden's name on it in my bag, and I grab it before heading back to his room. I ignore Noah's remarks as I enter the room again and close the door.

He had changed into fresh clothes while I was gone, and just laughs when I point out that he moved even though I told him not to.

"I didn't get you for Secret Santa either," I tell him, "but I saw this and wanted to give it to you."

I hand him the envelope and take a seat on the bed again as he opens it.

"Oh wow," he says as he holds the ticket in his hand. "This is amazing!"

I got him a ticket to one of those racetracks where they let you drive a car like a Lamborghini or Ferrari around a course at top speed.

I smile and bite my lip. "I thought you'd have some fun. I know you prefer your races illegal, but this might be cool too," I joke, and he smiles warmly at me, an emotion in his eyes that makes my heart squeeze.

"I love it. You didn't have to do this, but thank you."

He puts the envelope down on the dresser beside my necklace and holds out his arms. I practically scramble off the bed and jump into them.

I barely kiss him before there's banging on the door.

"Hey!" I hear Noah's voice. "Hurry up in there! We want to open presents!"

"Guess we should go before the children get antsy," he says, even though neither of us makes a move to pull apart.

"I am not a child!" comes Noah's voice from behind the door. "But I still want presents!"

We laugh as we pull apart and head into the living room, where everyone is gathered with the present from their Secret Santa.

As I sit down with Aiden and grab the gift with my name on it, I look around at all my friends and their happy faces. The twins are jumping all over each other to show Aiden what Santa left for them, and Aiden manages to look genuinely surprised. He even tells them he's jealous that the boys got video games and all he got was some chocolate and a tub of protein powder, and tells them it must be because they were extra good this year. Julian, Chase, and Mason are already devouring some of the snacks left in their stockings. Annalisa and Charlotte are reading the uses of each face mask, and Noah is complaining that his real stocking must be hidden somewhere because there's *no way* he could've gotten coal.

This may not be the most conventional holiday, and we might be away from home, but I already know that this is my favorite Christmas ever.

15

It's Friday night, and we all go to the carnival that the locals have been talking about. It's a pretty big event, with people from towns all over showing up to have a good time. There are a bunch of rides that, to be honest, look pretty rickety, but are holding their own, a bunch of games and stands, and seemingly more food trucks than there are people. The rain even stopped for the night, letting us enjoy the night wearing just sweaters.

"Congratulations! You're the winner!" the man at the make-shift stand tells Aiden as Annalisa and I pout since we were also competing.

"This game is rigged anyway," Annalisa mumbles as Julian hands her purse and jacket back.

"Amelia has two fingers taped together and she didn't do too bad." Julian motions to my dislocated finger, earning him a glare from his girlfriend.

"You get to pick anything on the top shelf." The game attendant waves at the line of medium-sized stuffed animals.

Aiden looks at me. "Pick whatever you want."

I beam at him and turn to the game attendant. "I'll have the dark-blue dragon, please."

I thank him when he hands it to me and clutch it to my chest as I turn to my friends.

"There's a whole collection of cute bears and dogs, but you go for the dragon," Aiden says.

"Dragons are badass." I defend my choice as we walk to the food trucks where the others are supposed to be. "Plus, it kinda reminds me of you, Aiden. I think I'll name him AJ, for Aiden Junior."

"How do I remind you of a stuffed dragon?"

"Because you're scary and fierce like a dragon, but on the inside you're cute and cuddly like this plush toy," I tell him as I hug AJ to my chest, resisting the urge to pinch Aiden's cheeks.

"I am not cute and cuddly," Aiden grumbles, but a small smile escapes anyway.

We laugh at him as we reach the picnic table Mason and Jason are sitting at, eating giant pretzels and arguing about something that's most likely trivial.

"Where's Jackson and everyone else?" Aiden asks.

"I don't know, we haven't seen them in a while. They went off to go on rides and stuff," Jason says as he wipes his mouth on his sleeve.

Aiden scowls at him but is interrupted from saying anything when there's an outburst from a crowd not too far from us.

"What's going on over there?" Annalisa asks as she sits down at the table and steals a piece of Mason's pretzel.

"Remember the mayor running for governor whose commercials we keep seeing? Mayor Kessler? It's him and a bunch of reporters," Mason explains. "Apparently, there's this whole controversy about his platform being based on being a family man and loving children, but he's having an affair or something. Vivienne Henfrey, the reporter from *Channel Five News*, especially hates him."

We all turn to look at Mason like he just announced that he's pregnant with the child of Satan.

"Why do you know that?" Julian asks what we're all thinking as Aiden goes back to studying the mayor.

Mason shrugs. "Jason and I are just sitting here, eating our food truck samplings. It's not my fault the drama is happening right in front of me and I happen to overhear it."

I follow Aiden's gaze as he looks over at the crowd. From what I can tell, the mayor is actually a pretty good-looking guy, with an easy smile that could effortlessly charm the pants off of potential voters. He seems very well put together, talking to carnival goers while also trying to disarm the reporters throwing accusations at him.

"What are you guys looking at?" Chase asks as he and Jackson join the group, taking a seat at the picnic table with us.

Mason fills him in quickly, but the conversation turns to Chase and Jackson's narrow escape from being hit in the face with puke on one of the rides.

"Some of the puke got on Noah and Charlotte, though! It was soooooo funny!" Jackson laughs, blissfully remembering the incident.

"Of course that's something that would happen to Noah." I laugh, feeling bad for them but also seeing the humor in the situation. "Where are they now?"

Chase breaks off a piece of Mason's giant pretzel, earning him a glare from his friend. "They walked back to the house to change."

Charlotte must not have been happy about getting puked on, but at least she was with Noah, who I'm certain made her feel better about the situation by cracking stupid jokes.

"Did you guys win any prizes at the games?" Jackson asks Aiden, but he doesn't hear. His eyes are laser focused on Mayor Kessler with an intensity that only Aiden can make look threatening.

I answer Jackson for him, and the conversation moves along, no one quite noticing that Aiden's calculating eyes are narrowed on the mayor.

"Is everything okay?" I ask Aiden softly as the conversation goes on around us.

He doesn't answer me, almost like he's zoned out of everything that's happening around us, and all he sees is the mayor. I don't even know if he's actually *seeing* the mayor, or if he's been transported somewhere else in his mind. That's how intense his gaze is; it's almost scaring me.

"Aiden—"

I'm cut off when he suddenly gets up and strides toward the mayor like he's on a mission, a palpable hate heavy in the air. I stand up, too, taking a couple steps to follow, but not going after him, instinctively knowing that this is something he wants to do alone. Everyone else notices, too, all conversation stopping as we watch Aiden, the muscles in his back tensed and his hands clenched into fists, with curiosity and alarm, holding our breath for whatever is about to happen.

Aiden doesn't slow as he steps around people and ends up right in front of the mayor. Aiden has a big presence; people just can't help but feel drawn to him, so it's not a surprise when the mayor stops talking to a reporter and looks right at him.

Mayor Kessler says something to Aiden that I can't hear, but I swear there's a flash of recognition in his eyes before Aiden does something that sends a shock through the whole crowd.

He raises his arm and throws a right hook that would make any boxer proud, sending the mayor sprawling to the ground.

There's an audible, collective gasp in the air as people realize what just happened, then rush to the mayor's aid as reporters turn on Aiden.

I hear my friends swearing and Jason's gasp of alarm in the background, and already know they're getting up, getting ready to disappear before men in suits descend on us. The mayor looks up at Aiden as Aiden calmly shakes his hand out, sends him one last glare, and turns around to casually walk back to me. I'm sure my eyes are bulging out of my face and my jaw is almost to the ground, but I shake it off long enough to grab his arm and haul ass out of the carnival before we're arrested for assaulting a political figure.

We walked to the carnival, which ends up working in our favor since we need to get out of here ASAP, and don't have time to sit in traffic trying to get out of the parking lot. We make it home in record time and go around to the back of the house instead of going inside. Other than our friends, no one else followed us.

Aiden didn't say anything on the walk, and no one asked him, since we were too concerned with getting back home. He sits down on the back-porch couch leisurely, like it's any other day, and we all stand around him, completely perplexed and waiting for answers.

When he doesn't volunteer an explanation, Annalisa says what everyone else is thinking. "Aiden, what the hell! Why did you just punch the mayor?!"

"Because he deserved it."

"But you don't even know him," I add.

"Exactly."

His cold response takes me aback. What the hell does *exactly* mean?

"Do you mind expanding?" Annalisa asks, crossing her arms and sitting down on the couch across from him.

Aiden looks at her, eyes slightly narrowed as if she's bothering him, and then his eyes flick over to his brothers. Jason and Jackson have personalities that can fill a room, but right now they look small and scared, concern for their brother plastered all over their faces.

"Are you . . . are you going to get in trouble?" Jason forces out, reminding me of just how young he is.

Aiden opens his mouth to say something but then closes it again, as if reconsidering, and his harsh expression softens.

"I'll be fine. I promise," he finally tells him, strategically leaving Jason's question unanswered.

Will the mayor press charges? Does he even know who Aiden is?

Aiden stands up. "It's late, time for bed, guys. Come on, Jason, Jackson, let's get you ready for bed. Good night everyone."

He ushers the twins into the house without a second glance.

I look at everyone else and then look back at Aiden's receding figure, knowing that something is definitely wrong with him. But does he want to talk to me about it? Or does he want to handle it on his own? Maybe I'll give him some time to himself with the twins. No one else is ready to go inside yet, but I feel itchy to check up on Aiden, so I say good night and leave them outside on the back porch. After getting ready for bed as fast as I can, I slip down the stairs and head over to Aiden's room. A quick glance out the sliding door shows Mason, Annalisa, Julian, and Chase still haven't moved from when we left them. I knock on Aiden's door and wait for him to hopefully answer and talk to me, instead of closing off like he used to do. When he opens the door, he doesn't seem surprised at all. He opens it wider and steps aside to let me in.

"Took you longer than I thought it would."

"How did you know I would come?" I ask.

He smirks at me but I can tell he's resisting the urge to roll his eyes. "It's kind of our thing. One of us running after the other after something dramatic happens to talk about it or figure it out. We may just be really nosy people," he ends with a joke, making me smile.

"Oh, we have another 'thing.' Don't let Noah find out. Yesterday, we each got stung by a wasp and he said 'Hey, maybe being stung by wasps can be our thing? Or even any other type of insect that can bite or sting?'" I laugh, recalling the incident and his hopefulness at finally having found a potential "thing." "Poor guy will not give up."

Sitting down on the bed, I cross my legs. "Back to the subject at hand, what happened back there?"

He sits down across from me. "I punched the mayor."

Thank you, Mr. I-State-the-Obvious. "Yes, I know that. Why?"

He's about to say something when I quickly interrupt him. "And *don't* say because he deserved it."

He gives me a look with a raised brow, as if to say, Really?

"He did deserve it," he mumbles before looking me straight in the eye. "Andrew Kessler is my biological father."

It takes me three full Mississippis to process exactly what he just said.

"Your biological father?" I repeat dumbly back to him.

"Yeah."

"The mayor of this city is the man who left you when you were a kid, while your mom had cancer and was pregnant with twins, because he didn't want to pay for all the expenses?! *That* man is the *mayor*? Who's *running for governor*?!"

I don't think I can wrap my brain around this. The man Aiden described was a deadbeat. He walked out on his family because he didn't want to deal with the bills. He left a son and a sick, pregnant wife at home to fend for themselves. But he's the mayor?

Oh my God. This whole time Aiden's been seeing commercials and posters and hearing about how Andrew Kessler is campaigning about being a family man, about fighting for low income families, about loving kids and caring for single parents, knowing full well that he's the biggest phony and hypocrite?

"That's him," he replies to my mostly rhetorical question.

"Are you—are you positive that's him?" I ask, not because I doubt Aiden, but just because I feel like that's something that should be asked.

Aiden's face hardens, his jaw sets with determination, and his fists clench in his lap.

"Of course I'm sure. That pathetic excuse for a man's face is engraved in my memory. He put my mom through hell. Everything I went through with Greg was because of him. He can change his last name to disguise his past, but he'll always be the same disgusting deadbeat."

Poor Aiden. I try to mask my facial expression so he doesn't see the slight pity I feel. I scoot over and wrap my arms around him, resting my head on his shoulder in what I hope is a supportive embrace. Aiden leans into me, allowing himself a rare moment to be vulnerable and comforted, his hand mindlessly rubbing small, slow circles on my back.

"What makes it worse is that he's fucking loaded now," Aiden says. "Does he not wonder about us? About my mom? About his kids, who he's never met?"

"I—I don't know, Aiden. What did you say to him when you went up to him? What did he say to you? Did you always plan on punching him?"

Aiden's head tilts to the side, contemplating my questions. "To be honest, I don't really know what I was planning on doing when I walked up to him. I was just really angry. When I walked up to him, I called his name, and he looked at me, studied me. I'm not sure if he recognized me or not. But he replied 'How can I help you, son?' And then my body just took over."

I pull him even closer to me, not really knowing what to say, but before I can even think of a reply, we hear a loud crash and a bang from upstairs. We look at each other and get up, rushing out of his room and upstairs toward the noise, which we can still hear. It sounds like . . . yelling?

We follow the noise to my room, Aiden slightly in front of me as if preparing to protect me from whatever is on the other side of the door. It's already slightly open, but Aiden pushes it open wide, and what we see leaves me completely shell-shocked.

Noah, who's only in his boxers, is lying on the floor under a very livid Chase, who's currently *punching Noah in the face.*

My eyes flicker from them to the other person in the room. Sitting in bed, clutching the sheets to her bare chest, is Charlotte, shouting in confusion and anger for them to stop, her cheeks tinged red with embarrassment.

I feel completely unable to do anything as my brain registers the scene that's unfolding around me. Aiden recovers quicker. He rushes into the room and breaks them up, pulling a livid Chase off of Noah, who seems to have let his emotions completely take over. Chase shakes Aiden off of him and storms out of the room without a second glance at anyone. We hear the front door slam moments later.

"What the hell is his problem?" Noah demands, shrugging on a pair of jeans that were discarded on the floor.

Aiden and I glance at each other. We both know exactly what Chase's problem is. I look at Charlotte, who's still slightly traumatized and clutching the sheet to her chest.

"Why don't we give you guys a minute?" I suggest, pulling Aiden out of the room and closing the door behind us.

We stand in the hall, staring at each other.

"You don't think they were—" I start, and Aiden's silent gaze tells me exactly what he thinks they were doing.

I sigh, and my shoulders slump as I frown at the floor. "Chase walked in on the love of his life and his best friend getting it on?"

Aiden shrugs. "That's kind of what it looked like."

Shit. Poor Chase. "Should I go after him? He couldn't have gotten that far, I can probably still catch up with him."

Aiden shakes his head. "I really don't think he wants to talk to you, or anyone else, right now."

My frown deepens. "So what do we do?"

Aiden puts his hand on my shoulder, his thumb rubbing soothing circles and leaving a trail of sparks from his touch. "Just be there for him when he's ready to talk."

The door to my room opens, revealing a fully clothed Noah. His cheek looks like it's starting to swell, but other than that there doesn't seem to be any damage.

Charlotte is sitting on the edge of the bed, also fully clothed, wringing her hands and wearing a nervous expression.

"Where did he go?" she asks me when I walk into the room.

"I don't know. I'm sure he'll be okay."

Noah runs his hand through his hair. "I don't even understand what happened. You guys weren't even supposed to be home!"

I exchange a glance with Aiden before answering Noah. "Aiden kind of punched the mayor in the face."

"What?" Charlotte and Noah ask in perfect unison.

"What does 'kind of' mean?" Noah inquires. "And why?"

"That's not important." Aiden waves him off. "Why was Chase in here in the first place?"

"I don't know," Charlotte says, looking completely defeated. "He just walked in and stared at us, like he couldn't believe what he was seeing. Then just came over and grabbed Noah, and started hitting him. I don't understand why."

She looks heartbroken. She knows why Chase reacted like that, even if she won't admit it, even if she refuses to think about it. Deep down, she knows seeing her with Noah like that hurt him, really hurt him. She knows something has shifted in her friendship with Chase. I honestly don't know if it will ever be the same between the two of them.

Noah sits down beside Charlotte on the bed. "I make fun of you guys all the time for not locking your door when you're getting it on."

"We're never getting it—"

Noah ignores my protest and continues. "But the one time someone decides to walk in on me is the *one time* I forget to lock the door."

He sighs and flops backward onto the bed, staring up at the ceiling.

"Does he hate me?"

No one answers Noah's question, because out of nowhere, Charlotte bursts into tears. The look on Aiden's and Noah's faces would almost be comical if not for the situation; they look horrified. Charlotte sobs into her hands, putting her feet on the bed and resting her head on her knees. Aiden and Noah both look at me, silently pleading with me to take control of the situation.

I throw them a bone. "Why don't you guys go see where everyone else is?"

The boys don't hesitate to run out of the room as fast as they possibly can, closing the door behind them and barely giving us a second glance. Resisting the urge to roll my eyes at their ridiculousness, I sit down beside Charlotte and put my arm around her. I don't say anything, I just let her cry and feel whatever emotions she needs to feel.

"I'm a horrible friend," she says once she calms down a bit.

"You're not a horrible friend, Char."

She puts her feet back on the floor and shifts on the bed to face me. "But I am! Chase is my best friend and he's never going to even be able to look at me again. He hates me now."

I always thought Charlotte was oblivious to Chase's feelings for her. Did she always know?

"I'm sure he doesn't," I reassure her as she wipes the tears off her face. "Why do you think that?"

"He walked in on me and Noah. And the way he reacted . . ." She sighs. "He has feelings for me, doesn't he?" she finishes in a small voice, looking down at her hands in her lap.

A small part of my brain wants to yell *Duh!* but the other part says I shouldn't be a hypocrite. Apparently, everyone knew that Mason was in love with me and I had no idea, or maybe I just didn't want to accept it, so I can't blame Charlotte for not knowing about Chase.

"Did you really have no idea?" I ask her gently.

"No? I mean yes?" She huffs out an agitated breath. "Maybe?"

A corner of my lip turns up. "Maybe?"

"Well, I don't know! Sometimes Drunk Chase says things, but we all know Drunk Chase is a different person. It was never confirmed. It still isn't."

"That wasn't confirmation enough?" I tease.

"I guess I'll have to have a real conversation with him when he gets back from wherever he went off to," she says.

What they'll talk about and what she'll tell him, I'm not sure.

"What about Noah?" I ask.

"I don't know."

She doesn't know? She was ready to fool around with him and she doesn't know how she feels about him?

"I know you're dying to ask, but no, we haven't slept together before. If Chase didn't walk in that probably would've been our first time together."

She tucks a piece of hair behind her ear, still looking down at her lap. It's so weird seeing Charlotte like this. She's usually so happy and cheery and filled with life. I don't think I've ever seen her look this sad or conflicted.

"It wasn't planned. It just kind of happened." She pauses. "Okay, I guess nothing really happened, but you know what I mean."

I nod. Everyone knows you don't need to be in love with someone to have some fun with them, as long as everyone consents.

"Do you think Noah has any feelings for you?" I can't stop myself from asking. I never thought Noah had feelings for Charlotte, but then again, I never thought to look.

She sighs. "I don't think so? I think we were just having some fun, and one thing led to another. But now Chase's feelings are hurt. What am I going to say to him?"

I don't know what to say to make her feel better, if there even *is* something I can say to make her feel better. I settle for what I think is best.

"You'll figure out what you want eventually. It may be bad right now, but everything will settle down. Chase won't stay mad forever. Just follow your heart."

She's not looking at me, but I look away from her so she can't see the hypocrisy in my eyes. If only I could take my own advice. I still have the weight of telling Mason about our parents *and* telling Aiden about my leaving hanging over my head, but I'm not planning on doing either of those anytime soon.

16

My grumbling stomach wakes me up earlier than I would like the morning after the whole Chase and Noah thing. Everyone is still sleeping as I tiptoe down the stairs to fix some breakfast, the early morning sun streaming through the windows lighting my way.

When I get to the bottom of the stairs I pause. There's a form lying on the couch, shifting as I get closer.

"Chase?" I whisper, not knowing if he's sleeping.

By the time I went to bed, no one had seen or heard from him since he'd stormed out of the house. We didn't know where he went, and he wouldn't answer our calls or texts. At least he's here now and I know he's okay, or mostly okay.

Aiden told me that the longer the night went on, the more pissed Noah was getting about the whole thing. Noah was fuming about it since he didn't understand why his friend would 'Cockblock him like that,' and 'Go apeshit on his ass for no reason.' Aiden confirmed what everyone kind of knew but never talked about, and explained that Chase walked in on his best friend getting it on with the love of his life. Noah felt really bad about it after that.

"Amelia?" Chase asks groggily, sitting up to look at me.

Once I get closer to the couch and can actually see him clearly, I throw my hands over my eyes to stop the sight from permanently scarring me. Chase is as naked as the day he was born.

"Why are you not wearing any clothes?!" Did he walk home naked?! I don't see any clothes thrown on the floor.

"I have no idea," Chase grumbles. "To be honest, most of last night and this morning are pretty spotty."

Peeping through my fingers to look at him again, I keep my eyes trained on his face.

"Jesus, Chase. Did you get black-out drunk last night?"

I toss a pillow at him as he mumbles an incoherent reply, before finally removing my hand from my face. That's when I realize he technically isn't as naked as the day he was born.

"What is that stuff all over you?" I ask him, but then my brain clicks in on something he said a long time ago about what happens when he gets black-out drunk.

"Are you covered in barbeque sauce and—" I lean in closer to him. "Are those Froot Loops?"

Chase looks down at his body as if noticing the mess for the first time.

"Huh. I guess my drunk ass couldn't find the Cheerios and settled for the next best thing."

I sigh and sit down on the part of the couch that isn't covered in BBQ sauce and Froot Loops. Chase is such a mess, and I don't mean just his outward appearance.

"Are you okay, Chase?"

He laughs a flat, emotionless laugh. "Of course I am. Why

wouldn't I be okay? I lost the girl of my dreams to my best friend. I'm just peachy."

"Chase." I don't even know where to begin. I don't know how to make this better, how to make *him* better. "They didn't know."

Chase slouches back on the couch, shifting the pillow to make sure it still covers everything, and turns his head to look at me. "How could they not know? Everyone else seemed to see it! Even Jason and Jackson asked me when I was going to marry Charlotte!"

"Noah and Char feel terrible about it." I try to comfort him, but that only seems to make him angrier.

"They don't feel bad about it! They feel bad that they got caught."

"Chase—"

"I know what you're going to tell me." He interrupts me, looking slightly defeated, the light dimmed from his eyes. "I don't own Charlotte and I can't tell her who she can and can't have sex with, but still. It *had* to be my best friend?"

I was thinking that, but I didn't have the heart to say that to him. He's hurting—it sucks to see the person you love with someone else, and Chase had to walk in on that firsthand without any warning.

"I just wish I could go back and tell Charlotte how I feel. I *know* I could make her happy if I just had the balls to say something to her. But now it's too late. She's with him now."

It hurts me to notice that he keeps referring to her as Charlotte instead of Charlie, his pet name for her, which she hates so much. Have things shifted so much that he doesn't see her as the same person anymore?

"Char isn't *with* anyone," I tell him. "She's her own person and can make her own decisions. But she doesn't know how she feels. It could've just been an in the moment thing. It's not too late to tell her how you feel. You're going to have to have a real conversation with her."

"It wouldn't mean anything." He sighs. "If she wanted to be with me, she wouldn't have been with him."

That slightly angers me. Chase, like Mason, goes around hooking up with random girls all the time, then doesn't understand when the girl he loves doesn't realize that he loves her!

"If you wanted to be with *her*, you wouldn't confuse her by hooking up with other girls."

"I told you why—"

"I know you told me why," I interrupt, sitting up straighter as I shift into talk some sense into him mode. "'You're not good enough for her and it'll ruin your friendship and you're trying to move on,' blah, blah, blah. It's too late to go back and change anything, but it's not too late to fix your friendship with Char. *And* Noah."

"But—"

"No." I wasn't done yet. "You already walked in on her and probably scarred her for life; you're going to have to talk things out anyway. Telling her how you feel can't possibly make things any worse or more awkward than they're going to be now."

"What if she chooses Noah?"

"First of all, we don't even know if Noah likes her, or if she likes him."

He opens his mouth to say something, but I continue anyway, deciding to be brutally honest because he needs to hear it. "*But* if she happens to choose him and they decide to give it a try, be happy for her. Charlotte doesn't owe you anything, Chase, but you're her best friend and I know she wouldn't want to lose you, just like you wouldn't want to lose her."

Chase looks down at his hands in his lap. "I don't know. I'll think about telling her, I guess."

"Good. And you owe Noah an apology. But think about what you're going to tell Char while you're in the shower. You smell like booze and barbeque."

The corners of his mouth turn up slightly in a small smile. "That you're right about."

He stands up and the pillow that was keeping him decent falls to the floor, along with whatever Froot Loops weren't glued to him. I throw my hands over my face.

"Chase!"

"Oh, sorry." He laughs, picks up the pillow, and covers his behind as he walks up the stairs.

"And burn the pillow!" I call after him, hearing his answering chuckle.

"Amelia?" A different voice calls, one that sends a warmth throughout my body.

Aiden comes out of his room, looking freshly showered.

"Shit, sorry. Did I wake you with the yelling?"

His room, Noah's room, and Annalisa and Julian's room are on the main floor, but Aiden's is the closest to the living room.

"No. It's eight thirty, I was already up. Who were you talking to? And what happened to the couch?"

I look at the couch and can't help but smile. "I was talking to Chase. He slept on the couch. It's kind of a long story."

"Ah. He was drinking last night."

"Guess it's not a long story after all." I laugh as I head into the kitchen, grab a roll of paper towels, and toss them to Aiden.

He catches them with ease and looks back at the mess. "Dammit. Please tell me he didn't finish all of my Froot Loops!"

I laugh as we kneel down and wipe off the couch, which, thankfully, is leather.

"We can always go get you some more," I tell him, because between the mess on the floor and on the couch, it's looking like Chase dumped the whole box.

We clean up the mess pretty quickly and manage to get the couch to stop being sticky, but right as we're going to make some breakfast as a reward, the doorbell rings.

"You keep working on those eggs, I'll get it," I tell Aiden as my stomach growls in protest.

The living room, kitchen, and small, front foyer is all in one big, open-concept area. When I look through the peephole, Aiden sees me step back in confusion.

"Who is it?" he asks, walking over to me.

There are three men in suits standing on the porch; the one in the middle is instantly recognizable.

"It's the mayor. What should we do?" I look at Aiden helplessly.

How did the mayor find us? Is he here to arrest Aiden? He wouldn't have come *personally* to arrest him, right?

There's another persistent knock on the door, and I look through the peephole again before Aiden has the chance to open the door. The two men with the mayor definitely look more like bodyguards than cops, which calms me down a bit. But still.

"Do you think he knows who you are?" I whisper to Aiden.

"Only one way to find out," he says, glancing at the door I'm standing in front of.

"Oh, sorry," I say sheepishly.

Aiden's the one who could get in trouble but I'm the one

worried about it; he looks completely unfazed. I open the door and am met with three blank but intimidating faces.

"It's about time," Mayor Andrew Kessler comments, glancing into the house behind me.

Well, then.

"Can I help you?" I ask him, slightly annoyed but still keeping my polite voice in check.

"Yes, actually. I'd like to speak with my son."

"Then you have the wrong house." Aiden steps out from behind me, not that I was doing much to cover him in the first place. Andrew smiles a smile that I can automatically tell isn't genuine.

"Aiden. Look at you. You've grown into quite the young man."

My eyes narrow at the mayor, and I can't see Aiden's reaction, but I'm sure it's similar to mine.

"What are you doing here?" Aiden asks in a tone that sends chills down my spine; it's the same one he uses on people who aren't me.

Aiden's an inch or two taller than his father. Andrew isn't out of shape in the least bit, with broad shoulders and a hint of some muscle, but Aiden definitely has more muscle on him with all the time he dedicates to working out. But their similar physiques is where the comparison ends. Aiden would never abandon his family.

"I wanted to talk," Andrew states, sounding much too calm for someone who's talking to the son he deserted years ago. "Are you going to invite me in or keep us standing out here like strangers?"

Aiden lets out a quick, humorless chuckle. "The second one."

He starts to close the door but Andrew quickly slams his hand onto it, stopping it from closing.

"I think it's best if we have a quick chat," he asserts, pushing the door open with authority and walking in, the two men who are with him following suit.

Aiden's facial expression doesn't change but his hand clenches into a fist and the muscle in his jaw twitches.

He closes the door and we follow Andrew into the house just as Annalisa and Julian walk out of their room. They look at the mayor standing in our living room with the two other men, then back at Aiden. Last night, Aiden told everyone (who was home and minus his brothers) who the mayor really was, so they look torn on how to react to the sight.

Julian eyes the two other men, who clearly look like bodyguards and still haven't said a word. "Is everything okay here?"

"It's fine." Aiden waves him off with a straight face. "Let's go talk on the back porch."

He leads the mayor and his two friends to the back, and I stay beside Annalisa and Julian as we watch them head outside.

It's driving me crazy not knowing how Aiden is feeling with all of this. This is the first time he's talking to his father since the man deserted him and his family, and now here he is, strolling into Aiden's life like he's a longtime golf buddy. I wish I could read Aiden's face like I can other people's.

Once Andrew and his friends are outside, Aiden turns to me. "Are you coming?"

Those three words catch me so off guard that I just stare at him dumbly. He wants me there with him, sitting in on his family drama?

"Amelia?" he asks again, waiting for me.

Shaking off my awestruck expression, I follow him outside and sit in the chair directly across from Andrew, separated only by a small, outdoor coffee table. His "friends" remain standing behind him until Andrew waves them off. They head down the porch steps and walk out of hearing distance but remain close enough to run back and intervene if something happens.

Why does a small-town mayor even need *bodyguards?*

Aiden closes the door to the house and sits beside me, and we all stare at each other in an intimidating silence.

I can't help but feel like a child who was called into the principal's office, about to be scolded. From what I can tell so far, Andrew Kessler is a very well-spoken, well–put together man who gives off an air of superiority and a large sense of entitlement. He has slightly long, slicked back, dirty-blond hair, bright-blue eyes, and well-maintained stubble that defines his already straight jawline. It almost pains me to admit that he's a handsome man, wearing an expensive-looking suit and with an even more costly watch adorning his wrist. A silver wedding band glints on his ring finger, and I know it's not the one from his marriage to Aiden's mom. His cheekbone has the slightest hint of a bruise, and I feel a twisted sense of pride in Aiden. Even so, it's evident that Andrew Kessler is one of those people who knows how to control a room, whose presence demands attention—which might be where Aiden gets it from.

"Listen, son, I think we got off on the wrong foot."

I didn't think it was possible for Aiden to get even tenser, but he does at hearing the word *son*.

"I'm not here to press charges," Andrew continues, "even though both my wife and campaign manager certainly think I should. But once I told them I would *never* do that to my son, they dropped it. We're family." He sends Aiden a pointed look, clearly wanting to punctuate some point he's trying to make.

Aiden's hand clenches into a fist, and I pry it open to hold it in my own. The last thing we need is for him to punch the mayor *again*. I doubt Andrew will take kindly to *two* black eyes during his campaign.

Aiden says nothing but Andrew doesn't seem to mind, completely content with steering the conversation.

"Speaking of family, where are my other sons?"

Aiden's hand tightens in mine almost painfully before he realizes it and lets go.

"Sons?" Aiden's voice is low. "You don't *have* any sons. At least not in this house."

Andrew tilts his head. "Last time I checked, I had three boys. You, and a set of twins."

The muscle in Aiden's jaw ticks. "Not if you had your way. They wouldn't be here if Mom listened to you."

As if instinctively knowing they were being talked about, Jason and Jackson appear behind the sliding glass door, looking out at us with worried faces. Andrew follows our gazes, and the twins, being spotted, scurry farther back into the house.

"Well, they are here." The corner of Andrew's lips turn up. "And they have my eyes, I see. Why don't you bring them out so I can meet them properly?"

Nothing about Andrew's tone or body language is threatening, but by the way Aiden's body reacts to his words, you'd think he was holding a gun to Aiden's head. I can tell it's taking everything Aiden has to stay calm and not punch Andrew in the face again. I can feel the aggravated energy radiating off of him.

"Do you even know their names?" Aiden snaps.

"Aiden, listen—"

"No, you listen," Aiden interrupts, eyes blazing. "You show up on our doorstep after wanting nothing to do with them, with us, and have the balls to play the we're family card? Unbe-fucking-lievable." Aiden stands. "Please see yourself out."

Andrew makes no move to leave. In fact, he looks entertained.

"Your reaction is normal, son. Please sit back down. I understand how you're feeling. You *should* be pissed. I left your mom while she was pregnant. I wasn't there for you when she died, and I wasn't there while you grew up. But those boys, *Jason* and *Jackson*, are still young. Obviously, you running into me at the fair was fate that we were meant to have a second chance. To be more of a family." Andrew leans forward, his elbows resting on his knees, and with a gleam in his eyes that I don't trust.

My scoff must've been out loud because they both look at me.

"Something to say?" Andrew raises an eyebrow at me as Aiden sits back down next to me.

I've never been one to hold back. "You're telling us that this kumbaya bullshit has nothing to do with the fact that you can't risk a scandal in the middle of your campaign? That you would've reached out to Aiden, Jason, and Jackson even if you weren't running for governor?"

Andrew's eyes narrow just a fraction before his expression smooths back out. "As I said, fate has brought us together." He pauses, carefully thinking out his next words. "Actually, I'm inviting you and your brothers to a gala I'm having tomorrow for my campaign. I know people would just love to meet my sons. I'll have suits in your sizes delivered here by tonight. I assume you don't have dress shoes here?" He pulls a money clip out of his pocket and my eyes bulge since it looks like it's holding enough cash to pay a year's worth of college tuition. Andrew pulls a few bills free. "This should cover shoes and then some." He pauses again, looking me over. "I guess you'll want to bring her as your date? Here's some extra for a dress and shoes for her." He pulls out more bills, holding the neat stack out to Aiden, who eyes the pile like he doesn't trust it not to spontaneously combust.

"Her name is Amelia. And no thanks," Aiden says plainly.

Andrew's laugh is one that I imagine rich people use when they're entertained by something they think is beneath them. "Right. I doubt you have enough money on you to pay for a suit and shoes yourself. Do you even know the going rate of a nice dress? You can't show up in jeans."

"No, I meant we aren't coming," Aiden clarifies. "In fact, it's probably the last thing I'd ever want to do, right after gouging my eyeballs out with a rusty spoon."

Andrew sets the stack of bills down on the outdoor coffee table and moves one of the decorative candles on top of it to keep them from flying away in the wind.

"But we're blood," Andrew starts, his analyzing gaze piercing Aiden's. "If we weren't family, then I would've pressed charges against you. But lucky for you, we *are* related, and as such, I expect you to show up to the gala, where I can present my sons to the world and show them that we're a strong, united family, one that can get over the past and make amends."

Aiden and I both see the threat for what it is: go to the gala, play nice, don't mention the past, and he won't press charges against Aiden.

"My wife, Katherine, is just dying to meet you." Andrew stands up, clearly deciding that the conversation is over, and so do Aiden and I. Andrew adds, "And so is your stepsister."

That throws Aiden off. "Stepsister?"

Andrew signals to his bodyguards, who make their way over to us. "Yes. Evianna. She's around your age, so I'm sure you'll become great friends."

Aiden's eyes meet mine, and we share a stunned look. Like Aiden needs *another* stepsibling in his life.

The back door slides open so fast it almost bounces closed again, causing us all to turn and look. Jason and Jackson are back, expressions of fear all over their faces. All they know is that the mayor whom Aiden punched last night is here in the house, and they don't want him to get in trouble.

Andrew's intimidating gaze sweeps over the twins. "Hi, boys. I'm your fa—"

"Not now!" Aiden interrupts, stepping between Andrew and his brothers, as if he doesn't even want him looking at them.

Andrew's eyes are cold and calculating. "They should get to meet their father."

Aiden tenses, his back is rigid and eyes hard. "You're not their father," he grits out. "And you have no legal claim over us after the divorce."

Andrew tugs on his expensive-looking cufflinks, completely unfazed by his son's intimidating demeanor. "You just need some time to adjust. We're family, remember?"

Aiden's jaw is set, a fire alight in his eyes that I've only seen a couple of times, when he's calculating how to make someone's life a living hell.

Andrew doesn't wait for us to answer. "We'll see ourselves out. I'll see you all at the gala."

Aiden follows them back into the house, as if to make sure that they go straight to the door and get away from him, leaving me outside with his brothers.

"Is Aiden in trouble?" Jackson asks me, worry for his brother written all over his face.

"Did you see Aiden's face? The one he makes when he promises pain? I think it's the mayor who's in trouble now," I joke.

Jason smiles at me, eyes shining with pride in his brother. "Yeah. That guy can go fuck himself."

My eyes widen at him. "Who told you it was okay to say that?!"

A small blush spreads across his cheeks. "Noah told me I can say that about people who are mean to me."

"Maybe don't say that in front of Aiden?" I suggest, resisting the urge to grin.

But Jason is totally right. Mayor Andrew Kessler can *definitely* go fuck himself.

17

After Andrew leaves, Aiden declares that no one is going to the fundraiser, and that is the end of that. Charlotte, Noah, and Chase are all stressed out because of their whole situation. The twins are worried about their brother being in trouble. Mason has been avoiding me ever since the fridge incident the other day, which just makes me feel even more guilty about the whole his dad is cheating with my mom thing, and I'm starting to realize that I need to figure out a way to tell Aiden that I'm leaving soon. And with everything so tense lately, Julian had the great idea of going paintballing to blow off some steam and have some fun. Under other circumstances it would've been fun, but now, I don't know.

Give a bunch of stressed out people guns and tell them to shoot each other—what could go wrong?

"I call me and Jackson as team captains!" Jason exclaims as we're putting jumpsuits on over our clothes.

The teams end up being me, Jackson, Mason, Annalisa, and Chase against Jason, Charlotte, Julian, Aiden, and Noah. Chase watches Noah showing Charlotte how to use her paintball gun but quickly looks away, kicking at the dirt floor.

Charlotte rode with me, Aiden, and Annalisa to the paintball arena and told us on the way what happened with Chase. After our talk this morning, Chase went up to shower then talked with Charlotte while we were dealing with the mayor. She told us that Chase basically told her that he's been in love with her since forever but was always too scared to say or do anything about it because he couldn't bear to hear her say that she didn't feel the same way.

And then she made those fears a reality. She told him, through tears, that she loves him but she doesn't have the same feelings he has for her. When he asked if it had anything to do with Noah, she said no, telling him that she doesn't understand her feelings for Noah. She doesn't think he believes her, but he didn't press the situation any further.

The conversation ended with Chase telling her that he still loves her and that he'll always be there for her, and that he doesn't want their relationship to be strained or awkward because of his confession. Of course she agreed, but she told us that he wouldn't call her Charlie during the conversation like he always has, and that hurt more than she thought it ever could've. Even if she still hates the nickname, his refusal to say it means something in their friendship has permanently shifted.

As for Chase and Noah's relationship, that's still up in the air too. Chase gave Noah a mumbled, half-assed apology that no one really thinks he meant. Before Noah could say anything, though, Chase stormed off. Noah's been trying to talk to Chase all morning, but Chase has been avoiding him, which I think is starting to annoy Noah.

Compared to all this drama, my Mason secret should probably stay well buried for now, as we've been through enough already on this vacation. I know Aiden still thinks I should tell him, but there's just so much going on. Can I *really* be the person who ruins someone else's vacation?

Now, my friends are in teams on opposite sides of the arena, waiting for the horn to blow, paintball guns in hand. The losing team is on cooking and cleaning duty for the next three days, so all of our adrenaline is pumping, everyone wanting to demolish the other team.

Since Aiden and I are on opposite teams, he promised me before the match that he'd shoot me last, you know, like the gentleman he is. I smiled at him and told him that I'd love to see him try.

The horn goes off and we scatter. We paired up so the team could split up, and Mason grabbed Annalisa and Jackson before I could even say a word to him. That left Chase and me together, which of course I don't mind. We're going to kick ass.

Not even two minutes in there are paintballs whizzing by my head, and Noah's diabolical laugh pins him as the culprit. Somehow, Chase and I get split up, leaving me on my own, but I come across Jason crouching behind a pile of tires, his back to me.

Can I shoot an innocent nine-year-old?

Jason hears me and turns around, gun raised to shoot, and I automatically shoot him right in the chest, pink paint splattering all over his torso. He takes off his mask and gives me the look of a wounded puppy.

"You would do me like that, Amelia?" He pouts.

"Sorry, bud, find me again next round for revenge!" I tell him with a devilish smile before running off.

I turn around the corner and run right into a solid chest that I would know anywhere. I back away and Aiden and I point our guns at each other, neither one of us able to keep a straight face in our standoff.

"Did you just shoot my little brother?" he asks me as he takes off his mask, his lips curving up on one side.

I take my mask off as well and smirk at him. "Maybe, but I thought you were gonna save me for last?"

He tilts his head to one side, as if thinking through his answer. "I was, but that was before I knew you were playing a ruthless game. I don't want to be on cooking and cleaning duty for three days."

We eye each other, and at the same time, aim and shoot at each other right in the stomach. Aiden looks at his stomach, now bright pink, and looks back at me, eyes bright and playful.

"You shot me!"

"You shot me too!" I defend myself, even though I heard his gun go off but didn't feel anything hit me.

"I purposely missed."

I look at the tree about five feet to my left, freshly painted bright blue.

"But . . . the gun . . . you shot . . . and the tree?" I stutter, and Aiden gives me a mischievous smile.

"I'll give you a ten second head start," he warns, his eyes alight and playful, so different from how he was just a couple of hours ago with his father.

"But you're already dead!" I point out, knowing there's no way I'll outrun Aiden. "And it's not my fault you can't aim!"

"One . . ."

I turn around and take off, and a few seconds later I feel strong arms around my waist and we both go down. If there's a way to gently tackle someone, that's what Aiden does, turning so that he takes the brunt of the fall into a pile of leaves.

"That was not a ten second head start." I laugh, dropping my gun and mask beside us.

"I'm a fast counter," he jokes, his hands tangling in my hair.

I love seeing this side of Aiden. Okay, *all* sides of Aiden are nice, but the playful side just melts my heart. He pulls me in and our lips meet as my heart explodes. He groans softly and his arms move to my waist, pulling me closer and letting me melt into him.

"Really, guys? We're having a very competitive game here," Julian says, and we break our kiss to look up.

He's standing with Annalisa, different colored paint smudged all over them. I roll off of Aiden and we both sit up, the front of my jumpsuit now smudged pink, just like how Annalisa's looks.

"Oh right. Like you guys, weren't just doing the same thing?" I smirk, and Annalisa sends me a big smile in response.

Aiden and I get up and he hands me my gun and mask as we hear yelling from around the corner. The four of us look at each other and run toward the noise to see what's going on.

"You already shot me multiple times! I'm dead! Stop shooting me!" We hear Noah say as we get closer.

When we get there, we see Chase and Noah, each covered in different colored paint.

"You started it!" Chase yells, shooting Noah in the stomach for what appears to be the tenth time.

"We were just trying to have fun but you're taking it personally!" Noah shoots him back.

"Oh, we can get personal!" Chase exclaims, dropping his mask and gun and tackling Noah to the ground, and not in the gentle way that Aiden tackled me. They roll around for a bit before Aiden and Julian step in to break it up.

Noah sits up. "What the fuck, man! If you have something to say just say it!"

Chase sits up as well, all the anger that he's been feeling suddenly coming to a boiling point. "You were going to sleep with Charlotte!"

"And?"

"And you're one of my best friends! You were going to sleep with the girl I'm in love with!" Chase shouts.

"I tried apologizing but you're being a salty little bitch!"

"You can't do something you know would hurt someone and then apologize and expect it to be all better!"

"I didn't know how you felt about her!" Noah defends himself.

Chase gets up and dusts himself off. "Everyone knew!"

He collects his gun and mask and storms off in the opposite direction, leaving the five of us staring after him, unsure if we should go after him or not. We were supposed to use paintball as a way to have fun and break the tension, but it seems like it just piled on even more.

Looking at the mask in my hand, I roll my eyes. Maybe next time we should go for massages or something.

18

The drive home is quiet and awkward. Aiden drives me, Annalisa, and Charlotte, and Annalisa gives Charlotte a rundown of what happened. Charlotte spends the rest of the ride frowning and looking out the window.

As we walk into the house, everyone disperses to do their own thing. Chase and Noah still aren't talking, Charlotte feels like she's caught in the middle, and no one else wants to feel like they have to pick sides. If a fight like this happened at home, at least no one would have to see each other. But we're staying in a house with each other for another week still, so there's nowhere for them to go to cool off or avoid each other.

After a shower, as I head into the kitchen to grab a snack, there's a knock on the front door. Since everyone is content to ignore the world, napping or showering or doing who knows what else, I open the door to find one of the large men who was with Andrew this morning.

"From Mayor Kessler," he says simply, holding out his arm to me. He's holding a clothes hanger covered by a large, protective bag. It's obvious that there's a freshly pressed suit in there, but the bag is black so I can't see what it looks like.

Taking the heavy bag from him, I discover that there are two smaller bags on separate hangers behind that one—I'm assuming a suit for each of the twins.

"There's a card for Mayor Kessler's personal tailor in Aiden's suit pocket. If any alterations need to be made, you'll need to call him in the next twenty minutes and bring the suit in tonight," he says, not waiting for me to reply before turning around and heading back to his blacked-out SUV.

"Thanks," I mumble sarcastically as I close the door and head to Aiden's room.

I knock tentatively and he opens the door a few seconds later wearing nothing but a towel, his hair still wet from his shower and water droplets still dripping down the crevices of his well-defined chest. Forcing my gaze from his body to his face takes an enormous amount of effort, but he doesn't notice since I thrust the suits out in front of me.

"A large man just delivered these for you."

Aiden holds the door open wider for me, grabs the suits, and closes the door once I'm in his room. He doesn't even bother looking at them before throwing them haphazardly on the bed and walking into the closet. I'm sitting cross-legged on the bed by the time he emerges fully dressed, and I try not to feel sad about that.

"Can you believe that guy?" he asks, shooting a look at the suits beside me. "He actually thinks I'm going to dress up in the monkey suit of his choosing and be his puppet. What's stopping me from exposing him for the piece of shit he is?" Aiden paces in front of the bed, ranting more to himself than to me. "He comes around here spouting all this 'we're family' bullshit. *Ha*. It's laughable how messed up that is."

"You haven't thought about going at all? It's being held at his house."

Aiden's eyebrows draw together. "No, I haven't."

"You're not the least bit curious about him?" I hesitate. "Isn't that why you picked Torywood Springs? To see him?"

Aiden's pacing stops and he looks straight at me, not saying a word.

"You *did* pick here because you knew he'd be here, right?" I press.

He sighs in resignation and sits down on the edge of the bed. "Yeah, I knew he'd be here."

I knew it couldn't have just been *fate*, as Andrew had said, that brought them together, but I didn't want to push Aiden.

"I found out he was the mayor here after my arrest," he confesses, looking out the back window at nothing in particular. "I saw a newspaper article about him running for governor, and recognized him. I couldn't stop myself from googling him afterward. I don't even know why I cared."

I try to put myself in Aiden's shoes. "It's normal to want to reach out to your parents."

He shakes his head, shifting to face me. "No, it's not that. I couldn't care less about having him in my life. In fact, I want *nothing* to do with him, and coming here did nothing but intensify that feeling."

"Then why *did* you choose here?" I ask softly. "Brian told us to go somewhere and you volunteered here before we even had a second to think."

He frowns. "I guess I was just curious, I don't know. When I saw that he's the mayor and got remarried, to some old money–type woman of all people, I couldn't believe it. I guess I just wanted to see with my own eyes that he really wrote us off, that he's living it up without a spare thought for the three sons he left behind."

I wrap my arms around his stiff shoulders and rest my head against his shoulder for support.

"I wasn't planning on talking to him. I wasn't even planning on punching him believe it or not. At the carnival when I saw him, I just—I don't know. I sound stupid."

"You don't sound stupid, Aiden."

"It was stupid to think this would give me any closure."

Lifting my head from his shoulder, I look him in the eye. "It wasn't a stupid idea. Andrew never was and will never be good enough for you, Jason, and Jackson, and now you know that for sure."

He nods, his eyes stormy and hard. "That, I know."

We both glance sideways at the suits sitting innocently on the bed. "So, should we burn those?" I'm only half joking.

A vibrating from the nightstand draws our attention, and Aiden reaches over to check his phone. He shifts suddenly, his face set with new determination. "No. I think I want to go."

I pause. "Wait, what?"

"It's from Andrew. Apparently he got my number."

He hands the phone to me so I can read it.

> *Heard the suits were delivered. Don't forget to be on your best behavior. Act like my son, not someone who gets charged for assault*

It's clear what Andrew's intentions are. "You're going so he won't charge you?"

A scowl mars Aiden's face. "He's not going to charge me. If I don't play whatever role he wants me to play then he's going to want nothing to do with me." He sets the phone down and turns to face me. "I guess you're right. I came here to get closure, and I want to see how he's living, what his life looks like now. If anything, it'll be the perfect opportunity to embarrass him."

I nod. I might not understand it fully, but I'll support him in whatever he wants to do. "Are you bringing Jason and Jackson?"

"No," he says quickly, then hesitates. "But would you come with me?"

My heart skips a beat. "I—yes, I want to come with you, but don't those events have a lot of media coverage? You know I can't get caught in a photo . . ." I trail off, not wanting to disappoint Aiden, but also needing to stay true to what I promised my mom.

"Oh shit. I'm sorry. That was selfish of me," he says, but he gives his head a frustrated shake and looks down at his hands.

I swallow hard. I don't want to disappoint Aiden, but is this something I'm able to do? I'm going to be leaving Aiden soon and ultimately betraying the trust we've just worked on fixing after he learned about the real me. He's inviting me into a part of his life I'm positive he doesn't want many people to know about, and I'm going to take that trust and crush it under my heel as I walk out on him when he'll probably need me most.

"Yes," I hear myself say, confusing my brain, which is shouting *No!*

"You don't have to," he says, but even I can tell that he sits up straighter.

"I want to," I tell him, putting as much confidence in my voice as I can. "We'll just avoid the photographers. No one will want to take a picture of two unimportant kids anyway. It'll be fine."

"I'd be lost without you," he says softly, and I feel like throwing up even though his words mean the world to me.

Before the guilt makes me physically sick, I stand up from the bed and pick up the suit bag from the wire hanger. "You should try this on."

Grumbling unhappily, he stands beside me in front of the bed. "I'll have to get shoes. And you need a dress. Are you sure you're okay running around finding a dress and shoes and everything?"

The "of course" leaves my mouth automatically. "Plus," I add, "we have a couple of hours before stores close. I'm sure we'll find something."

Taking the bag from me, he unzips it and pulls out a luxurious navy suit. His face contorts in disgust. "This is a four-thousand-dollar suit."

My shock is shadowed by my urge to laugh, but my eyebrows draw together in confusion. "You know how much a suit is just by looking at it?"

He turns the suit to fully face me. "No. He literally left the price tag on."

Yup. There's the price tag. And it's $4,470.80, to be precise. If Andrew Kessler can afford to spend that much money on a suit for a son he doesn't even like, he must be rolling in money.

Aiden drops the suit back on the bed with an angry scoff. "He makes me sick."

>> <<

Aiden tried on the suit Andrew got for him, and even though I didn't get to see, he said it was scary how well it fit him. After he finishes, we go shopping and bring Charlotte along with us, partly because she's an "expert last minute shopper," and partly because she needs a distraction. Chase has been avoiding her like I've been avoiding Mason, each of us out of our own sense of guilt.

We go to a store for Aiden first, who tries on one pair of shoes, more just to see if they fit, and buys them with the money Andrew left him.

We make it to a boutique an hour before it closes, and I let Charlotte run around picking out dresses for me.

"Don't look too excited," I tell Aiden sarcastically, who's looking around at all the dresses like he woke up in a foreign land.

He turns the full force of his smile on me and my breath hitches. "This isn't too bad. If you ignore where we're going, it's kind of like we're practicing for prom."

The smile on my face freezes when I sit on the weight of his words.

He wants to go to prom with me. He thinks I'll be *here* for prom.

I almost lost Aiden the first time because of all the lies I told him. Now here I am, telling him more lies. How much longer can I keep this secret from him? How much longer can I let him think he has a future with me when I'm supposed to be packing my bags to leave as soon as we get home? I'm such a shitty person.

Aiden misinterprets my reaction. "Not that—not that I assume you'll go to prom with me."

I suddenly can't meet his gaze. "No, yeah. Obviously I'd go to prom with you."

If I was around.

Before he can say anything else that breaks my heart, I turn around and walk to the dressing room where Charlotte's loaded up a bunch of dresses.

"This is so fun!" She smiles, looking wistfully at all the dresses. "I'm kind of jealous I'm not the one getting to put on a pretty dress, but dressing you up is still fun."

"Thanks for doing this, Char." I pick a red dress off the hook and analyze it.

"No problem! I can't wait to do this again for prom, except then I'll get to try on dresses too!" She laughs and leaves the room, yelling something at Aiden about how he can't see, but I'm left thinking over her words, my stomach sinking. Again with prom. Another person I'm letting down.

I close the door to the room and stare at the rest of the dresses, a frown on my face. This isn't fun anymore. How long can I keep pretending I'm a regular girl? How long can I ignore my problems by pushing them off? Even all the stuff with Mason. Can I really tell him about his dad's affair and then just vanish off the face of the earth?

"Do you have the first dress on yet?" Charlotte excitedly calls through the door, snapping me out of my musing.

"Sure, just one second!" I call back, ripping off my clothes and throwing on a random dress. I don't even look in the mirror before opening the door.

Charlotte's eyes are wide and shiny. "Yes. That's the dress." She claps her hands together and practically squeals.

"It's the first one I tried on," I say, feeling guilty that I'm not as excited as I should be.

"So? Have you even looked at yourself? Turn around so I can zip you the rest of the way." Placing her hands on my bare shoulders, she spins me around to face the mirror and my breath hitches.

"Whoa," is all I can manage. The dress is black and off both shoulders, leaving my upper chest bare, with a sweetheart plunge that's not inappropriate but not exactly modest either. It's tight all the way down, giving me curves where I didn't know I had them, and it loosens up about midthigh, flowing elegantly to the floor with a slit running up to my left thigh.

"'Whoa' is an understatement!" Charlotte's smile is so big it must hurt her cheeks. "I'm *so glad* I sent Aiden away so he didn't see this before you were properly glammed up. He'd jump your bones!"

"Char!" I laugh, my spirits lifting slightly.

The dress is gorgeous and I *feel* beautiful in it. It's dizzying and makes dark thoughts pop in my mind. *It's not illegal to feel happy. There's no reason you* shouldn't *wear this dress and pretend it's your prom, it's not like you'll get a real one with Aiden. It's not like you'll* want *to go to prom with anyone other than Aiden. Make the most of the situation.*

"I'm going to go get shoes!" Charlotte giggles, her excitement contagious as she turns and runs to the shoe section.

She leaves me staring at myself in the mirror, and I take a deep breath, decision made. For the millionth time since I met Aiden, I let myself be selfish. I'm going to let myself pretend that this is our prom, the one that I'll never get to have, and ignore the stabbing in my stomach, ignore everything telling me that I'm going to hurt all the people I care about, including myself.

» «

We get home without Aiden having a clue which dress we bought, as per Charlotte's demands, and I model it for Annalisa, who claps in delight and declares the rest of the evening a girls' spa night.

Charlotte makes face masks in the kitchen while Annalisa and

I are in my room gathering all our nail polishes together to have options, when Annalisa's phone rings. The look on her face when she examines the caller ID tells me something is wrong, but she answers the call out in the hall anyway.

"What happened?" I ask as she sits back down on the floor across from me.

"Nothing." She dismisses me, but then changes her mind. "That was Luke."

She actually answered the phone for her brother? I guess that's progress from having his number blocked and cursing the day he was born.

"He called me from jail. He was arrested a couple of days ago and charged with killing Greg. Second degree murder." She looks down and fiddles with her nail polish bottle.

"I'm so sorry, Anna," I say sincerely.

"Why? Don't be sorry. I'm not. He deserves this," she states fiercely, maybe too fiercely, the kind of statement that makes me feel like she's really only trying to convince herself.

My brief silence prompts her to keep talking. "He's a shitty brother, and he killed a person! A shitty person, but still! Plus, he killed my mom, so I say good riddance!"

She's definitely trying to convince herself.

"Why do you say he killed your mom, Anna? I thought her addiction did?" I ask gently, because I know it's a touchy subject for her, but I want to help her work through it.

She takes a deep breath, her tough façade slowly deflating.

"My mom may have had her faults, but she had a tough life. She was still my mom and I loved her."

I move closer to her and give her my full attention, knowing she's going to open up, which is incredibly rare for her.

"She was depressed and mostly absent from my life because of an incident from before I was born," she admits quietly, still not looking at me. "She was sixteen and pregnant, kicked out of her house, written off by her family, and left to fend for herself. She was a fighter, though, and managed to land on her feet and do pretty well for herself and Luke. But then I came along and fucked everything up."

"What? Anna! How could you even say that?! You didn't ruin anything by being born!" I say, slightly mad that she would think that about herself.

Her mom would've been twenty or twenty-one when she had Annalisa, which I get may have been hard for a young, single mom already, but it wasn't Annalisa's fault!

"I did ruin everything!" she says and looks at me, tears welling up in her eyes. "She was raped by some guy at a party, and that resulted in me being born. She never came out and said it, but I knew she looked at me as a constant reminder of that awful night."

"Oh, Anna. I'm sure she didn't feel that way about you," I tell her, not really knowing how to comfort her.

"I don't know, she was still my mom, but it was really hard for her, so she was pretty absent or high a lot of the time. She did her best when she could, and I wouldn't trade her for anyone else, but because of that, it was usually just me and Luke left to look after each other, and sometimes her."

She wipes her tears on her sweater and I stay quiet, hypnotized by her words and by the hardships that she's telling me about.

"When I started high school, she started getting really bad. I would come home and she would be passed out on the bathroom floor, the pots on the stove overflowing and burning, fire detector going off."

She sniffs. "I know it was pretty hard on Luke, but it was hard for me too! I knew that I could always depend on him. He was my big brother. He would always be there for me and make everything okay. But he didn't! He made it worse! He fell into the wrong crowd and he fell down the same rabbit hole as my mom with the drugs. He's the one who introduced her to heroin, sometimes they even did it together."

I feel the tears flowing down my own face but force myself to stay quiet.

"And then she overdosed," she continues. "I was the one who found her, too, and I was destroyed. My whole world died, and I had no idea what to do. I thought Luke would step in and be the hero I always thought he was, he'd make it better." A sob escapes her lips and tears start flowing again, and I wrap my arms around her, letting her feel whatever emotions she needs to feel.

"But he didn't! He left me! He left me on my own to navigate all the shit that was happening. If Luke's dad, who we barely even knew, didn't eventually feel guilty and pay off our apartment, I would've been on the streets."

The tears silently stream down my face. Annalisa is always so strong and confident and sure of herself and what she wants. It's so hard to picture her dealing with all of this, but I get why she's so strong. Going through all of that has hardened her, made her tough and ready to face whatever the world throws at her, and I'm so incredibly grateful to know her.

She pulls away from me and I let my arms drop, and both of us dry our eyes.

"When Luke told me that he was clean, I didn't want to believe him. I didn't want to think that I could get my brother back, the one I depended on, because I was scared that he'd screw up somehow and I'd lose him again. And that's exactly what happened! He got drunk and killed Aiden's stepdad! And now I won't get to see him for who knows how long."

She takes a deep breath, as if trying to clear her head and calm down.

"There's always a chance he didn't do it," I tell her, not wanting her to write off her brother just yet.

He's trying. For her. He's doing everything to try and get back into her life. It doesn't look too good for him right now, but if there's even the slightest chance that he's innocent and doesn't go to jail, deep down, Annalisa would love to have her brother back.

"I just don't know how to feel, I guess," she admits. "If he killed Greg then he deserves to go to jail. But I guess a part of me doesn't want to see him rot in there, you know?"

"Of course," I reassure her. "Despite everything, he's still your brother. And if you need anything, you have us."

"I know. You guys are all the best."

She smiles a sad smile, but then shakes her head, as if trying to clear her thoughts, and suddenly her mask snaps back into place, and the emotions she was just displaying are gone.

"So anyway, am I picking Midnight Blue or Deep Purple for my nails?" she asks coolly, as if the last forty minutes never happened.

I sense that she's done talking about it and don't push her, telling her Midnight Blue is definitely her color, and we paint our nails and tell jokes and kid ourselves into thinking that everything is okay in our world.

19

Sunday goes by in a blur, and before we know it, it's time to go to Andrew's house.

"And you guys made fun of me for bringing my curling iron." Charlotte smirks as she puts the final curls in my hair. "Always be prepared, that's what I like to say!"

I laugh and try not to move. "I apologize for doubting your packing skills."

"But if it wasn't for this event, you still wouldn't have used it," Annalisa says from where she's sitting in front of us on the bathroom counter.

Charlotte frowns, but she's not offended. "I'll remember that on New Year's Eve when you want to get all glammed up and try to get your grubby hands on my 'useless' curling iron."

"Hey, I never said it was *useless,*" Annalisa protests with a grin. "I said it would be useless on this *trip*. There's a difference."

"Nuh-uh!" Charlotte argues, putting the iron down. "All done, Amelia! Let me brush these out and you're good to go."

I'd vetoed wearing my hair in a fancy updo in favor of keeping it in loose curls, making it easier to hide my face behind my hair if I get caught by a camera flash.

"Thanks again, guys," I say as Charlotte angles my head to her liking.

I'm fully capable of doing my own hair and makeup, but I wanted this experience with my friends—a memory I can store and recall with fondness when I'm forced to leave them; something that will remind me that I had *real* friends when I feel alone wherever I end up.

"What are best friends for?" Charlotte replies like she was just reading my mind. "All done!"

She puts the brush down and turns me so I'm fully in the mirror. "You look so beautiful! Well, you always look beautiful, but you know . . ." Charlotte gushes, her huge smile mirrored by Annalisa's.

The sight of the three of us, standing side by side in the mirror, hits me right in the stomach. I've never had friendships like this. I probably never will again.

"Thanks—really, for everything." I bite my lip to stop myself from saying something that sounds like a good-bye, but in a way, it is. I'll never get this moment again. I take a snapshot of it in my mind and store it away, close to my heart.

"I want to see the whole thing together." Annalisa smiles and ushers me out of the en suite and into the bedroom. "Hurry up and put on your dress so we can zip you up."

Before I know it, I'm standing in front of them in my dress and heels, my clutch in my hand.

"I wish you'd let us take a picture of you." Charlotte frowns as she adjusts pieces of my hair.

"We don't need pictures," I tell her. "Let's just live in the moment."

"I can't wait any longer!" Annalisa turns and rushes out of the room. "She's coming down!" she yells to the rest of the house, and I laugh at her excitement.

"Are you ready?" Charlotte asks me, and I nod. This moment feels bigger than it actually is, but to me, it's the only time I'll get to be all dressed up with Aiden. Maybe we'll even dance.

Charlotte stands back and lets me head down the stairs ahead of her. My friends come into view as I descend the stairs, but my eyes land on Aiden's handsome face and stay there. His eyes are striking against the deep navy of his suit, and my heart squeezes as they lazily trail down my body, drinking me in in the same way I do him.

His broad shoulders fill out his suit perfectly, and it tapers in to fit his narrow waist. The black tie I know isn't a clip-on stands out against the white dress shirt. I've never seen Aiden all dressed up, but it's *definitely* a sight I could get used to. Aiden normally turns heads, but he's goddamn jaw dropping right now.

His eyes meet mine, and the heat and intensity in them steal my breath and make my heart pound against my rib cage. For some reason, I feel shy by the time I reach him, but I can't look away from his unwavering gaze.

"You're so beautiful," he murmurs, tucking a strand of hair behind my ear, and I think I stop breathing. Has Aiden ever told me that before?

"You look good too," I tell him before turning to face my friends, who are crowded around the base of the stairs.

"You look amazing, Amelia," Mason says. "Even more than usual, if that's possible."

Aiden shifts, and I look away from Mason to see Aiden's jaw clench.

"Thanks, Mason," I say, a pit forming in my stomach.

"You guys look *so good* together!" Charlotte squeals, her excitement contagious. "*Please* let us take a picture of you guys together! Please, please, please!"

Aiden, knowing why I don't take pictures, starts to protest, when in a split decision, I cut him off.

"Okay," I say, surprising Aiden and even myself a little. "One picture. Use my phone."

"Are you sure?" Aiden asks, his eyebrows drawn in concern.

My eyes trace his features, from his intense gray eyes, down his straight nose, to his high cheekbones and his straight jaw, covered in neat stubble.

"Yes." My memory can only do him so much justice.

I hand Charlotte my phone, and Aiden and I adjust our poses so that we're side by side, his arm around my waist. She snaps a few, then looks over the phone at us. "Get closer!"

Aiden tugs me and I almost fall into him, and we both laugh. My smile is genuine when we pose again, pressed up against each other, my hand on his chest and his on the small of my back, holding me close.

"You guys are gonna be the best-looking people there," Noah says from behind Charlotte as I take my phone back.

Aiden laughs, and it's a freeing sound. "We're already the best-looking people here, so we're used to the feeling."

It takes Noah a beat too long to get the joke. "Well, you—*hey*!"

Laughing along with everyone else, I quickly look through the pictures Charlotte took, the only ones of me on this phone. We look so carefree. So happy.

"Did it turn out all right?" Aiden asks, holding me hostage with his eyes, and I nod.

I'm glad I decided to do this, even though it's going to hurt me, knowing I had this and gave it all up. It's all worth it. All for this memory of Aiden, standing here, looking gorgeous, staring at me with a fire in his eyes like I'm the only person in the world—like he needs me as much as I need him. I promise myself I'll delete them later—but for now, for tonight, I'm going to keep them.

"Try not to cause too much trouble tonight," Julian tells us, leaning against the wall.

"And don't worry about Aquafina, she can't be as bad as Ryan," Noah adds.

I turn to Noah. "Who?"

"You know, Aiden's stepsister. Aquafina."

Aiden doesn't glance away from fixing his tie in the hallway mirror. "It's Evianna."

"*Psh,*" Noah waves it away. "Same thing, wrong bottled water company."

"Noah!" Annalisa chides, smacking him in the arm. "That's mean."

"What? You're gonna stand there and tell me that the name *doesn't* sound like an expensive bottled water brand?"

"That's not the point!"

"Okay, that's our cue to leave," Aiden tells me over the bickering, then looks at his brothers, who are playing video games in the living room. "Boys, don't stay up too late."

Neither of them glances up but they reply at the same time. "'Kay."

"Ready?" Aiden holds out his arm to me.

Putting my phone back in my clutch, I take his arm and let him lead me out of the house, glancing back to say bye to everyone.

» «

I'm in complete awe as Aiden joins the line of cars slowly moving up the large, mile-long driveway at Andrew's house. The word *house* isn't grand enough to describe the place Mayor Andrew Kessler calls home. Maybe manor or estate. It's the kind of house that has an east or a west wing.

"Unbelievable," Aiden mumbles, and I pull my gaze away from the window to look over at him.

"What?"

"When he left, we were basically living in poverty. He knew my mom died. He knew he had three sons out there. For all he knew, we were living on the streets. All the while he's living in this fucking McMansion he got by marrying some fucking rich broad."

I take in the $4,000 suit Andrew had no problem getting for Aiden, someone he doesn't even know, and wonder how far that money would've went back before Aiden started racing, how far it would still go for Aiden and his brothers. That money probably didn't even make a scratch in Andrew's account. He probably can't even tell it's gone.

"He's an asshole, Aiden. We already know that. It's not too late to turn around."

His grip tightens on the steering wheel. "We're doing this. Then I'm never seeing him again."

We follow the line of cars up the large driveway and around the fancy water fountain, stopping in front of the steps that lead to the front door, like all the cars before us had done. A well-dressed man opens my door and offers me a hand to help me out. I step out of the low car as gracefully as I can manage. As I wait for Aiden to hand his keys to the valet, I gawk up at the monster of a mansion.

"What do you think they possibly do with all this space?" I ask Aiden as he joins me.

"Host wild sex orgies."

Bursting out laughing, I take his offered elbow. I didn't think he'd be in the joking mood—at least, I think he's joking.

Together, we walk up the stairs and enter the grandiose front entrance. We stand in line behind a few people, all dressed in expensive-looking dresses, suits, and jewelry.

We get to the front of the line where a woman holding a clipboard and wearing an ANDREW KESSLER pin stands. Her smile is wide but falters when she notices it's two kids standing in front of her. "Name?"

"Aiden Parker," he states, looking down at her.

She flips through the pages. "I'm sorry, you're not on the—" She pauses as her eyes widen, then hastily flips all the sheets back in place. "Wait here, please."

We move over to the side of the wide entranceway, while Clipboard Lady whispers something to a man in a black suit wearing an earpiece.

Everything in the house looks so polished, clean, and elegant. I feel out of place even though this is the most expensive dress I've ever worn. They're the kind of rich who decorate their house with those little stands with vases on them, and even the stupid pottery is more elegant than I am, with delicate etchings and real gold flakes. The sudden urge to touch one consumes my mind. It looks so smooth and shiny and—

"Hey!" An angry voice makes me jump, and a bald man with an earpiece walks closer to me. "Don't touch that," he sneers. "It's probably worth more than your car."

I pull my hand back sheepishly as Aiden glares at the man with an intensity that would've made me wither into the floor.

Clipboard Lady comes to stand in front of us again. "Just one moment." She looks like she swallowed something sour, but she still keeps that smile on her face by sheer force of will.

The large man who dropped off Aiden's suit and never smiles appears beside Clipboard Lady. She gestures at him. "Mr. Vedenin will escort you to your father."

"Are we not allowed to mingle?" Aiden asks.

Her smile tightens. "Mr. Kessler made it very clear that he would like Harvey to escort you to him as soon as you arrived."

Aiden's gaze bounces from Harvey to Clipboard Lady then back. We're probably thinking the same thing: Andrew sent Harvey not as an esteemed escort, but as a prison guard.

There's now a line behind us, but Aiden's not in any rush to end his stare-off with the large man in front of him. Clipboard Lady shifts nervously. "If you please, I have people waiting."

Aiden addresses her without shifting his gaze from Harvey. "We'll find Andrew when we're ready. I'd like to mingle first."

With that, he guides me into the house, not caring about her protests or about the large man staring after us. Aiden expertly guides us around the people crowded in the large hallway, each person looking more expensively clad and important than the last, their flowery perfume and musky cologne mixing together so that I can't pinpoint who's wearing what, until we can no longer see Harvey or the other men in black suits and earpieces who were at the front entrance.

"Is it just me or does that Harvey guy give off a really bad vibe?" I ask, slowing our pace as we enter a large room. What is this? Is this a ballroom? Do modern homes even have ballrooms? The giant chandelier hanging in the middle of the room looks like it costs more than my house.

"It's not just you," Aiden says.

People are mingling while servers in suits walk by with trays, distributing hors d'oeuvres or flutes of champagne. A few large campaign ads are up on the wall across from the large floor-to-ceiling windows. The doors along the wall beside the windows are open, leading out to one long balcony that wraps around the outside of the room, where people are mingling and looking out at what I think is a garden. Ten or so men and women in white suit jackets are in the corner of the room playing soft classical music that fills the room.

"Whoa," is all I can manage. I feel like I've stepped into a scene straight out of *The Great Gatsby*, but modern, and even richer, if that was possible.

A woman walks by with a purse I *know* costs about $20,000 (because Charlotte is obsessed with it), and I think maybe I really *shouldn't* touch anything.

Aiden takes a deep breath beside me. Although he has his impassive mask on, I can feel the rage bubbling beneath the surface, begging for someone to say one wrong thing or make one wrong move so it can be unleashed. A server walks by with flutes of champagne and Aiden plucks one off and hands it to me, as if sensing that I'm just as overwhelmed as he is.

"I've never felt the urge to drink in my life, until right now," Aiden mutters as he takes in the scene in front of him, his posture rigid and his jaw clenched.

"I can't drive stick," I answer, taking a sip of the champagne he handed me.

He takes another breath, spotting something in the distance and following it with his eyes. "I know. Remind me to teach you one day."

"You're Aiden Parker," comes a voice from beside us.

The woman is familiar, but I can't place her until I read the reporters' pass dangling from a Channel Five lanyard.

"I'm Vivienne Henfrey from *Channel Five News*," she says, voicing what I already put together. She was the one hounding Andrew at the fair the other day.

"How do you know who I am?" Aiden asks, his expression giving nothing away.

"When you're dealing with someone as crooked as Andrew Kessler, you do your research." She reaches into her handbag and pulls out a business card. Her eyes remind me of a viper eyeing its prey. "I'd love to talk to you about your father."

Aiden stares at the card in her outstretched hand for a few beats, then takes it. "He's not my father."

She gives him a sympathetic smile, but everything about her screams of her ambition. "Of course. He hasn't been your father in years."

Aiden's gaze finds something in the distance again. "Sure," he says simply to her, and without taking his eyes off whatever he's trailing, he says to me, "Come on."

Leaving Vivienne behind, I set the champagne flute down on a random table and let him lead me in the direction he was looking, skillfully weaving around people. Even here, Aiden's presence is too much to ignore, and people move out of our way like they do in the halls at school. We exit the ballroom and walk through the house, where there are still tons of people mingling. Every tidbit of conversation we hear that's *Kessler's so great*, or *Kessler's so generous,* or *Kessler's an amazing guy*, makes Aiden's hand in mine tighten a little bit more.

We slip behind a security guard and head down a hallway that's definitely off limits. My footsteps are softened by the red carpet, and I can't help but stare at all the abstract paintings we pass. Was that one signed Picasso? Aiden pulls us to a stop in front of a room from which voices are drifting out from, and we move to the side so as to not be seen.

"How did you *lose* my son?" Kessler asks, his voice venomous.

"I'm not a babysitter," comes the flat answer, and I know it's from the large man, Harvey.

"You have to get him under control," comes another voice, a woman's. It sounds elegant even though she's clearly not happy. "We can't afford anything that would jeopardize you not winning this election. Do you know how royally fucked we'd be?"

"Yes, Katherine," comes Andrew's harsh reply, and I realize that's his wife. "I'm aware of the money we took and the promises we made."

"Those aren't the kind of people we can fuck over. Do you remember my cousin Vincent?" Katherine asks.

"No."

"Exactly!" she screeches, and I hear a glass being set down. I imagine she just chugged whatever alcoholic drink she had in her hand. "We have too much riding on this to let your stupid kid fuck it up."

"Calm down, Katherine. You know I'll do anything to win. I'm not going to let a kid I never even wanted fuck it up."

"I still can't believe you *had* him," she says like it's the most absurd thing she's ever heard.

"We've been over this. You know I only married his mom because I knocked her up. I'd never see him or his stupid bratty brothers if I didn't have to. I'm *never* going back to the life I had in King City. I'll do whatever it takes, so believe me when I say Aiden's not going to be a problem. I'll make sure of it."

I've always thought that Aiden's father was a terrible person, but hearing these words out loud is like a punch to the chest. The only indications that Aiden's pissed are his drawn eyebrows and the tick in his jaw.

"Well, then, where is he?" comes a new voice, low and masculine. "We're supposed to get ahead of this before it becomes a scandal. Introduce him as your estranged son you're reconnecting with. I can't do my job as your campaign manager if he's not going to cooperate."

"It's under control, Will," Andrew says forcefully.

"What are you doing?" A loud voice comes from directly behind us, making both Aiden and I jump at the unexpected sound.

"Vee? What are *you* doing here?" I ask her, astonished. We haven't seen her since the other day at the roller rink. Her long, sparkly, silver dress hugs her body and kind of makes me wish I was wearing it. Her brown hair is coiled professionally on top of her head and her deep-red lipstick is perfectly intact despite the almost empty glass of champagne in her hand. Her eyes jump over me and land on Aiden, at which she does a double take and stays there, drinking him in like she did last time. Jealousy boils in my veins.

"Evianna?" Katherine's voice comes from directly behind us, and Aiden and I turn again, caught in the doorway like deer in headlights between Vee and the adults.

"Aiden," says Andrew, his tone cool and authoritative, the sarcasm heavy. "Thank you for finally joining us. Come in."

With no other choice than to follow him into the room, we do, and Harvey closes the door behind us. We're in a large office. There's a heavy desk in the room, as well as a few leather couches. A large bookshelf covers the wall behind the desk, and I find the entire room intimidating since there are no windows in here.

"Aiden, this is my wife, Katherine." Andrew gestures to a regal woman in a burgundy floor-length dress. She's quite striking, in a beautiful but intimidating kind of way. "And her daughter, Evianna." Andrew gestures at Vee, and Aiden and I stare at her openly.

"*This* is your 'criminal, trailer-park thug of a no-good son'?" Evianna's eyes are wide as she takes in Aiden's gorgeous frame in a new light, and I know she's trying to match the image Andrew's painted with the tall, could-be underwear model in front of her.

I want to punch her.

"Where are your brothers?" Andrew asks, not even bothering to deny that he called Aiden those names, and as usual, completely ignoring me.

"I left the '*stupid brats*' at home." Aiden emphasizes Andrew's previous words. "I didn't want them to be a part of your game. In fact, neither do I."

Andrew's head tilts. "Then why did you come?"

Aiden glances at me, and I know he doesn't really understand why himself, but I hope he got the closure he was looking for, because from the sound of it, Andrew's still the same self-absorbed asshole he was when he left Aiden and his mom all those years ago.

"I've known a lot of really shitty people over the course of my life," Aiden starts, "but none of them come even remotely close to you."

"I'm sorry you feel that way." Andrew doesn't sound sorry in the slightest.

"I didn't come here with the intention of wanting anything from you," Aiden tells him. "But now, I think I want everything."

Andrew shares a glance with his wife. She gives him an approving nod. They were prepared for this.

Andrew's tone is confident and a little cocky. "We have enough money to make sure you and your brothers never have to work a day in your life."

I know Aiden's not missing the fact that Andrew only refers to Jason and Jackson as "your brothers," and not "my sons."

"I don't want your money."

"Then what—"

"I had a conversation with Vivienne Henfrey, earlier." Aiden cuts Andrew off, looking right at home even though we're in the middle of a snake pit. "She really doesn't like you."

Andrew's "we're family, son" manner falls, and I see him for who he truly is as he sends Aiden a venomous look. "A lot of work and money has gone into this campaign, Aiden." He's trying to stay calm, trying to remain in control of the situation. "A lot of people are counting on me. From the way this campaign is going, I *will* become governor. People love me, they think I'm a champion for the underdog, fighting for them and their children. You understand, then, why I can't afford a scandal right now."

"What kind of scandal are you talking about, Andrew?" Aiden asks him, knowing full well what he's talking about but wanting to hear him say the words.

Andrew's lips turn up at the corners, his eyes cold and

calculating. "If you're anything like me, you're a smart man. Smart enough to know that *all* of our unfortunate pasts should just stay where they belong. We wouldn't want them to ruin my reputation." He glances at me for what must be the first time since we entered, and I don't miss how pointed of a look it is.

"And why should I give a fuck about your reputation?" Aiden challenges, and anyone other than Andrew would've shriveled up into nothing.

Andrew doesn't hesitate. "I'm a very powerful man, Aiden. And I know a lot of people—people who don't mind getting their hands dirty. Remember, it's not just about *you*."

Another pointed look at me. Goose bumps break out on my arms.

Aiden doesn't hesitate. "Is that a threat?"

Andrew tugs on his expensive-looking cufflinks, completely unfazed by his son's intimidating demeanor. "You can interpret that statement however you want. It won't make it any less true." Andrew straightens. "I always knew I was destined for something greater than being stuck in that tiny house with a dying woman and a bunch of ungrateful kids. I'm not going to let some *punk* ruin my goals."

Aiden straightens as well, his back stiff, and I can feel his resolve to not hit Andrew dissolving into nothing. I quickly put my hand on his arm, which is seconds away from causing some serious pain, even though I, myself, want to punch Andrew. I've stayed quiet until now, trying to let Aiden handle it the way he wants to, but now I'm pissed off. Andrew not only insulted his dead wife, but Aiden, Jason, and Jackson, all while threatening him to get him to stay quiet about the truth of who Andrew actually is.

I put as much venom in my words as I possibly can. "So what? You desert your sick, pregnant wife and young son? Con Katherine into marrying you since she has money? Run for mayor, for governor, lie to the people, and pretend to be something you're not so that you can fill the void in your life? That void that you just can't seem to fill, because you know that no matter what you do, no matter who you pay to like you or intimidate into fearing you, no matter how much money you have, you'll never come close to amounting to anything. You'll *always* be a piece of shit coward and a sorry excuse of a man."

Andrew narrows his eyes at me, his lips tilting up at the corners the slightest bit, almost as if he's intrigued by me. He addresses Aiden but keeps his eyes trained on me. "Your *girlfriend* has quite the mouth on her. Make sure to keep *Amelia* in line as well, or I'll send someone to do it for you."

When he stresses my name like that, I know he's the kind of powerful man who can quickly become a big problem, can easily do more damage than good. A shiver runs down my spine. Aiden's whole body tenses, and I *almost* let him do whatever damage he wants, but quickly squeeze his arm and address Andrew before he can react.

I send him a sinister smile. "You know where to find me, but it'd be so much more fun if you didn't send someone to do your dirty work like a little pus—"

"Hey!" Andrew cuts me off. "That's enough from both of you. Get out of my house. If either of you cause any problems for me or this campaign, I will send someone to *deal* with it. Understand? I tried, but if you don't want to play this game, fine, stay quiet then, and that's the only way you all stay safe."

Aiden stares at Andrew, a challenge in his eyes and not seeming the least bit threatened by his father. "Go fuck yourself," he says. "Come on, Amelia."

Without looking back, we leave the room, hand in hand, our anger fueling us as we exit the private hallway and join the crowded halls again. I can't believe the *nerve* on Andrew. To say all that horrible stuff about Aiden and his family. To threaten them. Maybe I really *should've* let Aiden hit him, at least it would've made him feel better.

We reach the large front hall where we entered, and although there still are people around, it's not as busy as it was before. I catch a glimpse of the bald security man with the earpiece and we stare each other down. There's a tick in my jaw, then I reach out and knock over the vase I was instructed not to touch earlier. It falls to the floor and shatters.

Aiden's head swivels over to look at me, and for a second I freeze. Everyone is staring at us in shock. I can't believe I just did that! But then Aiden smiles, a real smile that reaches his eyes, the first one since pulling up to Andrew's house, and he laughs. A smile spreads on my own face, and before I even know what we're doing, we both reach out to another vase on a stand beside the one I just broke, and without looking away from each other, simultaneously push it off.

The sound of the vase shattering is drowned out by the security guard yelling, "Hey!"

Aiden and I burst out laughing and rush out of the house, my heart light for the first time since hearing Andrew's voice today. We dodge the people coming up the steps and run all the way to the valet, where Aiden produces his ticket.

"Guess we shouldn't have done that when we don't have an

escape waiting." Aiden laughs, his eyes light and shining as they focus on me.

A quick glance behind us at the house makes it clear no one's following us to yell at us. "It certainly does undercut the drama, but at least they're too busy cleaning it up."

Aiden's smile is genuine as he pulls me into him, wrapping his arms around me and holding me close, his chest rumbling in time with his chuckles.

20

We spend the next day walking down the beach and into town, shopping until we can't shop anymore, and trying to get our minds off of what happened last night. Aiden didn't really go into detail with our friends, but they know it didn't go well. By the time we get back from shopping, we're all exhausted.

I'm in Aiden's room lying on the bed, eating a Nutella sandwich for dinner while scrolling through my laptop and waiting for him to come back with more sandwiches.

I'm so deep down the rabbit hole of watching random YouTube videos that I only notice that Aiden has been gone for much longer than it should take to get more sandwiches when my stomach growls.

He better not have gotten distracted and forgotten about my Nutella.

When I open the door to go find him, he's standing right in front of it about to come in, one hand holding a plate of sandwiches, the other pressing his phone to his ear.

"As always, it's been a pleasure talking to you, Andrew. Go fuck yourself." He hangs up the phone and I stare at him with wide eyes.

"That was Andrew," he says flatly, stepping around me and into the room.

"I gathered as much." I close the door and turn around to look at him. "What happened?"

I sit cross-legged in front of him on the bed and take the sandwich that he holds out to me.

"Oh, you know, just some thinly veiled threats. The usual." He takes a bite of his own sandwich and rolls his eyes. "He was all, 'I'm a powerful man with powerful connections, keep that in mind if you try to screw me over.' 'Promise to stay quiet and not cause trouble and I'll keep everyone safe,' *blah, blah, blah*."

Everyone safe.

"He called you for the sole purpose of making sure you kept your mouth shut?" That must not have gone well. "What did you say?"

His jaw clenches. "He's pissing me off. Threatening me and my family? And have you noticed that black SUV with the blacked out windows that's been parked across the street since last night? Surveillance? Really?"

I feel the color drain from my face. "Someone's been watching us? Are you sure it's Andrew and not . . . ?"

He knows where my train of thought is headed and immediately comforts me.

"It's not Tony, I promise." He puts his warm hand on my thigh and my heart automatically calms down. "I saw that it was Harvey when he rolled down the window to have a smoke."

I take a relieved breath. "Okay. What are we going to do about Andrew?"

He lifts an amused eyebrow. "We?"

"Of course *we*." I give him a duh look. "What's the plan?"

Aiden finishes his sandwich and cleans his hands. "I told him I was absolutely going to give Vivienne Henfrey the inside story. She already hates him so he knows she'll take this story and run with it."

"How did he react?"

He chuckles. "Not very well. Lost his composure for a bit and taught me a few new swear combinations. Even if I don't talk to the journalist, it was fun to see him sweat for a while."

Why is he playing this off like it's no big deal? "Aren't you worried he'll make good on his threats?"

Aiden's smirk intensifies, his eyes smoldering with a combination of mischief and confidence that only he can pull off. "Are you worried about me, Thea?"

I smack his chest. "Of course I'm worried!"

He grabs my waist and without warning flips us over so that we're lying down, with him on top of me. I pray my face isn't heating up.

"Don't be," he says soothingly. "You have enough to be worried about. I wouldn't do anything that might risk Tony finding you. I just don't want Andrew to think it's that easy."

"I'm still going to worry," I say. "The way he said *Amelia* totally freaked me out."

"He's just being an asshole. He knows I care about you and he's using that against me." He pauses, then pushes my hair out of my face. "You know, I couldn't have done any of that without you last night." He smiles and looks deep into my eyes, a gleam in his that's only there when he's truly happy.

"I didn't even do anything," I answer breathlessly.

"You did *everything*," he replies confidently and then he lowers his head and kisses me deeply, so intensely that my head feels like it's spinning, that the world feels like it's melted away, and all that matters is me and him and this moment.

My hands travel up and down his back, feeling the muscles contract under my touch, secretly delighted that I can have such an effect on him. His hands tighten on my waist and he flips us over so that I'm on top of him, my body pressed tightly against his. His hands are all over me, leaving a trail of fire on my skin as he goes, and I know that I've never wanted anyone as much and as badly in my life as I want Aiden Parker.

We gently pull apart and he gazes into my eyes, a lazy smile on his lips, and his thumbs gently running across my jaw. "I love you, Thea."

Wha—? I feel my face physically freeze in a look of shock and worry.

He loves me?

I suddenly and ungracefully roll off of him and sit up, not daring to look at him.

Oh my God. I fucked up so badly.

I feel him sit up quickly and he puts his hand on my arm. "Thea?"

My face must be contorted in a panicked look because I feel him stiffen. "What's wrong?"

I say it without thinking about it, needing this emotional weight off my chest before it explodes. "I'm leaving in the new year when we get back home."

He freezes. "What do you mean?"

"I mean that on January 3 I'm picking up my things and moving. I'll become a Jennifer or an Erica or some other name that isn't mine and start all over again." I look away from him and into my lap, not wanting to see the look of betrayal in his eyes.

"What? They can't just force you to move for no reason! You're safe here, and if you weren't, I'd be the first damn person getting ready to protect you!"

The fact that he thinks I don't have a choice in the matter breaks my heart. Really, physically, breaks my heart. With every word he says it feels like someone is stabbing me in the chest with a knife and I can barely even look at him.

"I think it's a good idea to leave," I whisper, staring at my hands in my lap.

I feel him freeze beside me as he registers what that means. "What?" he asks in a flat, emotionless tone.

"I have to leave, Aiden. You all mean too much to me to stay here. Where I go, people get hurt. People *die*. And I'm not going to be selfish and put everyone in danger without them knowing, without them even having a choice in the matter! As much as it hurts, the best thing for me to do in this situation is to just leave."

There's anger in his eyes, betrayal. "Were you even planning on telling me or were you just planning to steal my heart and disappear without a second glance?"

He stands up and runs his hands through his hair, and I scramble off of the bed to stand in front of him.

"I—I wanted to tell you! I was going to—"

"Yeah? When?" He turns around to face me, eyes blazing. "You were going to give me an hour's notice before hopping in your car and waving a big fuck you to everyone?"

The knife in my heart twists. "None of this was supposed to happen! I wasn't supposed to make friends! I wasn't supposed to fall in love—"

"So you do love me?" he interrupts, his cool gray eyes set with determination, holding me prisoner.

"How could I not?" My voice breaks at the end, and it's taking all that I have to not completely break down.

"Then don't leave." He steps closer to me but I back away, as if scared that his proximity will destroy any resolve I have.

"I can't." My heart's shattering into a million pieces.

"Why the hell not?"

"You know why, Aiden. I just told you. People get hurt because of me, people I care about. It's inevitable. And I can't afford to risk it, especially not now. My mom had decided a while ago, and now after the mayor, his threats, I have to go. I've been too selfish, but it's time I put you above my own wants. You and everyone else. I can't risk it, not this time."

His eyes are laser focused on me, the intensity burning a hole straight to my soul.

"You told me that you contemplated just ending the running and hiding and just giving yourself up to Tony. But you didn't. You said you were strong. You said that you didn't take the easy way out. So prove it. Be strong *now*. Don't take the easy way out by leaving. Stay here with us, with *me*."

I force myself to hold it together, at least until I'm no longer in his presence, even though there's a hole in my chest where my heart should be and it feels like someone is squeezing my throat.

"I can't, Aiden. I just can't. If your dad knows who I am—if it's that easy to find out, then Tony'll be a step behind. I can't risk it. I can't."

I turn my back on him and quickly leave the room before the single tear that escaped during my reply turns into full blown sobbing.

21

Tuesday, December 30, is not New Year's Eve, but that doesn't stop Erin from throwing a New Year's Eve party at her house that night. She texted Mason and invited us to her Pre-NYE party, because, according to Erin, "There's always a reason to get wasted if you look hard enough." She even gave us the number for a local babysitter to watch Jason and Jackson, because apparently her Pre-NYE party is "fun as fuck" and she forbade us from missing it. Before we even agreed to go, we asked if Vee was going to be there, and Erin told us that Vee had a family event and wouldn't be able to come.

After thinking about it, we decided it would be cool to go to a party that wouldn't be crashed by Silvers starting fights, and that Vee wouldn't be at either. Aiden didn't want to leave his brothers but the guys convinced him that out of all of us, he needs to have some fun. Plus, it's not like he's leaving them *on* New Year's Eve, and the babysitter had great references and was apparently a pro at *Return of the Zombie Aliens Part Three and a Half*, which earned her bonus points with Jason and Jackson.

So that's where we currently are, at Erin's massive house right on the beach, with what appears to be her whole school and the entire town's supply of booze.

"That group of guys has been staring at us for the last twenty minutes. Do you think they'll come talk to us?" Charlotte asks with a tilt of her head in their direction.

I casually look in the direction she hinted, and there's a group of four guys staring at us. I guess a couple of them are conventionally good looking, but none of them are Aiden.

"Do you want them to?" I ask.

Charlotte shrugs and looks at her beer. "I don't know. Maybe."

I'm not having the greatest time at this party. With everything still unresolved with Aiden and still not having told Mason about our parents, it's too hard to have fun, and I don't think Charlotte or Annalisa are either. Charlotte's still stressed about Chase and Noah, since they're still not friends, and Annalisa's conflicted about her brother.

"They better not. Aiden would bite their heads off if they tried getting with you," Annalisa says to me.

I look down at my drink, my already sad mood worsening.

"Doubt it," I murmur, but I don't think either girl hears me over the loud music.

Things are tense between Aiden and me, and the whole house knows it. I get that he's upset, I really do. It breaks my heart to think about how betrayed he must feel, but I have to stand my ground. He has to see why I really have no choice in the matter, and that I think it's best to leave rather than stay and put everyone I love in danger—including him, especially him.

"How awesome are Erin's friends?" Mason stumbles over, already one too many beers in.

He slings his arm around my shoulder. "How great is it to go to a party and not worry about seeing Dave's ugly fat face."

I shiver, recalling the first time I met Dave at a party, when he wouldn't take no for an answer. I'm definitely glad he's not here.

"You look like you're having fun," Annalisa tells him, dodging the splash of beer from his cup when he turns to face her.

"Yeah, but you guys don't. Why are you all such Debbie Downers over here?"

Annalisa glares at him but doesn't answer, and I shrug off his arm since it's starting to get kind of heavy.

"We're not Debbie Downers." I defend us, secretly glad that maybe old Mason is back, and that the regular tension present whenever Mason and I are around each other is finally starting to lessen.

"You so are! Come on, k-bear! You used to be fun! But then you get in a secret fight with Aiden that no one will talk about and you become a downer. Let's go get in on the beer pong action in the kitchen!"

Before I can even process what he said, he's pulling me along with him and I have no choice but to comply. As we're walking to the kitchen, we pass the living room, where I easily spot Aiden. He's with Julian talking to some of Erin's friends, and my heart squeezes with longing and hurt.

Almost as if he senses me, he turns his head and his intense gray eyes narrow in on me, and it's suddenly like the world has converted into slow motion. His eyes are unreadable as they study my face, but then lock on my hand in Mason's as he leads me past the room. His eyes stay locked there until we pass the living room, and suddenly the world speeds up again to regular time, and I feel like I can release the breath I didn't know I was holding.

"Hey, Trey!" Mason calls to some guy in the kitchen. "Me and my girl wanna take you up on that beer pong challenge!"

I do a double take. My girl? He better mean "my girl" in the way I call Annalisa my girl, and not in the way Aiden calls me his girl.

Or I guess *called* me. Past tense.

We end up losing beer pong, badly. Apparently, drunk Mason has zero aim, and I'm useless once I feel Aiden burning a hole in the back of my head after he comes into the room. He's making me nervous. All I can think about is him. He's in the corner talking to some guys, but I feel his eyes on me, his face as stoic and unreadable as the day I met him.

I can't take this anymore. I can't bear the thought of him treating me like he did when he first met me, even if I deserve it.

I'm walking through the crowd of people to go talk to him when I see him put his phone to his ear, and a flash of annoyance and anger crosses his face before it's neutral again. He leaves the room, still talking on the phone, and I stop trying to get to him, feeling my whole body deflate.

I don't think he even noticed me.

"Hey, k-bear! Where ya goin'?" Mason steps in front of me, blocking my last remaining glimpse of Aiden. "I just challenged Trey and his girlfriend to a rematch!"

"I'm not really feeling it right now, Mason. But I'm sure Chase would love to take my spot."

I need to know where Aiden went. It's killing me to not know how he's doing. I know I have no right and I should probably leave it before I make things worse, but feelings don't just go away because your brain tells them to.

I try to step around Mason but he takes a step to block my

path. "You're not still thinkin' 'bout Aiden, are you?" he asks with a frown. "'Cause he's not thinkin' about you."

I blink at him, taken off guard. "What?"

"Listen, k-bear. I don't know what happened between the two of you, but you know Aiden. Once he's done with a girl, he's done. Remember Kaitlyn?"

Mason is standing there completely harmless, but he might as well have just stabbed me in the chest, twisted the knife, pulled it out, and then stabbed me again.

"What Aiden and I have is different than anything he might've had with Kaitlyn," I say, knowing in my heart that it's true, even if Mason's words planted a tiny seed of doubt in my mind.

"Maybe," he says, "but I'm pretty sure he was flirting with a bunch of girls earlier, and if not tonight, then it's only a matter of time till he does."

That's good. He's moving on. Once I leave it'll be like I was never here. That's a good thing. It's a good thing. Maybe if I keep saying it over and over I'll actually start believing it instead of feeling like turning into a sobbing mess.

Even drunk, Mason notices my I'm trying really hard not to cry right now face, because he says, "Oh, but don't worry, k-bear. You'll always be my number one."

"That's very reassuring, Mason. Thank you," I say just to be polite, but it comes out flat and deflated.

Mason is either too drunk to notice or doesn't care, because he beams his perfectly straight, white teeth at me. "Anytime! Now how 'bout that beer pong rematch?"

I manage to slip out of playing beer pong by switching out with some random girl, and go sit out on the beach to watch the calming waves. A body sits down next to me, but I instinctively know it's not Aiden, even though I wish it was.

"This party would've been a lot more fun if we all weren't bummed out," Annalisa says, resting her palms on the sand behind her and leaning back.

I laugh humorlessly. "I guess this whole thing was a dumb idea, huh? All coming here accomplished was starting fights and causing tension between people who were the best of friends."

"It's not your fault. Clearly we just can't handle being together for long stretches of time without drama finding us," Annalisa says matter-of-factly. "Honestly, all of this would've happened whether or not we were together anyway. It was only a matter of time."

"I guess," I sigh. "Maybe not the drama and threats from Aiden's dad, but I guess everything else."

"I know. Andrew Kessler needs to calm his balls," Annalisa scoffs. "He called Aiden again an hour or two ago."

I snap to attention when she says that. "What did he want?"

Annalisa sits up and rubs the sand off of her hands. "Julian told me that Andrew told Aiden he has one more chance to reconsider talking to the reporters or else he'll have to take 'drastic measures' to stop him."

My eyebrows draw together. "What does 'drastic measures' mean?"

Anna shrugs. "Beats me. He was already a shitty person to begin with, and no fancy suits can cover that up, so I wouldn't underestimate him."

"What did Aiden say?"

"He told him to go fuck himself and that his meeting with Vivienne Henfrey tomorrow night is happening whether he likes it or not," she answers, smiling at Aiden's confidence.

Good. I hope Aiden takes down his disgusting deadbeat dad, even if I won't be there to help him. I'm glad he decided to do it after all, but it makes me more resolved than ever to leave.

» «

Erin's Pre-NYE party is apparently so big that the cops come to break it up pretty early, much to everyone's dismay. By the time we stumble back to the beach house, it's only one in the morning.

The babysitter tells us that the twins are upstairs sleeping before Aiden pays her and drives her home (since he didn't have anything to drink). The rest of us (mostly the half who are happily intoxicated) decide one o'clock is the perfect time to cook up a feast and continue drinking.

Annalisa, Charlotte, and I barely drank, but since we don't trust the guys to operate heavy kitchen appliances while drunk, we stay up and cook for them.

"Isn't this ironic?" Noah plops himself down on the stool at the kitchen counter. "The men sitting around drinking beer and the women in the—"

Annalisa cuts him off by pulling a knife from the wooden block and pointing it at him from across the kitchen, her eyes narrowed.

"Finish that sentence with a joke about how women belong barefoot and pregnant in the kitchen. I dare you."

Noah gulps, his eyes wide. "I was gonna say something about

the women looking so pretty and being so nice and generous and taking care of us . . ."

Annalisa rolls her eyes but smirks anyway and puts the knife down on the counter. "That's exactly what I thought."

Mason takes a seat on the stool beside Noah, beer in hand. "What are you making for our feast? I want a full, four-course meal!"

"You're getting grilled cheese," I deadpan, already buttering the bread.

He frowns. "But we want—"

Annalisa picks up the knife again, and like she did with Noah, points it at him from across the kitchen.

"Grilled cheese. That's what you were going to say, right?"

Mason eyes Annalisa and compliantly nods. "I love grilled cheese."

Annalisa smiles triumphantly and holds up the knife to inspect it. "Wow, this knife is great at getting the Boys to do whatever we want."

Julian puts his arm around her as he opens the fridge to grab another beer.

"It's not the knife, it's the crazy, murderous, I'm not afraid to cut you alive and wear your skin as pajamas look you have in your eyes," he jokes, and she laughs as she play hits him and wiggles out of his embrace.

We make so much grilled cheese that we finish two packages of bread. There's a pile of sandwiches on the stove so that Aiden is able to have some when he gets back.

I'm sitting on the floor eating my own grilled cheese while playing a board game with Mason, Annalisa, and Noah, trying to ignore Aiden in the other room.

"Earth to k-bear! It's your turn." Mason taps me on the forehead.

"Oh, sorry." I shake my head and roll the dice so I can move my piece across the board.

"It's okay, you were probably just distracted by my godlike abs." Mason smirks at me, and any girl who wasn't already in love with Aiden would've melted.

"You're wearing a shirt, Mason," I inform him with a laugh, content with pretending that any tension we've had the last few days doesn't exist.

He swiftly pulls his shirt over his head in a way that would've been shot in slow motion if this was a movie. "Not anymore." He smiles cheekily.

"Oh no. Mason's taking his clothes off. Now you know he's drunk." Annalisa shakes her head with an exhausted smile.

"Like we didn't already know that," Noah says. "Dude, put your shirt back on."

"Why?" Mason smiles innocently. "Amelia likes it, right, k-bear?"

Mason is not unattractive in the slightest—he could probably get a professional modeling contract if he tried—but he's just not the guy I'm interested in looking at shirtless.

"Put your clothes back on, Mason." I laugh as I finish my sandwich.

"Don't lie, k-bear. We all know you want it," he teases, flexing his pecs so that they bounce in a mesmerizing manner.

"Oh yeah, Mason. The only reason I told you to put your shirt back on is because it's the only thing stopping me from jumping your bones," I say incredibly sarcastically.

He either consciously chooses to ignore the sarcasm or is too drunk to notice it, because he smiles widely with a mischievous gleam in his eyes.

"Nothing's stopping you right now!" He smiles.

My eyes widen as he takes me off guard, leaning over and sort of tackling me, pinning me under him, and starts *tickling me.*

"*Mason!*" I manage to yell between forced giggles, incapable of pushing him off of me. "Stop!"

All of a sudden, his weight is lifted off of me, and I wipe the resulting tears from my eyes as I sit up. Aiden is standing over us, having pulled Mason off of me, and he looks incredibly pissed off.

"What the hell, man?" Mason complains. "What's your problem? We were just playing!"

"You're my problem," Aiden deadpans, his eyes bold and fiery.

Mason stands up to face Aiden, and I exchange a nervous glance with Noah and Annalisa.

"It's not my fault you grew tired of Amelia like you did with every other girl before her," Mason spits out venomously.

"That's not what happened," Aiden practically growls.

"Either way, it's clearly over and Amelia is up for grabs." Mason smirks maliciously.

I stand up, feeling taken aback that Mason would talk about me like that, like I was an old CD or used baseball bat that Aiden no longer wanted and was therefore passed down to Mason.

"She is not 'up for grabs,' she's a fucking person." Aiden reads my mind, looking like he's trying very hard to remain calm.

"Well, either way." Mason squares off with him. "You fucked up and lost your chance."

What is happening?!

Noah and Annalisa stand up and move beside me, not really knowing what to do.

Aiden's eyes are trained on Mason. "You're supposed to be my best friend, but you sense the tiniest sliver of tension and you're already trying to steal my girl?"

"She shouldn't even be with you!" Mason exclaims. "I was her friend. I was nice to her when she was the new girl. You were nothing but a closed off asshole to her and she still chose you!"

Aiden's eyes narrow to deadly slits, all the muscles in his body tense. "You know nothing about my relationship with Amelia."

"But I know Amelia. And I know she'd be happier with me."

Aiden releases a humorless chuckle, one that conveys he in no way finds Mason amusing. "Believe me, you do not know Amelia."

"Guys, please. Let's just cool off," I cut in, then turn to look at Mason. "You're drunk. Why don't you sober up and we can talk about this like adults in the morning?"

I look at Aiden. "You know he's drunk. I know it's not an excuse, but let's just take a walk before you say *something you'll regret*," I tell him, putting emphasis on the last part as a reminder that he needs to keep my past a secret and not reveal it in a petty ego competition.

He whips his head over to look at me, taking his steady glare off of Mason for the first time. "I would never," he promises, looking all the way into my soul, trying to convey the seriousness of his words.

Julian walks into the room with Charlotte and Chase, and they immediately notice the tension.

"What's going on here?" Julian asks.

Noah sips his beer. "Mason decided to grow a pair at the wrong time."

Mason's head swivels over to look at Noah. "Says the guy who's still trying to sleep with the girl his best friend has pined over for years."

Noah practically slams his beer down. "*I didn't know!*"

"*Everyone knew!*" Mason counters.

This is getting out of hand now. It already was, but now things are really heating up. We need to calm down before shit hits the fan and explodes all over us.

"Okay, everyone needs to take a breather," I announce. "If you're drinking, pick a sober buddy you're not currently fighting with and go for a walk."

"Great idea," Mason says to me, downing the last of his beer. "K-bear, you're my buddy."

Aiden steps in front of me before Mason can grab my arm. "Really, Mason? After what we just said?"

I move around Aiden so I can see what's going on.

"All we talked about was how I'm a better man for Amelia. So, yeah. Really." On the last word, Mason shoves Aiden for emphasis.

Caught off guard, Aiden is forced to step back to catch his balance, but he recovers quickly.

"Don't start a fight you can't win," Aiden threatens in a low voice, the double meaning not lost on anyone.

Julian steps up. "Mason, just calm down, man."

While Mason and Aiden are in a stare-off, Julian puts his hand on Mason's shoulder, which sets off an inevitable chain reaction. Mason immediately turns around and pushes Julian away from him, then in one motion, turns back around and swings at Aiden.

Aiden expertly dodges the punch, but now he's pissed—even more than before. He tackles Mason and they fall to the floor in a tornado of punches and insults. It's less a fight and more Aiden trying to restrain Mason—he's drunk, and Aiden's still a good friend. He knows it wouldn't be a fair fight and Mason's not really in his right mind.

Somehow, Mason slips Aiden's grip and ends up on top of him, getting a hit in on his face, all the while insulting him. Of course, this *really* angers Aiden, and I can tell he's going to stop playing nice.

I barely take a second to think. All I see are two of the most important boys in my life physically fighting over something unworthy of either of their time—me.

Aiden flips them over so that Mason is pinned under him, and is about to throw his first *real* punch, which I'm sure would knock Mason out cold, when I instinctively reach out and grab his right arm, stopping him from landing the hit.

"Aiden, come on," I beg, not letting go of his arm.

He looks at Mason, who's on the floor with a bloody split lip, and then back at my pleading eyes, as if contemplating if it was worth it.

He sighs and shrugs my hand off his arm, and shoots Mason a chilling glare as he gets off of him. Nevertheless, Aiden still holds out a hand to help Mason up, which Mason swiftly swats aside.

He stands up on his own and drags the back of his hand across his mouth to wipe away the blood, all while staring Aiden down. "I wasn't done kicking your ass," he slurs, grabbing Aiden by the collar of his shirt.

Damn it, why won't he just calm down?!

Since I clearly just love jumping into the middle of fights, I move to pull them apart. Some part of my mind registers Aiden, Julian, Chase, and Noah yelling at me to stop, but it's too late. I come up behind Mason, and when I try to pull him away, he draws his arm back to throw a punch at Aiden, his elbow slamming into my face at full force.

"*Son of a—*" My hands automatically fly to my face as a nauseating pain radiates from my nose throughout my face.

I feel multiple pairs of hands on me but I shrug them off, focused only on the coppery taste of my own blood, which I have no idea where it's coming from. A pair of hands land on me that send sparks up my spine and I stop resisting.

"Amelia, stop squirming. Let me see," a calm, deep, and comforting voice demands.

I force myself to straighten up and look at Aiden, keeping my hands on my face, as if trying to shove the blood back where it came from.

"This hurts like a fucking bitch, geez," I complain, my eyes watering from the pulsing sting.

"Come on, let's go take a look at it," Aiden says in an authoritative tone, ushering me up the stairs and into the bathroom in my room.

As we're walking, Mason continuously says he's sorry, and one of the other guys orders him to go for a walk with them to cool off.

Aiden closes the door to my room as we walk in, as well as the bathroom door once we're inside. He puts his hands on my waist and effortlessly picks me up and places me gently on top of the counter. If I wasn't so focused on trying to stop the bleeding, I would've blushed or swooned or something.

He gets two small towels and wets them both with warm water.

"Move your hands, Thea," he gently commands, and I obediently comply.

He hands me one of the towels to clean my hands, and uses the other to gently mop up the blood on my face. When he pulls the blood-soaked towel away, my eyes widen in horror.

"Please tell me I didn't break my nose," I beg, eyeballing all the blood.

That much blood means it's broken, right? I knew someone who got a soccer ball to the face and their nose never healed properly, and now they have trouble breathing through it.

He gently moves my head around to examine my nose. "No, I don't think so. At least it stopped bleeding."

We make eye contact and my heartbeat elevates.

"Why are you being so nice to me? I thought you hated me?"

Aiden smiles sadly. "Were you not present during that whole thing ten minutes ago?"

"Well, mostly," I joke and motion to my face, which is probably swelling. "But I thought you hated me?"

Aiden's lips pull up in one corner. "I don't hate you."

He doesn't hate me. I feel like since our fight I've been having trouble breathing, but now the polluted air has cleared and all I smell is fresh air and flowers. Or I guess technically right now all I smell is blood, but at least I can breathe again.

"How are you so calm right now?" I can't help but ask.

His eyebrows draw together. "What do you mean?"

"I don't know. Usually you get all 'What did I tell you about jumping into fights. You could get hurt,' blah, blah, blah," I say in my best Aiden voice.

"First of all, I don't sound like that." He takes the bloody towel from my hands and throws it in the sink.

He puts his hands on the counter on either side of my legs, trapping me between his strong arms.

"And I guess I've come to learn that you're a lot stronger than we give you credit for," he says in a low voice, his lips so close to mine.

Before I can even process the weight of his words or his closeness, he ruins the moment by leaning back and adding, "Plus, I wanted to make sure you were okay before lecturing you. I mean really, Thea? What were you thinking? Every time you jump in you end up getting hurt. Why can't you just let other people deal with it?"

I catch him eyeing my—now bloodstained—taped-up fingers and move them out of sight.

"I was thinking that I didn't want you guys ripping each other to shreds over something so stupid. Are you even okay? Is Mason?"

I was so preoccupied with my stupid bloody mess that I haven't even considered if they're okay. Aiden looks fine, not even a scratch on him.

"We're okay. Let's not change the subject." He dismisses my question. "Next time, if you see someone fighting, don't jump in, okay? I was handling it."

I stop myself from exploding on him. Don't jump in? That's like asking Nutella to stop being so delicious. Basically impossible. To Aiden, I say, "You were not handling it. You were going to eat him!"

"I was not going to eat him."

"Obviously, I mean figuratively, not literally. You were eyeing him like you were trying to decide which size platter would best fit his head."

"Can you really blame me? If it was anyone else their head would've already been on that platter before I even thought about it."

I frown and look down at my lap. "He was emotional and drunk. He didn't mean it."

He narrows his perceptive eyes at me. "Didn't he though?"

"I mean—I don't know. Maybe? I don't really want to think about it."

Aiden runs a frustrated hand through his hair. "Why are you so damn content to ignore the way Mason's been acting this whole trip?"

I shrink into myself. "How has he been acting?"

"Like a giant, fucking, self-absorbed, entitled prick!"

I shrug, feeling like nothing I say can be a good enough excuse. Because I know what I have to tell Mason, and that I'll ruin his life, and I can't do it.

I can feel Aiden's frustration rising, but he takes a calming breath. "I know you. You're so perceptive. You can't really not notice what's going on."

"I just . . . I don't know." I think about the last few days. Really think about them, and try to be honest about what I'm feeling. "Every time I look at Mason, I think about Brian and my mom. And then I feel guilty for knowing and that it's *my* mom who's helping break his family . . ." I trail off, not meeting Aiden's gaze.

"You're mistaking guilt for not understanding he's putting moves on you. I get that he's going to be in a bad spot when he finds out, but you can't let that excuse him from being a shitty friend," Aiden says.

I know he's right. "It won't matter soon anyway."

He clenches his fists and I can tell he's trying hard to stay calm. "Because you're leaving," he finishes for me.

I'm suddenly desperate for him to not hate me. I don't blame him for being mad—I understand, really. But when I got elbowed in the face, he and I went back to normal for a bit instead of being all tense and upset with each other. I really miss him, more than I thought I ever would.

"I told you, Aiden. I really wish I didn't have to, but I have no choice."

"But you do have a choice! It's all your choice! It's your life! You can't just vanish and leave me with no way of ever seeing you or contacting you again."

"I'm just trying to protect you! Protect everyone!" I defend my decision, hating that we're going to have this fight again.

"It's not your job to protect us." His eyes are blazing, shoulders set with determination.

"What do you want me to do, Aiden? Stay here knowing that I'm putting you in danger? People *died* last time! How could I live with myself if something happened to any of you because of me?"

"I'm not asking you to put us in danger. We won't be in danger. We'll be careful, like we have been. You don't have to do this alone anymore, Thea." His voice softens, his eyes more vulnerable, slightly pleading. "I'm asking you to give us a chance. I know the risks, and I'm choosing to take them. Don't leave. Don't cut us off. Don't give up on us."

I sigh, wishing on everything in the entire universe that my life was normal and I could just be with Aiden.

I look away from him. "Aiden—I don't—"

"Come with me tomorrow," he interrupts, gently taking hold of my chin and turning me to look at him. "I have a meeting with Vivienne Henfrey, and I want you there with me. You won't be on camera, but off screen for support. I'm going to do it and then we'll deal with the consequences together. All in, remember?"

My whole body heats up, and all I can do is nod in reply.

"Good," he says softly. "Now let's get some ice for your nose."

22

Everyone else has already crashed, so we try to make as little noise as possible fixing up my face. Without even thinking about it, Aiden grabs my hand and leads me into his room, and I fall asleep in his arms, savoring every single moment with him.

Hours later, I'm woken up by the sound of my phone ringing on the nightstand. I check the caller ID and with a heavy heart, I wiggle out of Aiden's embrace without waking him up.

"Hello?" I whisper as I pad into Aiden's bathroom and close the door.

"Thea. How is everything?" Agent Dylan, the man assigned to my case, asks me.

"It's all right, how about you? Anything on Tony?"

If they just catch and arrest Tony, then that solves all my problems. I can stay here and be with Aiden and my friends and not have to constantly look over my shoulder. I can be a normal teenager.

"Actually, yes. But not his location just yet," he adds, as if knowing to make sure I don't get my hopes up. "There have been a few developments in the case—and it's information we think you deserve to know."

He then proceeds to tell me that Tony Derando isn't Tony's real name. His name is Anthony DeRosso. He's been accused of and charged with multiple felonies, and has been accused of raping several women over the years in different states before he got married. Once he was married, he settled down in one place and stayed mostly under the radar except for some petty thefts and crimes, and had his daughter, Sabrina. Apparently, the experts at the FBI believe that Sabrina's death pushed him completely over the edge. But information has come to light recently that tied him to some earlier crimes, and now they have a countrywide warrant out for his arrest. It's bigger than me now; it's about all the women he's hurt in his life. Somehow, I find this comforting, knowing that it's not just my life Tony's ruined.

"Why didn't you guys tell me this before? I'm assuming you didn't just find this out?" I ask him.

"There's new evidence—meaning the case is bigger, we have more resources now. We'll find him," Agent Dylan says.

I resist the urge to laugh, instead rolling my eyes. Yes, I'm resting very assured. That's why I'm popping sleeping pills like breath mints.

"I'm just calling to check up on you," he continues, "and to let you know that your relocation process may take a week or two longer than we initially thought."

I crack open the bathroom door and sneak a look at Aiden, who's still sound asleep. He looks so peaceful, so young and innocent, but at the same time fearless and strong. At least I get more time with Aiden and my friends, even if it's just a few weeks.

But can I *really* just give him up? Can I really never talk to him again? Can I kid myself into thinking that I'm not missing something so vital to me? Will I be okay to live the rest of my life knowing that I'll probably never be this happy again? Never talking to Aiden again is going to feel like I'm missing the air I need to make me whole.

My eyes drink Aiden in, from his messy hair to his perfect jawline, covered in stubble, to his sculpted and powerful naked chest. Could I live with myself if something happened to him or my friends?

I know how I feel, and I know what I need to do to keep people safe, but maybe some rules can be broken; maybe I won't have to feel like I'm drowning.

» «

After I finish up in the bathroom, I crawl back into bed with Aiden.

"Hey," he says in a deep, sleepy voice.

He shifts so that I can rest my head on his shoulder as he wraps his arm around me and pulls me closer.

"Did your phone ring earlier?" he asks as I trace mindless patterns on his chest with my finger.

"Yeah, it was Agent Dylan."

I tell him about Tony's real name and about his past, but leave out any mention of my leaving.

"It's going to be okay, Thea," he reassures me.

I choose to not respond to that statement, instead checking the time on my phone.

"Hey, it's almost four o'clock. What time is the meeting with Vivienne?"

Aiden sits up, rubbing the sleep from his eyes. "It's at six. I guess we should get up and get something to eat now."

Aiden jumps in the shower, and I go to my room to do the same. Since Aiden's room is right off of the living room/kitchen area, everyone turns to look at me as I leave his room in his oversized T-shirt and boxers, my clothes from last night crumpled in my hands.

Annalisa sends me a knowing smirk. "Looks like someone made up."

I self-consciously fix my hair, as if that would make it look like less of a walk of shame. "I guess." I blush, even though we were completely innocent last night.

"Your face looks worse," Noah, ever the gentleman, points out.

Annalisa swats him on the arm in response.

"Thanks for the observation, Noah," I say as I walk up the stairs to shower and change.

Mason didn't look at me the entire time.

When I'm ready I head back downstairs, and the atmosphere is tense. Aiden is on one side of the house and Mason's on the other. Chase and Noah aren't talking to each other, either, so it's just an awkward atmosphere in general. Tonight is New Year's Eve, too, and we'll probably all be too mad at each other to properly celebrate.

Mason is the first one to notice me. He stands up immediately from the kitchen island where he was eating with Chase.

"Amelia. I'm so sorry. The last thing I ever want to do is hurt you and I didn't mean to hit you last night, I just—"

"It's okay, Mason," I interrupt. "It's not your fault, I basically walked into your elbow."

He comes closer to me, stopping a few feet away from me. Aiden turns his intense gaze on us, but he stays where he is.

"I really am sorry, k-bear. Seeing your face like that kills me," Mason says.

"Geez, you guys are making me feel like such a pretty, pretty princess right now," I joke.

"No! That's not what I meant, you're still gorgeous," he adds quickly, and I swear I hear Aiden clear his throat.

"I know, Mason. It's all right, really."

I already forgave Mason. If Aiden forgives him, that's a different story. But I don't blame him for my swollen and bruised face. His arm was swinging back and I walked into it in classic Amelia fashion. He didn't try to hit me. He tried to hit Aiden, but again, that's kind of for him and Aiden to sort out, and by the looks of it, they haven't.

"We should get going," Aiden cuts in, standing up and looking at me expectantly. "We'll stop and grab something to eat first since we have no food here."

"Yeah, we should go shopping," Julian, who's currently looking in the fridge, adds. "Might as well go now. Keep me company, Mason?"

I'm assuming Julian is trying to get some one-on-one time with Mason so he can see what's going on in his head, and talk some sense into him. Maybe he and Aiden will make up before dinner, and Chase and Noah will make up, and we can all start the new year as best friends again.

Is that hoping for too much?

23

Since it's winter, even though it's only five o'clock, it's already starting to get dark outside. I'm sitting in the passenger seat of Aiden's car as he pulls out of the driveway, Julian's truck right behind us since he's heading the same way into town.

"What do you want to eat?" Aiden asks me.

To get to the main part of town from the beach house, you have to drive through about twenty minutes of deserted, hilly, open road. What restaurants do they have in town? They don't have what I really want.

"Will you and Mason ever make up?" I blurt out in response.

Aiden doesn't take his eyes off of the road. "I've never heard of that type of food. Is it Italian?"

"Aiden! Come on."

I get that he's pissed off at Mason, but they've been friends for so long, I'd hate for this to ruin it.

"Maybe. Maybe not," he answers calmly. "Do you like him?"

What?

"He's my friend, of course I like him."

Aiden's knuckles tighten on the steering wheel. "That's not what I meant."

I sigh and turn my body to face him properly, putting my hand on his arm. "I like Mason as a friend. I love *you*, Aiden."

He looks at me, the expression in his eyes light but heavy at the same time. "But you're still leaving."

"I have to. I don't have a choice."

"But I'll never hear from you again," he says softly.

"No. I won't let that happen. You're stuck with me, Aiden Parker."

The car jerks, but Aiden quickly recovers. "What? What do you mean?"

I smile at him, hoping he sees the love and confidence in my eyes, hoping he knows how huge this is for me. "I can't never talk to you again. FaceTime, phone calls, maybe even visits. I don't care. I can't just throw us away. I can't never see your face again." I hesitate at his silence, feeling stupid for making it sound like a huge revelation when it really isn't. "I know it doesn't sound like a big deal, but—"

"Are you fucking kidding me? It's a huge deal! I'd get to see you!" The expression on Aiden's face fills my heart with so much joy and excitement. He smiles so big it reaches his eyes and transforms his whole face. "Are you sure it's safe, though? I don't want to put you in danger. If staying away from you is what will keep you safe, then I'm prepared to do that, even if it's the last thing I want to do. Even if it'll kill me."

"We'll find a way," I promise, not only to Aiden, but to myself. Maybe I'll be losing all my friendships, but I'll get to keep Aiden.

Aiden laughs and hits the steering wheel with excitement.

"Yes! I wish you told me while I wasn't driving because I really want to grab you and kiss you right now."

I unbuckle my seat belt and lean over to give him a quick kiss. "When we get out for tacos, I promise."

He laughs. "Is that what you finally decided you want?"

I sit back down and buckle up. "Been craving them since I woke up."

He looks at me, his beautiful smile never faltering. "Then tacos it—"

I don't hear the end of Aiden's sentence, because there's a sound of a horn honking at us from behind, like a warning.

And then there's metal hitting metal, the squealing of tires, more honking, glass shattering, my screams. I can barely see what's happening, I can barely comprehend it. The world is spinning and spinning and there's metal crunching and grating and I feel my skin being sliced again and again and again.

The car stops moving but the world is still spinning. There's a ringing in my ears and a pounding in my head and I'm so disoriented I can't tell up from down or left from right. Distantly, my name is being called, demanding that I answer. The voice is angry. No, it's scared, scared because I'm not answering. I groggily shake my head, the world slowly coming into focus.

"Thea! You're okay, you're all right." It's Aiden, but he's upside down?

Oh wait, I'm upside down. I'm strapped into the seat, but the car is on its roof.

"I'm going to cut your seat belt off, okay? I need you to not land on your head," he instructs, more frightened than I've ever seen him in my life, but still managing to keep calm, his face set in determination.

I make some type of noise in agreement. Will the pounding in my head ever stop?

"It's going to be okay," he repeats, and even I know it sounds like he's only trying to convince himself.

"Put this foot there, and that one there, and your arms here and here," he positions my limbs so that they're all braced against something.

"I'm going to try to catch you, but try to catch yourself as much as you can, okay?"

"Umm-hmm," I reply, my head starting to clear.

How can he catch me? He's lying on his back on the ground—or technically roof—with his lower body flat on the ground sticking out the window, and there's barely any room in here.

"Okay, one, two, three!" My seat belt is cut loose and I'm right-side up again.

I don't think it hurt, but then again everything kind of already hurts anyway.

Aiden's covered in blood, but I can't tell where it's coming from. Do I look like that? He backs out of his window and helps me follow until we're outside. We lie down on the grass and try to catch our breath to calm our racing heart rates.

"Are you okay, Thea?" His hand reaches for me, his fingers intertwining with mine.

I roll my head over to look at him. Behind him, there's a steep hill, a path of thin, broken trees and debris leading to the road. A car just hit us hard enough to push us into a ditch.

"I think so," I answer, squeezing his hand. "Are you?"

Relief floods his face. "Now I am."

"Not for long." A third deep, intimidating voice cuts in.

A man in a black suit walks around from behind us. There's a black SUV parked at the top of the hill, the same one that's been parked outside our house for the last couple of days, except now the front end is totaled.

Aiden sits up, the tenseness of his muscles telling me he's on high alert, and he pulls me up with him to face the new threat—Harvey.

"What do you want?" Aiden spits out, his demeanor completely different from how tender it was just moments ago. "Is this Andrew making good on his threats?"

"Your father didn't get where he is without getting his hands a little dirty, you know," Harvey says, reaching into his suit jacket and pulling out a gun. My eyes go wide, and I'm too stunned to cry. Aiden stiffens, and I know even he can't get us out of this one. We're both injured, disoriented, tired, and weaponless, and this man is perfectly fine *and* has a gun.

He's going to kill us.

"He warned you. All you had to do was either play along or keep your mouth shut." The man points the gun at Aiden, and I scream.

"This message is from your dad." Harvey swivels so that the gun is now aimed at my chest. "Remember it for next time, Aiden."

I blink, but before I hear the shot, Aiden, from the ground, kicks Harvey in the kneecap and his leg buckles, making the shot go wide. From that opportunity, I quickly roll out of the way as Aiden tackles the man to the ground.

He must be powered by adrenaline because he is way too strong for someone who's covered in blood and was just in a car that flipped down a hill multiple times. They grapple for the gun and it slides out of Harvey's hands.

While they fight, I crawl over to where the gun went, feeling around for it in the leaves. Leaves crunch behind me and I whip around. It has to be more of Andrew's thugs who've come to assist Harvey in killing me to send a message.

Searching the ground with more fervor than before, I can barely think over the heavy pounding of my head and heart. *Find the gun! Find the gun! Where is the goddamn gun?!*

Turning around again to face the new threat, I take a deep breath when Mason and Julian appear, one holding a large, heavy wrench, and the other a thick tire iron.

They move quickly to help Aiden, but Harvey, who must have about a hundred pounds on Aiden, gets the upper hand. He drags Aiden up by wrapping his arm around his neck, and holds him against his chest. He pulls out a knife and presses it to Aiden's neck, and my heart stops.

Without looking away from the scene, my hand wraps around the object I need.

"I wouldn't move if I were you," the man directs at Mason and Julian.

He's not facing me, he doesn't think I'm a threat. Mason and Julian are the ones with the weapons, after all. They stop where they are, considering their options.

"The cops are on their way," Mason cautions. "Just drop the knife."

Harvey tilts his head at Mason. "I was told not to kill Aiden, but that I could if I had to. I guess I have to."

Harvey moves quickly, and the hand holding the knife starts sliding against Aiden's neck. I don't even think. I see a flash of red and suddenly there's a loud bang, a man yelling in pain, two bodies collapsing to the ground.

Lowering the gun I just fired, I rush over to Aiden, yelling his name over and over and over.

"I'm okay," comes his voice, and I've never been so happy and relieved and scared at the same time.

He sits up and rubs his hand across his throat. The knife cut him on the side of the neck, only about an inch long and not deep from what I can tell. Throwing my arms around him, I sob into his neck, not caring if I'm hurting myself or him, just needing to hold him, to make sure he's okay. He wraps his arms around me and holds me close, and I can feel his elevated heart rate, beating in unison with mine.

Mason and Julian are there as well, making sure we're okay, telling us that help is coming, that'll we'll all get to go home.

"Where the fuck did he go?" Julian asks, looking around the wooded area.

I sit back and turn to where Harvey fell, but he's no longer there. I did shoot him in the side of the stomach, so he wasn't dead when he dropped. We all look up when we hear the SUV peel away before we can do anything about it.

"Are the cops really on their way?" Aiden asks.

"Yes, we called them when we saw him run you off the road," Mason confirms.

Aiden turns back to me, taking the gun from my shaking hands and wiping it down on the part of his shirt that's not covered in blood.

"Listen to me, Thea," he orders, low enough that only I can hear. "I want you to get out of here. Go home, get cleaned up and go to the hospital if you have to. Tell them you fell down the stairs or something. But you were never here, got it?"

What? Why is he telling me to leave him right now? "What the hell, Aiden? Why would I do that?"

He finishes wiping off the gun and grabs it with his hands, smudging his blood all over it in the process.

"I shot him in self-defense. Why are you wiping my prints off?" I ask.

He aims the gun in the opposite direction of us and fires once at nothing.

"What are you doing?!" I demand, seriously concerned. Are his injuries worse than I thought? How hard did he hit his head?

"Gun residue." He gestures to his hand then drops the gun. "Just in case." He looks me in the eye, talking clear and straight so that I understand. "You didn't shoot anyone. I did. You were at home where you fell down the stairs. Right, Julian? You were with her?"

Julian shoots Aiden a curious look but nods slowly, not knowing why Aiden is sticking to this story but dedicating himself to it anyway. "Saw the whole thing. You know how clumsy she is."

I can't believe this right now! Why are they doing this?

Aiden puts the gun down and helps me stand up, wrapping his arms around me in a tight hug.

"I just got you back," he whispers lowly in my ear. "This is going to be on the news, and I'm not risking Tony seeing you and trying to take you away from me."

My heart beats heavy in my chest, a pit forming in my stomach.

"I want you far away from this, okay? It's my mess, let me deal with it. I love you," he says, his eyes raw and staring straight into my soul.

I nod at him, tears clouding my vision. "I love you too."

He kisses me. It's rough but soft, and scared but confident all at once, but it makes me feel like I'm lighter than air, like I can do anything and be anyone, and it wouldn't matter because Aiden loves me.

"Go," he commands when we pull apart.

Mason hands Julian his wrench, then plops down in all the blood and starts rolling around.

"What are you doing?!" I ask him, horrified that he would do such a thing.

"It's obvious that Aiden wasn't in that car alone. I'm already all busted up from our fight yesterday, anyway."

He looks at Aiden and nods, and Aiden nods back at him.

"Come on, Amelia." Julian grabs my hand and leads me up the hill toward his truck.

Looking back at the two boys sitting on the ground beside a wrecked car, I feel nothing but love and appreciation for both of them.

We get in the car and Julian hightails it out of there, taking backroads instead of the main ones, trying to put as much distance between us and the crime scene.

As we drive away, the distinct sound of sirens shriek in the background.

The End

Acknowledgments

As always, the first person I want to thank is you, the reader, the person who picked up this book and gave it a chance. Thank you so much to my readers, fans, friends, and Violets. If it wasn't for you, I wouldn't have realized that writing is something I enjoy doing, and this story would not have existed. Thank you from the bottom of my heart for following me on this journey and for allowing me to follow my dreams. I will forever be grateful for your love and support.

Thank you to my mom, Carmela, for being the greatest mom to ever walk the planet, for always believing in me, and for being my biggest fan. Thank you for reading to me every night without fail before bed, and for teaching me the power of a good story.

I'd like to thank my dad, Bruno, for supporting me unconditionally, for always believing in me without fail, and for letting me take your Challenger for "research purposes." Thanks for answering all my dumb technical questions like "Can I hit someone with a toilet tank lid without it breaking?" without any context, and still not thinking that I'm crazy. You're the greatest.

Like the first book, I want to acknowledge my brother, Michael. You literally did nothing and still don't know what this story is about, but I love you anyway.

Thank you to my boyfriend, Mario, and his family, for being so supportive and for being my number one fans. If there was a record for the most copies of *She's With Me* purchased by a single family, I'm positive you guys would hold it. I'm so grateful to have you all in my life.

Thank you to my grandparents, zias, zios, cousins, neighbors, family, and friends who have always supported me. Yes, it's kind of awkward having all your family and friends read a romance and imagine the kissing scenes being read in your voice, but I wouldn't have it any other way. My first-ever book signing was basically one hundred of you guys crowding an Indigo store and it was the best thing ever; it meant so much to me.

On that note, thanks to all the Toronto readers, Wattpad staff, and everyone else who came out to my one and only book signing. It was literally one of the best days of my life and I'll never forget it.

To the Wattpad community and Wattpad Stars, thank you for always being such a great support network, always being so quick and willing to help a Wattpad Star in need, and for always being available for a writing sprint. Also, thanks to all of the Stars and fellow Wattpad published authors for sharing my books with their audiences—you guys are the coolest.

The first draft of this book is so different from the awesome version you're reading right now, and that's because of the input of my amazing editors. Thanks to Adam Wilson, for pointing out all the plot holes and overall story notes, and to Rebecca Mills, for being the absolute best copy editor around. And of course, thank you so much to Deanna McFadden. Your help, notes, suggestions, and input have been absolutely invaluable. This story was able to reach its full potential because you were here cheering me on and helping me hone my craft. I can't wait to work with you all again on the next book.

Thank you to my talent manager, I-Yana Tucker. I legitimately could not imagine my writing journey without you. Not only are you the best talent manager, but you're probably my biggest cheerleader. I always thought you were exaggerating when you told me you talk about *She's With Me* all the time, but people from Wattpad tell me that you honestly *do* talk about it all the time! Thank you for being a champion for me and my work, and for planning the above mentioned amazing book signing! I'm so grateful to have you through this experience.

Also, a big thank you to everyone at Wattpad HQ and Wattpad Books—editors, publicists, marketing, graphic designers—involved in working so hard to make my book ready for publishing and promoting it out in the world.

To all of you, and everyone I probably forgot, thank you for believing in me. I'm so grateful to have all of you in my life, and it's because of you that I was able to make *Stay With Me* a book I'm so proud of.

Still With Me

EXCLUSIVE EXCERPT

1

When I was in elementary school, I thought being normal was probably the worst thing I could grow up to be. I must have been six or seven, and we had to pick what we wanted to be when we were older from a list of preapproved careers to do a project on. They didn't have the option I wanted, so I picked doctor and went home to complain.

My dad was thoroughly confused when I explained that I didn't want to be a doctor or lawyer or teacher, but I wanted to be a hairdresser exclusively for gorillas, who also juggled part time in a traveling ukulele band.

He tried throwing logical facts at me, but I was undeterred by the fact that gorillas probably don't need hairdressers, or that I didn't know how to juggle or play ukulele, and that no one even wanted to see a juggling ukulele band in the first place.

Then he hit me with the that's not a normal career path speech. I replied, in my cutesy, little kid way, that being normal sounded boring, and I'd much rather have interesting things happen to me, even if they made my life harder. Now, looking back, I would do anything to slap six- or seven-year-old me silly, and eat my words out of existence.

My dad wanted me to have a normal, boring life without any hardships. I scoffed at the idea. It's funny how in the end, he was the one who set into motion a chain of events that ensured my life would never be completely normal again.

There have been multiple attempts to end my life made by two different men, all within the last year. There's Tony, the man who's quite possibly a real psychopath, and the reason I've had to move three times and change my identity each time in order to keep myself safe.

Then there's Aiden's biological dad, Andrew Kessler, who's ruthless and clearly has no problem getting someone to murder a teenage girl in order to send a message to his estranged son, who threatened to blow the whistle on his true, shitty past.

My mother is having an affair with the father of one of my best friends, and I have no idea if or how I should tell Mason. Plus, there's the whole Mason's most likely in love with me thing that I really don't even want to think about addressing right now.

Annalisa's half brother, Luke, is going to stand trial for murdering Aiden's stepfather, which he claims he doesn't remember doing because he wasn't sober at the time, and Annalisa is just now realizing that she can't bear to not have Luke in her life.

Noah and Chase are in a weird, we're friends but not really stage because Chase walked in on Noah in bed with the love of his life, Charlotte, who really doesn't know if she even likes either of them as more than friends.

My middle (and favorite) finger is dislocated from punching Ryan, Aiden's now ex-stepbrother, in the face, my nose is swollen and bruised from walking into Mason's elbow, and there are a bunch of cuts and bruises on my body from Aiden's dad's attempt to *murder me*.

And to make all of that worse, I'm being relocated as soon as the agents assigned to my case finalize our new location and identities. King City is the one place that feels like home, where I have friends I love and a *boy* I love. But Aiden already knows all about me, and I decided to break *some* small rules so that I don't have to completely give him up, namely the no contacting anyone from your old life rule. But what my mom and the agents don't know won't hurt them, and I'll be supercareful. When the time comes to leave, I won't feel like my heart is being ripped out; I'll still have Aiden.

But in the meantime, while I'm still here in King City, not only do I have Kaitlyn and Ryan trying to make my life miserable, but my best friends are all in the middle of their own drama, and I have two grown men trying to kill me.

Nice.

Honestly, Julian's the only one in this group who has his shit together and is living a relatively normal life, except for the fact that he hangs out with all of us.

After the accident, Aiden and Mason give the cops a pretty convincing story about what had happened, mostly sticking to the truth but omitting any mention of me or Julian. As far as I know, the detectives don't see any discrepancies in their story.

Harvey, the man who ran Aiden and me off the road and tried to shoot me, wasn't found, but Aiden didn't deliver a kill shot, so they believe he's injured. They ran the prints on the knife that he held to Aiden's throat, and they were matched to a Harvey Vedenin, who, to no surprise, has been arrested before. It's also no surprise that Harvey Vedenin is a known associate and bodyguard of Andrew Kessler, which gives validity to Aiden's story. Of course, there's no undeniable evidence to actually prove that Andrew Kessler was behind Harvey's actions, but we know the truth.

Aiden did end up speaking to Vivienne Henfrey, the reporter who made it clear she is not a fan of Kessler's, and she practically begged Aiden to go on air. He and Mason stayed at the beach house a few extra days to sort everything out, and the rest of us went back home, and Jason and Jackson stayed at Mason's house.

I watched Aiden on the news from home, my heart exploding with pride seeing his handsome and determined face, sharing a part of his life that I know he'd rather bury so far inside of him that his subconscious doesn't even know it's there. I know how hard it was for him to share his past, but he was confident as he told the world about how he is the son of Andrew Kessler, even though Andrew originally claimed to have no children. He explained how Andrew left when his mother was sick and pregnant, and how he hasn't tried to contact his family since his wife died. But Aiden was on the news, looking bold, brave, and confident, his words elegant and captivating, making the listener hold their breath just to make sure they didn't miss a single word of his story.

He was the same Aiden as usual—cold, stoic, and deadly beautiful, looking even more intimidating with the bruised jaw and ten stitches on the side of his forehead. But the world couldn't help falling in love with him, right there and then.

That's the thing about Aiden. He has that presence and charm, even on camera, and even when he's not trying, that just makes people gravitate toward him, that makes people like him, makes them want *him* to like *them*, even when everything about him screams, Don't mess with me.

Vivienne took Aiden's story and old family photos and ran with it, destroying Kessler's platform and family friendly agenda with it. She basically proved that Kessler is the biggest hypocrite on the planet, and doesn't actually care or live by any of the issues he was campaigning for. Obviously, Kessler denied everything. His team worked quickly and efficiently at his response and recovery from this new revelation of information, and as far as I know, has no plans of dropping out of the race for governor.

We were all together when we heard Kessler say he has no intention of dropping out, and Charlotte asked, "He'll never recover from this, right? People will think he's an awful person or a phony or a hypocrite and won't elect him if he chooses not to drop out? Right?"

Annalisa snorted when she replied. "Well, you never know—worse people have done worse things in this country and have still been elected to high places of power, so . . ."

We all deflated a bit after that, knowing it was true, but at least he's under more public scrutiny, and won't make any attempts to take my or Aiden's life anytime soon.

Hopefully.

Now it's Monday morning, and we have to go back to school and face the gossip mongers who have nothing better to do than gawk and stare at us. It doesn't help that there are all sorts of rumors already swirling around before we even head to school.

A few days before school, Makayla Thomas, Kaitlyn's best friend, saw me at the grocery store, and told everyone that my face is fucked up from botched plastic surgery. I couldn't help but roll my eyes when Charlotte told me about that rumor. Of all the things Makayla could've come up with, she went with the most basic and uncreative thing. But still, this means everyone's going to try to get a look at me, but that's nothing in comparison to what Aiden's going to face when he steps in the building.

He doesn't open up; it was a miracle when I got him to tell me the most insignificant detail about himself, and that was when he liked me. Having a bunch of stupid teenagers openly staring at you and stage whispering as you walk by isn't something I think he'll especially enjoy. I haven't seen him since the accident because he just got back last night, but I wouldn't blame him if he decided to skip the next few days.

As I walk into the school with Annalisa beside me, I already feel the stares on me. I fidget with the necklace that Aiden got me for Christmas, feeling calmed by its weight. It's a pocket-knife disguised as a necklace that has a secret button to press to release the blade. Obviously, I know I shouldn't be wearing it to school, but I didn't wear it the night Aiden and I went to meet with Vivienne Henfrey, and we were run off the road and almost killed. I could've really used it then, so I decided I'd much rather have it on me now, just in case.

Annalisa holds her head high, a scowl on her face, staring down the people who gawk at us without shame until they bow their heads in submission. If I wasn't her friend, I'd be terrified of her.

We round the corner to get to my locker, and I stop short. At my locker waiting for me is Aiden. It's been almost a full week since I've seen him in person, and a sense of peace comes over me at seeing him standing there, waiting for me, looking at me like I just made his whole week. Everyone else and their stares and whispers at seeing me or Aiden fade away as I walk over to him.

2

Aiden pushes himself off of the locker he was leaning on and studies me as Annalisa and I approach him.

"How's your face?" is the first thing he says to me once we're close enough.

Wow. He's so romantic. The corner of my lip turns up. "Not as bad as yours."

He smiles at me as he shakes his head, immediately pulling me in for a hug, and I melt as he rests his chin on the top of my head.

I've talked to him over FaceTime during this past week, but this is the first time I've actually been with him in person since that hectic night where we were in a car accident and almost killed by Andrew's orders. Being in Aiden's arms now, hearing his steady heartbeat and feeling the tight muscles in his back, I can say with absolute certainty that nothing can substitute for the feeling of actually being with him in person.

"Are you okay?" he whispers to me.

There's something about sharing a traumatic, life threatening experience with someone that brings you immediately closer to them. When you think about it, Aiden and I kind of saved each other's lives. Actually, not kind of. We did. Harvey's gun was pointed at me when he pulled the trigger, but the shot went wide because of Aiden's quick thinking. Harvey started slicing Aiden's throat but stopped when I shot him, and I'm so grateful my aim was good that day.

Being with Aiden now, I instinctively know that no matter what happens in my life, he'll always be close to my heart.

I nod to answer his question. "Are you?"

He pushes a piece of hair behind my ear and pulls back to meet my eyes. "I'm better now."

My heart flutters, and I remember when he said something similar to me after we got separated at the Tracks when the cops busted the races, which seems like forever ago.

Annalisa clears her throat. "I wanted to know how you were, too, in case you were wondering."

I laugh and pull away from Aiden so that Annalisa can have her turn with him.

"I'm glad you're okay," she says when they pull out of their hug.

Just then, Noah and Julian come around the corner and pull Aiden into one of those bro hugs.

"I knew we'd find you here," Julian says to Aiden with a quick glance in my direction.

"But would it kill you to answer a text message every once in a while?" Noah complains as he gives Aiden a shove.

Aiden rolls his eyes and steps aside so I can open my locker.

"Hey, how are the twins handling all of this?" Annalisa asks. "Have you explained everything to them yet?"

Aiden sighs and runs his hand through his hair, which I just noticed is getting kind of long now.

"I mean, just like with the whole finding Greg dead outside our house thing, I didn't exactly tell them *everything*. But they know who Andrew Kessler is now, and they don't really care for him. So since we're staying at Mason's for a bit, Brian and Natalia have been really good with keeping them occupied and getting them ready for back to school."

Ever since Aiden's arrest, Mason's dad has legal custody over Aiden and his brothers, Jason and Jackson, until Aiden turns eighteen and is allowed to file for custody. I'm guessing it's working out pretty well for now, since Aiden's been dealing with a media frenzy and it's helpful to have actual adults around that you can depend on.

The warning bell rings, so we all start moving toward class. As we walk, Aiden grabs my hand in his bigger one, and I smile as I look up at him.

"Hey, just a heads-up, don't make plans this Friday." Noah smiles not so innocently.

Aiden sighs, already knowing what he's talking about. "I told you, I don't want a birthday party."

"You're turning eighteen in two days! You're getting a birthday party! My house. This Friday. Be there." Noah stresses the importance of each word.

"Noah, the last time you threw a party, you ended up in the hospital," I point out, and I know none of us want a repeat of that. Especially right now.

He looks at me thoughtfully, then says, "You can't just stop trying to live because something bad happened. We're just gonna pull up our big boy and girl pants and throw the best damn party that Aiden deserves. And *no one* is going to talk me out of it." He looks at us with narrowed eyes, challenging any of us to disagree.

It's Aiden's party, so really, he gets the final say. He sighs, mumbling something that sounds like "Fine, whatever," under his breath, making Noah smile triumphantly.

As we walk, something about Noah's words resonate with me. Bad things happen in life—especially mine lately—and we can't let that stop us from living. I am going to get through this senior year and have a normal life if it kills me, which it honestly just might. With my new resolution coursing through my veins, I feel more determined than ever.

"What classes do you have after lunch again? History, spare, then math with me?" Aiden asks me as we walk up the stairs.

"English, spare, then math. Why?"

"We have a sub for math." His eyes light up mischievously. "What do you say we get out of here after English and go do something?"

"Like what?" I ask, trying to hide my absolute delight. Alone time with Aiden? Don't have to ask me twice! We haven't had any real alone time since before the accident.

"Your choice."

"So if I wanted to get pancakes . . . ?"

"Then you're getting pancakes." He smiles a bright smile that transforms his whole face, and I feel my heart squeeze.

"Then how can I say no?" I'd never say no. Who knows how much time I have left with him?

"Good. I'll meet you at your locker after fourth period." He kisses my forehead quickly, an act that for some reason feels so much more intimate and sweet than a kiss on the lips, and leaves in the opposite direction with Julian.

Noah and I have the same class, and Annalisa's class is near ours, so we continue to room 341, the class that started all of this.

"Well, damn. I've never felt more like a fifth wheel in my life," Noah grumbles. "Anna and Julian were on one side of me making out, and Amelia and Aiden were on the other side of me making out. But no one's over here making out with me before first period."

"We were not making out," Annalisa and I defend ourselves at the same time.

"Yeah, yeah." He dismisses us. "Maybe it's time I find a nice girl and settle down. Any suggestions?"

"Kaitlyn," Annalisa says flatly.

We both swing our heads over to look at her.

"That's not even funny," I deadpan.

"No, I'm not talking about Noah," she explains, tilting her head in the direction she was looking. "I meant Kaitlyn is coming."

I follow her gaze, and sure enough, the she-devil herself is marching right in our direction.

3

I can practically feel the excitement coursing through Kaitlyn's veins at getting to pick a fight with me. She must have gone stir crazy over the break without having me to annoy the shit out of. She and Makayla stop in front of me and cross their arms over their chests in what seems like practiced synchrony, barely even noticing Annalisa and Noah at my side.

Kaitlyn has the same icy, blue eyes and permanent scowl etched on her face as always, but she looks different somehow. Tired, maybe.

"I'm glad you tried to fix your face over the break, it needed a lot of work done." Kaitlyn sneers. "But I thought people get plastic surgery to make themselves look *better*, not worse. You should consider suing your doctor."

Back at it again. Is it bad that I'm almost excited to trade insults with her? This feels somewhat normal, innocent even, at least in comparison to what we've just been through. "You must've sued the shit out of your doctor, then, Kaitlyn. I mean, I'd be pissed if my face came out like that."

"Kaitlyn's face came out great!" Makayla jumps to her defense, earning her a glare from her friend and an amused eyebrow raise from Annalisa, Noah, and me.

"I didn't get plastic surgery, dumbass," Kaitlyn hisses at her second-in-command before turning back to me. "Well, either way, that monstrosity you call a face is distracting everyone here. I could get you a paper bag to wear if you'd like?"

I narrow my eyes at her. "My face was good enough to steal your man."

Ohhhh shit.

Boom.

Mic drop.

I didn't actually steal Aiden from her, he's made that abundantly clear. But *damn*, that felt good. I swear I see her eye twitch and a vein in her forehead pop, but she does a good job trying to remain calm and unfazed. Wow, maybe her New Year's resolution is to try not reacting explosively.

Annalisa's laughing beside me, and Noah is practically glowing with pride.

"Ryan is twice the man Aiden is."

Doubt it. "Not that I don't thoroughly enjoy our time together, Kaitlyn, but is there a reason I'm spending my morning talking to you?"

Her blue eyes laser focus on me. "I hate you. I more than hate you, I despise you. You've had a good first semester, running around thinking you're the queen of the school. But that ends now. This is my school. I'm running the show."

She takes a step closer to me, and I force myself to square my shoulders and stay where I am, not backing down. The shadows under her eyes that she's concealed with makeup are more prominent this close, and she seems different. Older, maybe. But still the same, entitled attitude.

"Ryan thinks there's something off about you, more than in the sense of you being a stupid little bitch, and I agree. Andrew Kessler is going to ruin Aiden's life, and we're going to ruin yours." She gets even closer to me, if possible, and this time I do step back. "Secrets don't stay secrets forever. Stay out of my way."

I open my mouth to lob back a snarky comeback, which is what I'm known for, but my mind draws a blank. I'm honestly a bit rattled. All the time she's spent hanging out with Ryan has clearly changed her. She seems more focused and calculating, less likely to explode and go off with just the right comeback. She's always been kind of scary, but now she seems more threatening, if possible.

Something on my face must give away how much her words just affected me, because Noah steps in and gently pushes her away from me. "Lay off, Kaitlyn."

She gives him a calculated smile that doesn't reach her eyes. "Don't act like I killed someone. *I'm* not the one who has a murderer for a brother, am I, Annalisa?"

Oh. No. She. Didn't.

Annalisa's head snaps over to Kaitlyn so fast *I* get whiplash. "What?" she says lowly, almost as a warning.

"Ryan told me that the Luke Montley who's going to rot in jail for killing his dad comes from your white-trash family," she basically sings, loud enough for the whole hallway to hear.

Annalisa and Luke have different last names, so when his

name came out in the news, no one harassed her since they didn't know he was her brother. Even though Annalisa doesn't have the greatest relationship with her brother, we all know how much this is affecting her, and how bothered she is with her brother spending his life in jail.

I put a hand on Annalisa's arm, warning her not to react the way Kaitlyn wants her to react.

"Does your brother get his jollies from killing innocent old men? Is that what you do in your spare time, too, Anna?"

Suddenly, whatever was holding me back before disappears from my mind since it's no longer me Kaitlyn's threatening, it's my friend. Brushing past Noah, I get so close to Kaitlyn that I can count each eyelash.

"Tread very carefully here, Kaitlyn," I warn in a low voice, making sure she understands every word I'm saying. "I know your mom's the principal and you think you're untouchable, but I promise you, push the wrong buttons and nothing's stopping us from pushing back."

"I'm just stating facts," Kaitlyn says confidently, no fear in her eyes at all.

Annalisa moves around Noah, assuring him she won't do something stupid, and I step back so that she can stand in front of Kaitlyn. It looks like it takes Annalisa a great deal of strength to stand so near Kaitlyn and be somewhat calm. She's basically fighting every instinct in her body that tells her to destroy Kaitlyn.

"Talk about me or my family again, and I will find you, and I will make sure that no amount of reconstructive surgery is able to fix your face after I'm through with you."

The tone that Annalisa uses sends shivers down my spine, and she's not even talking to me. To Kaitlyn's credit, she looks completely unfazed by Annalisa's promise. It's probably something she's heard before, plenty of times, from Annalisa. Kaitlyn actually smiles, as if she just won some game that Annalisa and I weren't even aware we were playing.

"Just stay on your shitty side of town and we won't have a problem."

The corners of her lips tilt up in a malicious and triumphant smile. Satisfied, she turns around and walks off, shoving a kid out of her way and into a locker without a thought as she continues down the hall, Makayla at her side.

"Whoa, someone took an extra dose of their evil psychopath pill this morning," Noah says as we watch Kaitlyn disappear around the corner.

I don't hear what Annalisa replies, my brain focusing on what was just said. *Secrets don't stay secrets forever.*

Here I was, excited to trade insults with Kaitlyn like the good old days and feel back to normal in our routine, our *simple, safe* routine in comparison to murder attempts and political scandals, but obvious Kaitlyn's stepping up her game. Does she know something? Is she close to exposing me? If she doesn't already know and digs deep enough, she's going to stumble onto a secret that's much bigger than she, or anyone, could've ever imagined.

about the author

Jessica Cunsolo's young adult series, With Me, has amassed over one hundred million reads on Wattpad since she posted her first story, *She's With Me*, on the platform in 2015. The novel has since won a 2016 Watty Award for Best Teen Fiction, and has been published in French by Hachette Romans, in Spanish by Grupo Planeta, and in English by Wattpad Books. Jessica lives with her dog, Leo, just outside of Toronto, where she enjoys the outdoors and transforming her real-life awkward situations into plotlines for her viral stories. You can find her on Twitter @AvaViolet17, on Instagram @jesscunsolo, or on Wattpad @AvaViolet.

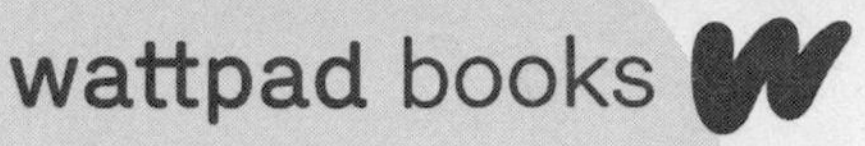
wattpad books

wattpad books
I'm a Gay Wizard
IN
THE CITY OF THE NIGHTMARE KING
V.S. SANTONI
wattpad books
HISTORICALLY INACCURATE
SHAY BRAVO

JESSICA
Stay
wattpad books
wattpad books
THE BRO CODE
ELIZABETH A. SEIBERT

wattpad books
THE BAD BOY & THE TOMBOY
NICOLE NWOSU